Max considered herself the greatest of the dragons flying in the German Luftwaffe

She wondered what treasure would be added for her performance during yesterday's bombing mission?

"Perhaps a van Gogh," she purred.

Whatever Goering or Hitler had set aside, it wouldn't arrive for days, certainly not until she was finished with her next mission and would make her request for some jeweled Russian eggs.

Warring on the side of the Germans in the last war and, in particular, throughout this one had done much to enrich her hoard. Indeed, during the previous four centuries she lived in the Alps, she'd only been able to loot merchants and traveling knights. Her take from those four hundred years was a pittance compared to her haul from the wars.

"May the wars go on forever," she hissed. She stretched on out the floor of the largest vault, closed her eyes, and thought of Vincent's *Starry Night*.

—from "Focke-Drache" by Jean Rabe

Also Available from DAW Books:

Hags, Harpies, and Other Bad Girls of Fantasy, **edited by Denise Little**
From hags and harpies to sorceresses and sirens, this volume features twenty all-new tales that prove women are far from the weaker sex—in all their alluring, magical, and monstrous roles. With stories by C.S Friedman, Rosemary Edghill, Lisa Silverthorne, Jean Rabe, and Laura Resnick.

If I Were an Evil Overlord, **edited by Martin H. Greenberg and Russell Davis**
Isn't it always more fun to be the "bad guy"? Some of fantasy's finest, such as Esther Friesner, Tanya Huff, Donald J. Bingle, David Bischoff, Fiona Patton and Dean Wesley Smith, have risen to the editors' evil challenge with stories ranging from a man given ultimate power by fortune cookie fortunes, to a tyrant's daughter bent on avenging her father's untimely demise—and by the way, rising to power herself—to a fellow who takes his cutthroat business savvy and turns his expertise to the creation of a new career as an Evil Overlord, to a youth forced to play through game level after game level to fulfill someone else's schemes for conquest. . . .

Under Cover of Darkness, edited by Julie E. Czerneda and Jana Paniccia
In our modern-day world, where rumors of conspiracies and covert organizations can spread with the speed of the Internet, it's often hard to separate truth from fiction. Down through the centuries there have been groups sworn to protect important artifacts and secrets, perhaps even exercising their power, both wordly and mystical, to guide the world's future. In this daring volume, authors such as Larry Niven, Janny Wurtz, Esther Friesner, Tanya Huff, and Russell Davis offer up fourteen stories of those unseen powers operating for their own purposes. From an unexpected ally who aids Lawrence in Arabia, to an assassin hired to target the one person he'd never want to kill, to a young woman who stumbles into an elfin war in the heart of London, to a man who steals time itself. . . .

ARMY OF THE FANTASTIC

EDITED BY
John Marco
and John Helfers

DAW BOOKS, INC.
DONALD A. WOLLHEIM, FOUNDER
375 Hudson Street, New York, NY 10014

ELIZABETH R. WOLLHEIM
SHEILA E. GILBERT
PUBLISHERS
http://www.dawbooks.com

First Printing, May 2007
1 2 3 4 5 6 7 8 9

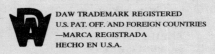

DAW TRADEMARK REGISTERED
U.S. PAT. OFF. AND FOREIGN COUNTRIES
—MARCA REGISTRADA
HECHO EN U.S.A.

PRINTED IN THE U.S.A.

ACKNOWLEDGMENTS

Introduction copyright © 2007 by John Marco

"Focke-Drache," copyright © 2007 by Jean Rabe

"Over the Top," copyright © 2007 by Rick Hautala

"The Blood of the People," copyright © 2007 by Fiona Patton

"Brothers in Arms," copyright © 2007 by Tim Waggoner

"Unnatural," copyright © 2007 by Thranx, Inc.

"Blood in the Water," copyright © 2007 by Tanya Huff

"Iowa Under Siege," copyright © 2007 by Mickey Zucker Reichert

"Teeth in the Sand," copyright © 2007 by Russell Davis

"The Twain Shall Meet," copyright © 2007 by Bill Fawcett

"Airborne," copyright © 2007 by Jody Lynn Nye

"Demon's Touch," copyright © 2007 by James Barclay

"Dispatches from the Front," copyright © 2007 by Kristine Kathryn Rusch

"Wildest Dreams," copyright © 2007 by Michael A. Stackpole

CONTENTS

INTRODUCTION

by John Marco

WHEN I WAS a boy, armies and soldiers stirred my imagination. They still do. Growing up, like most kids, I would play with my little green "army men" under the porch of our house, staging my mock battles in the dirt, crouched down on my knees while I made the strange sound effects that every battle needs to be truly authentic. My armies had guns and tanks, of course, but I wasn't constrained by logic, and it didn't matter if a giant snake crept onto the field or if a pterodactyl came swooping down upon my plastic figures. During those hours under the porch, I lived in a wonderful dreamworld where anything was possible, where armies of men and beasts fought a war that lasted almost to my teens. I'm nearly forty now, but I still love stories about dragons flying into battle or brigades of ax-wielding orcs. Give me a tale about World War II and I'm happy, but put a dragon into the mix and I'm in heaven.

We live in a world of fantastic armies. Now we can fly a stealth plane across the world unseen, just to deliver a bomb through a bedroom window. Such a thing sometimes seems magical, but of course there's no sorcery there—it's good old technology marching onward, making war efficient and lethal. Men don't fight with swords anymore or ride horses into combat. They certainly don't ride unicorns. But what if they did? What if the world was filled with magical beasts who fought alongside us? Or against us? That's the kind of thing that makes my blood race, the kind of story I want to read. Some people would call that escapism, but I'm not so sure. Stories—even fantasy stories—have a way of getting under the skin and staying with you. And maybe even teaching you something.

I didn't anticipate the chance to coedit this anthology. Like so many good things, it came to me unexpectedly. If you know me and my work, then you know the kind of books I write. Long ones. I've had only brief flirtations with short story writing, and here's why—for me, writing long books is easy. Time consuming, yes, and frustrating at times, but it's short stories that are really hard, because there isn't the same room to stretch. When I'm creating a fantasy world, I need elbow room. And yet the wonderful writers in this book all rose to that challenge, bringing their fantastical armies vividly to life. Each of them took the theme and made it their own. Their stories are unique and thought-provoking. Writers don't write short stories to get rich. They write them because they want to write them. There are things we do in life because we have to, and other things we do because we want to. Those are the best things in life.

If you're a dragon fan (and what fantasy reader isn't?), then you're going to love flying along with Max, the bomb-running, art-loving dragon of Jean Rabe's masterful "Focke Drache," set in WWII Germany. It's unlike anything I ever read before, and the perfect way to start this collection.

For action, take a ride with Jody Lynn Nye's flying centaur in "Airborne," or go to sea with Tanya Huff's selkies in "Blood in the Water."

For a more reflective look at war, check out Rick Hautala's ghostly "Over the Top," or Kristine Kathryn Rusch's poignant "Dispatches from the Front: Number Sixty-one," a story that takes an unsentimental look at war through the eyes of a weary journalist.

The thirteen stories in this collection will take you to a Hawaii you never knew existed and to magical realms that never truly have. In all of these places, the armies of the fantastic are on the march, waging wars both vast and personal. It has been a thrill for me to read these stories and now to present them to you. Thank you, writers, for your work and talent. And thank you, dear readers, for coming along for the journey.

FOCKE-DRACHE

by Jean Rabe

THE DRAGON WEIGHED nearly five tons and stretched ninety-eight feet from nose to tailtip. One hundred and twenty teeth filled her cavernous mouth, serrated and impossibly sharp to help her tear her prey apart. Her curved talons were a foot long, backed by leg muscles that would have made her as strong as a Tyrannosaurus rex, if any had still existed in the world. Her smallest scales were the size of large coins, the biggest the size of motorcycle tires—all of them a dull smoky black, the same color as her saucer-shaped eyes.

Her wings, scalloped like a bat's, had a span that measured seventy-five feet—more than double that of the Focke-Wulf Fw 190F she flew behind. She critically studied the plane as the wash from its propellers teased the barbels hanging from her jaw.

The plane's armament consisted of two 13-mm MG 131 cannons in its top decking and two 20-mm MG 151 cannons in its wing roots. It normally toted an eleven-hundred-pound bomb on the center line of its fuselage rack, but a wiring problem made that impossible today, and so the dragon maladroitly clutched the bomb in her right claw.

While the dragon admired the plane's lines and maneuverability, thinking it almost as agile as herself and possibly one of the better aircraft German engineers had produced, she remained disgusted that this particular marvel of the Luftwaffe had a short in its fuselage rack.

The bomb felt awkward and heavy in her grip, and she transferred it to her other claw. Its bulk kept her off balance, and so she had to compensate and beat her wings faster and harder, tilting herself to the right now so she could fly level.

She'd done this before, carry bombs, but that was in the previous war. The bombs were not so large then, and the planes were slower and more colorfully painted—and therefore more interesting to watch. She remembered liking the red ones the best, the ones with three wings. She'd flown with the most daring of pilots then, a part of the famed Flying Circus. The pilots had to be brave in those decades to trust their lives to the primitive contraptions of wood and canvas. The planes were sturdier now, so the pilots did not have to be so adventurous or inventive. They, like she, simply had to follow orders.

The three other Focke-Wulf Fws on this mission were miles and miles ahead of her and her wingman, long out of sight because of their incredible speed. She couldn't match these planes in that respect, but they couldn't match her size and ferocity, and none of the pilots could match her cunning. Her role in the Luftwaffe, despite the production of ever-faster planes, seemed ensured.

She wondered if her wingman in the imperfect

Focke-Wulf railed at the notion of flying at half speed to accommodate her. A part of her hoped so; she had little respect for men that had not earned at least the Knight's Cross. Not one of the pilots on this mission had such a medal. In the Great War she flew with several men who had that medal and more; some of them had even won the coveted Blue Max.

When Sturmbahnfuhrer Baron Gerhard von Rolf ordered today's mission, he asked her name. She told him "Max," as that was what she'd been going by during this war. He could not have pronounced her dragon name anyway.

Max—she liked the sound of it and what it implied, forty kills. She'd had three times that many during the previous war alone.

She cast her gaze down, finding the landscape more interesting than the smooth lines of the plane. They traveled northeast, mirroring the course of the Psyol River. It was old water, meandering in wide cuts and moving slowly, almost doubling back on itself here and there. In the setting sun the water glittered red-orange and made her think of the dying embers in a campfire. The banks looked wrinkled, like the tanned skin on an aging farmer's face or the thick bark on the white oaks that used to stretch up from this part of the country. They'd all been cut down, the precious trees, used for furniture in the holes men called homes. Pity—she remembered liking the scent the white oaks gave the air.

Now she could smell only the exhaust from the imperfect Focke-Wulf.

At the point where the river narrowed, the other Focke-Wulf Fws returned, circling wide to the sides and coming up behind her, cutting their speed to match hers. She heard them chatter on their tinny radios, her keen hearing picking through the sound of the wind against her wings and the noise of the planes' exhaust.

The others had been "flying observation," as one of the pilots reported. High and apparently unobserved, they'd found the targets and noted the absence of troops. The Russians clearly were not expecting them. It had been a brilliant move on the sturmbahnfuhrer's part to send only four planes. Less noise from the Junkers Jumo engines, less chance of them being heard. They needed surprise on their side, and according to the sturmbahnfurher, they would need each bomb to find the mark.

July 1. This day would mark the opening salvo of Operation Citadel, and Max intended it to be successful to please Sturmbahnfuhrer Baron Gerhard von Rolf and Adolf Hitler. The happier they were, the richer she would be.

Another loop in the river, and the target came into view. A factory and warehouse complex on the outskirts of a Russian village. The factory consisted of three wood-and-stone buildings, and the Focke-Wulfs would concentrate on them. Her target was the long, low warehouse sheltered by trees and rusted construction equipment.

Four bombs, four buildings.

The neglected appearance of the site would lead the casual observer to think the buildings abandoned. But spies had reported otherwise, and the dragon's keen eyes and superb sense of smell caused her to agree. There was a hint of oil in the air, and not the kind used in the Focke-Wulfs' engines. There was cordite, gasoline, and the sweat of men who had gone too long without proper baths. Through a gap in the metal roof of the warehouse she spied the cab of a truck.

She knew about this part of Russia. The villages supported several small flour mills, tobacco works, hemp-crushing mills, and distilleries. There were tanneries and soapworks, and the factories manufactured iron.

This complex had been an ironworks; she could tell by the detritus along the edges of all the buildings. It was all thoroughly rusted, meaning the place had ceased operation . . . though it likely had a new and deadly purpose as a hidden munitions factory, or a staging area filled with guns and bullets and bombs. The scents of the cordite, fuel, oil, and more fit her guess. Whatever was stored below, the Russians would surely mourn its loss.

And that would make Sturmbahnfuhrer Baron Gerhard von Rolf and Adolf Hitler very happy indeed.

She swooped lower, gliding now and angling toward her warehouse, spotting a camouflage net covering a machine-gun nest north of her target, and another one to the west. Her wingman flew cover for her, while the other three planes headed toward the "abandoned" factory buildings and began their assault. She heard the keening whistle of the first bomb dropping, followed by the second and the third, then the thuds they made that sounded almost imperceptible against the blasts that followed.

Deafening.

Hurtful to Max's ears.

She forced the pain to the back of her mind and continued her downward spiral, watching now the men streaming out of the supposedly empty warehouse beneath her and her wingman, who was laying in a field of suppressing fire to keep them away from the hidden machine guns. Secondary explosions from the three factory buildings rocked the ground and sent some men to their knees, the stored munitions igniting and sending up gouts of flame and great puffs of smoke, all of it punctuated by screaming shards of metal careening in all directions. A siren sounded, drowned out by more small explosions.

Not quite close enough yet, Max thought.

A little more.

It must be perfect.

Max made one more spiral, then released the bomb. It struck the building squarely on the roof, falling through as it detonated. She slammed her eyes shut and beat her wings faster to take her away from the explosion, flexing her claw as she went and glad to be rid of the damned bomb. As secondary explosions sounded behind her, she streaked toward the western machine-gun nest. She spied movement under the net and saw two gun mounts swivel, then noted a line of bodies on the ground nearby, courtesy of her wingman.

Inhaling, she craned her neck down and exhaled a stream of fire that incinerated the camouflage net and the men hidden underneath. She could barely hear their cries what with the flames roaring and spreading to boxes of ammunition that exploded, spitting shells in all directions. The cacophony continued as Max turned and banked, spying more men running, these heading pell-mell toward the woods. She slowed and waited until they thrashed into the brush, then she made toward them and breathed again, her furnace breath setting the trees and the men on fire.

Above and behind her came the rat-a-tat-tat of machine-gun fire from the Focke-Wulf Fws working on the other machine-gun nest. Lesser explosions continued, and the air grew thicker with fire and smoke, laced with the heavy odors of chemicals and fuels that must have been stored in the buildings.

She rose and circled the blazing complex, spying a few men below and leaving them for the Focke-Wulfs. There wasn't enough of a concentration to warrant expending her energies on another blast of fiery breath. One of the buildings had folded in upon itself so much that all the dragon saw were twisted metal beams in a blackened pile. Her target had been the largest, and muted blasts continued to sound inside it. Through the roiling gray clouds she saw bright flashes, as if from giant camera bulbs.

The Russians would surely feel this loss.

But if Hitler's plan succeeded, today's mission would be but a pinprick in the great bear's side.

Max had been at the Battle of Stalingrad, which ended in February. More than three hundred thousand German soldiers died or were captured. The Soviets had pushed toward Kharkov, but a German counterattack, in which Max played a pivotal role, stopped them.

Operation Citadel would improve morale throughout Germany, the dragon knew. It would be an opportunity for the Fuhrer to claim a clear victory in Russia and pay back the enemy for the failed Battle of Stalingrad. In three or four more days the maneuvers would begin in earnest. The Germans would cut off a nearly one-hundred-mile-long bulge in the Eastern Front between Orel and Kharkov. The village of Kursk would be a pivotal point.

It all was to have begun in May, but bickering among the sturmbahnfuhrers and generalstabsoffiziers stalled it. And so—despite months of careful preparations—things had been put off. Until now.

Max gloried in the stench that rose from the melted factory, the odors of the munitions, burned tires, and charred flesh. She drank in the hurtful sounds of screaming men, continuing explosions—so soft compared to everything else, the crackling fire in the woods, two distant sirens keening, the whoosh of the Focke-Wulf Fws as they streaked away. Her wingman flew with them, all of them soon lost from sight.

It was early in the morning of the following day before Max reached her lair. She'd flown there directly after her mission, her claws still tingling from carrying the damnable bomb for so long. She had to admit, however, that it had been an effective weapon, inflicting more destruction than even her furnacelike breath was capable of. Too, she delivered her bomb with more accuracy than the Focke-Wulf Fw pilots had, and took out a larger target. She'd been more daring than they, spiraling in closer and striking at the very center of the warehouse, demonstrating that she was more maneuverable than the planes, and more skilled than the pilots. Certainly more experienced.

She considered herself without a doubt the greatest of the dragons flying in the German Luftwaffe, the oldest and largest and wisest. Not that there were all that many dragons remaining—ten that she knew of. There'd been half again that many four years ago come September when the blessed war began. Two died to Russian tanks last winter. Two more—one of them a clutchmate—were shot down over the English Channel during the Battle of Britain. And one dragon, a young bull with no stomach for war, abandoned Europe for Greenland a few months ago. Max would never abandon Germany. She enjoyed the rush of combat, and she thrived on the danger and excitement, looking forward to each mission. More than that, she loved the spoils.

The light that spilled in through the opening in her lair highlighted one of her favorite pieces—a Cubist landscape by Albert Gleizes. Hitler had presented it to her personally during the first year of the war, and she'd had it hung in this outer chamber. He had pledged her more and more treasure with each successful mission, and he'd been true to his word, a redeeming quality in the dictator. She'd talked to him at length about art that first day, discovering he shared her passion for it. In the ensuing months, and during subsequent conversations and presentations of treasure, she'd learned Hitler was a frustrated artist, who despite his inability to master the techniques, appreciated the works of others, in particular the Old Masters.

Three years ago, when he was in Paris, he directed his Third Reich troops to collect the greatest works in the city and bring them to him and Hermann Goering. Many of the paintings and sculptures were displayed in Munich in the Nazi Museum; other pieces he kept in his villa and office and in hidden places such as the castle Neuschwanstein in the Alps near Austria. Still more he gave to Max (and, she suspected, to some of the other Luftwaffe dragons). But she liked to think he gave the best pieces to her.

Her lair was at the edge of Steinberg, Austria, in a salt mine that had been worked in the early 1300s and long since abandoned. At her request, Hitler sent engineers and contractors to build a cavernous, elaborate, wood-paneled vault deep in the mine where Max's paintings could be safely stored and displayed. She traveled down the shaft to visit the vault now, tucking her wings close to her sides so as not to touch the walls, where various pieces by lesser artists hung, including a still life Hitler had painted years ago. Her tail deftly flipped a switch that turned on the lights. Max's lair stretched so far underground that the treasure repository was invisible to Allied eyes and certainly secure from their bombs. A humidifier, the hum of which she found soothing, kept the climate perfect and constant to ensure the art's condition.

Among her collection were works by Degas, Renoir, Botticelli, Guardis, Dürer, and Van de Velde. She had an especially fine study done in 1763 by Francois Lagrénée, *Portrait of a Young Girl* by Edouard Manet, and *Moses and the Israelites* by Mihaly Munkacsy.

Some of these paintings had been looted by the Nazis from castles throughout Europe, including pieces by Guercina da Cento, Courbet, Rembrandt, Egon Schiele, and Picasso. She had drawings behind glass, including one hundred and thirty-nine from the Koenigs Collection. Centerpieces included a group of six apostles rendered by Hans Holbein the Younger, and an elegant, though small, pastoral painting titled *Les Jeunes Amourex* by Francois Boucher.

Max's treasures went beyond paintings. She had five pieces of the crown jewels of the Holy Roman Empire, and more than one hundred intricate gold sculptures that once belonged to Queen Helen, and reportedly had been excavated from the Troy ruins by Heinrich Schliemann, a noted German archaeologist.

Gold bars stacked a man tall stretched across one chamber wall. Nearby were bins filled with hundreds of thousands of English pounds—which Max had no clue what to do with, but certainly would not give up. Too, she had crates containing plates for counterfeit pounds and American dollars.

In the rearmost chamber were gold and silver crucifixes, a bin filled with diamonds and other precious stones, a silver reliquary festooned with enamels and gems, a stamp collection Hitler told her was worth more than three million gold marks, rock crystal flasks and vases, a liturgical ivory comb too small for her to pick up, and a variety of priceless baubles that supposedly had belonged to German warlords from the ninth and tenth centuries. The pinnacle of her collection, a piece presented by Hermann Goering two weeks past for her part in a raid on a hidden Russian air base, was an illustrated version of the four gospels from the ninth century, held in a silver-and-gold binding that was covered with gold filigree and gems.

These two German wars were not her first mercenary assignments. Max had dabbled in the Bohemian Revolt and fought throughout the three decades of the Thirty Years War in 1618 to 1648, which she considered far bloodier and more destructive than this present war or the one before. It was a series of small wars—not one as the name implied, starting in Germany and spreading through the rest of Europe. And though it began with the religious passions of the Reformation, fueled by Protestant and Catholic royalty, dynastic rivalries became involved and Sweden and France tried to limit the power of the German Holy Roman Empire. Max recalled a commander claiming that six million Germans died in those decades. But not a single dragon succumbed.

Max's oldest treasure came early in those battles. A sculpture from Asia Minor in the year 240, she called it "Portrait Head of a Balding Man." And though she didn't consider it overly aesthetically pleasing, she knew it to be historically significant. Her greatest prize from those years had been named "The Imperial Eagle Beaker," roughly as tall as one of her talons. Free-blown glass with gold leaf and enamel decorations, it dated to 1599 and was either Bohemian or German. Max didn't care about its origins, she just admired it. Slightly smaller stood a goblet displaying the arms of Liechtenberg, definitely Bohemian, and likely made between 1500 and 1530—Max had a keen eye for dating baubles. From about the same time came the shield of Henry II of France, likely made in 1555 from designs provided by Étienne Delaune of Paris. The shield was embossed with gold and silver, and when Nazi soldiers brought Max more bits for her collection, she usually had one of them polish the shield so she could see her scaly visage in it.

There had been other conflicts that enriched her horde, including the Franco-German War when Bismarck, the chancellor of Prussia, tried to unify all of Germany under the Prussian flag in 1870. He menaced and infuriated France, and Napoleon III declared war in response. But Napoleon was captured, and in the end, King William I of Prussia was named emperor of Germany. The next four decades were uneasy, and Max had hoped for more hostilities. But that didn't happen until the Great War.

In the Franco-German conflict, Max acquired a goblet etched with the arms of the Holy Roman Empire, crafted in 1711 and displayed in a glass case specially built just to house it. She didn't risk touching it because it was so small and fragile. But she admired it every time she came to the lair. Another goblet—Max had so many she found it difficult to recall the histories of each—bore engravings to commemorate the wedding of Frederick II and Princess Christina in 1733.

She wondered what treasure would be added for her performance during yesterday's bombing mission? She'd told Sturmbahnfuhrer Baron Gerhard von Rolf that there was room for more paintings on the walls and that one room of the vault remained entirely empty. Max hinted about another Rembrandt or a van Gogh, the latter of which was absent from her collection. She had difficulty forcing down her anticipation for the reward, imagining all the possibilities and dwelling again on the notion of a van Gogh, or perhaps a Monet, as she enjoyed the French Impressionists. But she already had a half-dozen Monets.

"A van Gogh," she purred.

Whatever Goering or Hitler had set aside, it wouldn't arrive for days, certainly not until she was finished with her next mission and would make her request for some jeweled Russian eggs.

Warring on the side of the Germans in the last war and, in particular, throughout this one had done much to enrich her hoard. Indeed, during the previous four centuries she lived in the Alps, she'd only been able to loot merchants and traveling knights. Her take from those four hundred years was a pittance compared to her haul from the wars.

"May the wars go on forever," she hissed. She stretched on out the floor of the largest vault, closed her eyes, and thought of Vincent's *Starry Night*.

Three days later Max flew northeast again, following the Psyol River, this time with a bomb clutched in each of her front claws. The weight of both pained her, and she'd been forced to stop twice, carefully setting the bombs down to rest her wings and talons. Two other dragons were with her, both younger and slightly smaller, each charged with carrying one bomb. They were different than the bombs designed for the Focke-Wulf Fws. Though smaller, they were practically as heavy, and her two wingmates complained about them also.

"Hateful things, these bombs." The smallest dragon, an inky black with shiny yellow eyes, sat back on his haunches and nudged his with a talon.

Max shuddered, her eyes daggers aimed at him. "Be

careful," she hissed, "lest we never reach our target and be blown to pieces because of your carelessness."

The dragon let out a sigh, the sound of a dry wind rustling dead leaves. "Such a heavy thing," he said. "Good that I carry only one. Sorry you must carry two."

The third dragon silently regarded them. She was ·also black but with a smattering of gray scales on her shoulders and along the veining in her left wing. She stretched like a cat, picked up the bomb in her right claw, and nodded skyward.

Max flexed her talons and picked up her bombs. "Time to go."

The air was chill and achingly thin as high as they climbed shortly before dawn. It was misting, and though it was summer, the rain hit Max like slivers of angry ice. Her hide was tough, though, and it only bothered her eyes. The younger dragons flew slightly beneath and behind her, observing Drache-protocol, as Max considered it. She'd prodded them last night about their hoards and rewards, bringing the matter up as casual conversation.

The results were acceptable.

The younger dragons had received herds of goats and cattle for their efforts, plus occasional crates of gold bars. Nothing of the Old Masters and no archaeological relics. They wouldn't lie to her, she being their superior, and they'd not asked her about her own hoard. She wouldn't have lied to them if they had asked. Max understood deception, especially because it was a part of the war. But she felt no need to practice it—deception was a trait that belonged to men.

Still, there were seven other dragons in the Luftwaffe, two as old as she. They wouldn't settle for meat that they could acquire easily on their own. Perhaps one of them had her coveted van Gogh. She would look into the matter later.

The clouds were thick and heavy, and Max and her wingmen skimmed through the lowest layer as they mirrored the course of the winding old river. This high, sound carried well, and Max picked out the harsh buzz of fighters and bombers, too distant to detect the scent of their fuel. She caught sight of them long minutes later when she passed over the factory complex she'd helped bomb a few days ago.

It was a squad of Messerschmitts flying cover for nearly two-dozen Focke-Wulf Fw bombers. She recognized two of the latter planes from the previous run.

"We join these planes," Max told her wingmates.

The dragons tucked their wings into their sides, and angled themselves like arrows, plummeting toward a city on a fork of the Psyol. The Focke-Wulfs got there first, dropping their bombs on the buildings, seemingly without discrimination. A school near a factory was struck, and across from that a church was leveled. Children ran in terror, mingling with a scattering of soldiers in the street, all of them cut down by more bombs and by the machine guns of the Messerschmitts. The factory was in flames in a heartbeat, and sirens were erupting everywhere. More bombs struck a second factory, and beyond it a railway station. Max remembered from the briefing that the train was one of the important targets. The tracks buckled and looked like insect legs reaching crookedly up from the ground.

There were tanks on a wide street on the other side of the burning school. Max thought this odd, given that Operation Citadel was to be a surprise. Why would a city be so guarded? There were no reports of Russian troops in this area. Was the German intelligence faulty? The bombing a few days ago would have alerted them . . . but they would not have had time to bring such support here. Eight tanks, all of them craning their turrets skyward, began firing. Suddenly Russian troops poured out of several buildings and onto the streets, all of them running to the southwest, loaded down with packs, rifles, and machine guns.

"I do not understand—" the youngest dragon howled to Max. "This was to be undefended. In the briefing—"

Max snarled, cutting off the rest of his words. She continued her plunge, but angled now toward the tanks, rather than the hospital and a third factory to the north, which had been the dragons' original targets. The booming fire of the tanks was hurtful, as were the sounds of the bombs that the Focke-Wulfs continued dropping. In the distance, she heard what she thought was thunder, but realized after a moment it was battle sounds from over the rise, where more German forces fought. Operation Citadel was extensive, certainly not confined to this city or the land that spread away from the Psyol River basin.

A shrill whistle sounded, and she risked a glance over her shoulder, seeing a Focke-Wulf careening down, struck by a shell from one of the tanks.

Closer, she told herself.

Just a little closer.

She passed above one tank, and then another, dropping one of her bombs on the third tank in the line, and streaking over the rest of them, coming up and around in a tight bank. The bomb found its mark, crippling the tank she struck and the ones on either end. Smoke billowed out of the hatches.

The youngest dragon copied her, though he wasn't as precise in his efforts. His bomb struck the street behind a tank, creating a crater the tank slid into, effectively stopping it. Men spilled out of the hatch, only to be killed by a spray of bullets from a passing Messerschmitt. The young dragon continued following Max, jaws working and obviously asking her for direction. But she couldn't hear him above the machine-gun fire of the Messerschmitts and the "booms" sounding from the four remaining tanks.

Smoke billowed from bombed buildings and two downed Focke-Wulfs, and the scent of charred wood and flesh wafted up from the village. Overhead, lightning flashed, echoed by soft thunder.

Russian troops! More of them! Max gasped. And all those tanks! How could the Russians have known the Germans were coming here this day? It was fortunate the Russians had no dragons on their side. Of the enemy, only the British employed dragons, three of them that Max knew of, relegated to defending London and its environs. Save for the young bull who fled to Greenland, dragons were found only in Europe and China in this age, and the ones in China were worshipped and never asked to participate in wars.

The Russian soldiers looked like ants scurrying down the street to meet the charge of the German ground forces. So many of them, they flowed between the buildings in such numbers she couldn't see the cobblestones beneath their feet. She dipped toward them as she swung back to the tanks, spreading her wings wide and exhaling her fire breath, catching more than a dozen soldiers who died too quickly to scream. She heard the young dragon breathe behind her, a sense of pride swelling that he mimicked her.

A moment more and she flew over the tanks again, blessedly releasing the other bomb, flexing her sore talons, and destroying two more tanks. Two remained, and she trusted her other Drache wingman would manage those. She looked for the other female, seeing only the young male behind her.

"Where?" Max shouted to the male. "Where is J'shalathar're?"

He looked as confused as she, then his mouth gaped wide in surprise.

Max followed his gaze as she banked beyond the tanks and the troops, turning south toward the approaching German ground forces. The third dragon stretched broken and twisted between two squat buildings, a hole in her chest from a tank round. Black blood pulsed from it, and though J'shalathar're still lived, she wouldn't for long. Her fixed eyes looked skyward, seeing nothing, Max was certain.

Nine dragons left in the Luftwaffe.

Roaring in rage, Max turned back to the remaining tanks. The two turned down a street, rolling over debris from a bombed building, the tank in front raising its turret and swiveling to get a bead on Max.

She inhaled sharply and dove on the lead tank, releasing her furnace breath and watching it engulf her target. She breathed again on the second one, pulsing her fire down the turret and into the air slits, roasting the men inside. She heard their screams, brief and horrible, heard the young dragon behind her breathing on the tanks, too, then asking what to do next. The bombs gone, the dragons could not effectively go after the hospital and the third factory.

"What?" he shouted to her. "What now?"

Max didn't answer him, just flapped her wings harder to take her higher. She felt machine-gun bullets striking her stomach. They bounced off her scales, feeling like fly bites to a man. She was furious over the death of the female dragon. Not because there was now one fewer dragon in the world . . . when there were so few dragons remaining to begin with . . . but because the dragon had been in her "squad" and was her responsibility. The dragon's death was a black mark on Max's otherwise impeccable record.

Max did not mourn J'shalathar're, nor feel the slightest measure of sadness. Neither did Max mourn the deaths of the Russians in the tanks or on the street, or the ones beneath her now that she incinerated with another blast of her breath. She didn't mourn the Germans in the downed planes, or the ones dying on the ground to the approaching Soviet troops. She didn't mourn the innocent children. Grief did not exist for her and her kind. Dragons and men were either "here" or "not here," dead or living, no emotion attached to either state. Max was not capable of mourning.

She was capable of desire, however, and had a strong desire for success and victory. She understood loss—but only in the material sense of gaining or losing territory or treasure or a wingman that would have helped contribute to her success. She also understood loyalty, and she'd sworn hers to Germany many decades past. In exchange for her service, she was paid in gold and art—wealth she understood above all else.

She thought of van Gogh as she arced over the city toward the oncoming German troops. She would fly cover for them. In the distance she spotted fusiliers, heavy infantry units, entering the city from the south, east, and west roads. They were *fahrtruppen*, fast troops, those on foot running hard, trucks speeding up the road between their lines. She heard orders barked, sounding like a whisper given the machine guns, rifles, and the thrumming of an antiaircraft gun from somewhere behind her. She picked through the noise and the droning sound of the Messerschmitts and Focke-Wulfs, trying to hear just what the commander was saying. A dozen *kettenkrads*, tracked motorcycles, raced behind the trucks, adding to the dissonance and keeping her from hearing any distinct words.

She passed over a light truck in the lead that had a *granatwerfer* mounted on the right side of the hood. The window was knocked out on the passenger side, and a soldier leaned through the open space, fitting a grenade into the mortar's tube, then firing it. He reached for another. She didn't have to look to know he was launching them at the Russian soldiers flowing down the street and to the edge of the city. Midway over the mass of German forces, Max turned again, the young male flying at her side now. Wingtip to wingtip, their massive bodies cast a shadow over the soldiers and trucks, making grayer a countryside already gloomy from thick clouds that cut the sun.

"*Aufklärung?*" the young dragon called to Max.

"*Nein.* We are not flying reconnaissance. We are Focke-Drache," she replied, the strength of her words clearly heard above the racket from the trucks and guns. "Like the Focke-Wulf bombers, we are ground support now."

The young male nodded his understanding, and the pair escorted the German force into the city.

At the edge of the first residential district, Max opened her maw and reduced the first line of Russians setting up a border defense to ashes. She listened to the sounds of popping flesh as her wingman roasted the ones just behind. She heard cheers from the Germans streaming below and behind her, then all she made out was the harsh spitting sounds of machine guns, the whine of mortar shells, and the explosions from the Focke-Wulfs' bombs.

The minutes stretched into an hour as the fighting continued. It shouldn't have been like this, Max knew from the briefing. It should have been strategic bombing, followed by the German soldiers capturing key points in the city and shooting anyone who resisted. They'd expected some Russian soldiers, but not hundreds, not tanks, not antiaircraft guns mounted on buildings at the corners of the city. They'd not expected to lose any bombers, or Messerschmitts . . . three of which were down due to the antiaircraft. They certainly hadn't expected to lose a dragon.

They hadn't expected any of this.

Max strained to pick up any conversations below but could discern only the occasional shouts and the never-ending screams. She breathed and breathed until there were no more flames in her belly, and she landed atop the hospital to rest. A moment later she tore at its roof with her impossibly sharp talons, slicing through pebbled tar paper and wood and bricks until she spied people through the hole she'd made and began grabbing and squeezing them.

All around her, the city burned. No more bombs fell; Max knew the Focke-Wulf Fws had dropped everything they had and were now relying on their machine guns. People still screamed, Germans and Russians, interspersed with sounds of breaking glass and falling brickwork, mortars blasting, and the squeals of tires. The intensity of the sounds continued to pain Max, and she was not able to shove it all to the back of her mind. So she ground her massive teeth together in response to the agony, and tore at the hospital more ferociously. She would have continued in her grisly work until the hospital was leveled, but the noise above her grew louder, and she looked up to see what was adding to her misery.

"Yaks." She spit the word out like it was a rancid cow.

Flying in tight formation overhead were twenty Yakovlev fighters, accompanied by a dozen Lavotchkin-type planes bent on chasing the Germans from the sky.

Max roared to her wingmate and pushed off the hospital, knocking over what was left of one of its walls in the process and burying people running in the street. She focused on her heart and her stomach, stoking the natural furnace inside her and searching for some spark to fuel her fiery breath.

She'd flown against these fighters once before. They were not as well engineered as the Messerschmitts or the Focke-Wulfs; they lacked the speed and armament, though they were maneuverable. She looked for the older Yaks, as she remembered that these were made of wood. Quickly spotting one, she made for it, not bothering to tell her wingmate which targets were better.

The Yaks were elegant in their simplicity. To her eye, the wings looked almost stubby compared to the Messerschmitts', and the colors were much drabber— mud brown with bands and splotches of black and dull yellow, as if a colorblind man with no sense of artistry had been conscripted to paint them. Far worse than the bland colors of the Focke-Wulfs.

Because the Yaks had slowed when they approached the city to engage the Messerschmitts and Focke-Wulfs, Max had little trouble catching one. Her talons sunk into its wooden wings, shredding the horrid paint scheme. With a great cracking sound, she ripped the wings off and hovered, clutching them, allowing herself a moment to soak up the minor victory as the broken Yak fell onto a mass of Russian soldiers below. Then she dropped the wings and shot toward the next Russian plane. This, too, was one of the older models, the wood splintering before the pilot could react. She craned her neck over the cockpit and gave him a toothy grin, noting the terror on his face as she tore off a wing and then pushed off the craft, sending it down to explode against the cobblestones.

She felt rain falling hard now, and felt the spit of machine-gun fire against her hide—one of the Yakovlev fighters headed straight at her, firing as it went. These guns had more power than the ones held by the ground troops, and so some of the bullets penetrated her scales. No serious damage, but they stung and put her in a foul mood and helped power her furnace. She opened her maw as wide as possible and breathed at the plane. The fire rushed out to engulf it, steam billowing from contact with the rain, then smoke roiling in all directions as the Yak exploded.

She shot straight up at that moment, avoiding the pieces of metal and wood that spun away, and nearly colliding with a pair of Lavotchkin fighters. Lashing out with her tail, she struck a Lavotchkin's wing and set it off balance, sending it into the fighter next to it. Higher she went, the rain cleansing her eyes of smoke and grit. She opened her mouth and let it cool her tongue and throat. Still higher, until the sounds below were softer, then she leveled off and glided, relishing the cool summer breeze and the rain. Her chest ached from where the bullets pierced her. She could tell they hadn't gone deep, but knew they would forever fester and remind her of this day.

One more glance skyward to drink in a bit more rain, then she looked down and took in the battle, pleased to see her wingmate climbing toward her and away from the planes. The sky over the city was full of aircraft, the paint schemes and wing designs making it easy for Max to tell the sides apart. The Messer-schmitts were the fastest and were spitting bullets everywhere, taking down one Yak after the next. But the Yaks outnumbered the Germans and were not without their own victories.

Max couldn't see just how many planes on either side had crashed. But she'd been responsible for five planes; bringing her total in this war to thirty-eight. Two more, and she'd have the treasured number the pilots aimed for during the previous war. The Great War, she recalled them naming it. The war when the planes were more colorful and the pilots more daring. When they gave out the medal she coveted and should have received.

No matter, she'd get her forty kills and then some today, and she'd demand a van Gogh and a dozen Russian jeweled eggs for her participation. She picked two Yaks on the outskirts of the city, on the edge of the aerial battle where there would be less chance she'd be peppered with bullets. A nod to her wing-mate, and they dove toward the targets, catching sight of another Russian squadron streaking in from the north.

She stretched her talons forward and slammed into one, latched onto the wings, and let her great weight knock it down. She watched the pilot struggle with the controls, yanking back on the stick with all his strength. When the tallest of the city's buildings loomed into view, she released the plane, and the Yak plummeted into what was left of the hospital.

Then Max stoked her furnace breath and went after Russian soldiers on the ground. Time to support the German *panzergrenadier*, the armored infantry that was fighting its way into the heart of the city.

She and her wingmate gave the battle everything,

fighting until their wings ached and threatened to keep them out of the sky. There was no more fire inside her by the time the retreat was sounded, and though she'd never backed down from a battle before, she had to this time.

In the days to follow she bombed villages and military targets, flew with Focke-Wulfs and Messerschmitts along the Psyol River and deeper into Russia. Always, they were driven back. The sound of the retreat cry was more painful to her than all the bombs and machine-gun fire.

"*Ruckzug!*" she heard each day. "Retreat!"

She learned in the months following Operation Citadel that because the Germans had delayed in launching the offensive, the Russians had months to prepare, gleaning bits of information from spies. The Russians laid more than four hundred thousand land mines behind the front line, and dug more than five thousand kilometers of trenches. They gathered a massive army, with more than a million men, more than three thousand tanks, more than twenty thousand pieces of artillery. And more than two thousand planes.

The Germans had put so much effort into this strike that Max almost felt sad, almost felt the twinge of grief she knew men often expressed during wartime.

By fall only a half-dozen dragons remained in the German Luftwaffe. Max continued to fly with various squadrons, always carrying bombs now, and always following orders to the best of her ability. She understood loyalty.

She'd retreat to her lair from time to time, admiring her paintings, including a van Gogh, which was hung from a wall in the previously-empty vault. In a case beneath it were four jeweled Russian eggs and a Blue

Max medal. It had been Goering's, and he'd presented it to her.

By the following spring, she knew there'd be no more treasure coming to her lair during whatever remained of this war. Hitler and his officers were spending their efforts on planning, not presenting the dragons gifts.

She stretched out in her deepest vault, admiring the brushstrokes on the van Gogh.

But there would be another war, and she would add to her art collection then. Men could never get along for any extended period of time. Religion, wealth, land . . . they'd find some reason to start fighting. And she would offer her services to help one side, hopefully the German side—for a price.

She would wait. She had patience, and she had centuries left to live.

OVER THE TOP

by Rick Hautala

IF ANYONE THOUGHT about it at all, people visiting the *Aisne-Marne* Cemetery in *Bois-de-Belleau*, France, that day in late April would have assumed the older man and the little girl were father and daughter. No one ever would have believed the truth.

The girl's name was Sally Edwards. She lived in the small town of North Platte, Nebraska, where her mother was a schoolteacher and her father was a truck driver. She was twelve years old, but—because she was so short and frail—she looked no more than ten. Unlike the few other children who were visiting the cemetery and running all around, Sally didn't have an overabundance of youthful energy. She walked quietly with a slow, almost stately pace, her head slightly bowed.

The man's name was Alan Edwards. He was tall and slender with thinning light brown hair, and he walked with a vigor that belied his true age. The most striking thing about him was his eyes, which shone like twin chips of blue ice. The tears that gathered in

27

them from time to time as he surveyed the cemetery further enhanced the distant, dreamy effect.

It was late in the afternoon. A gentle breeze carried the damp, mulchy smell of growing things and made the leaves flutter like thousands of tiny green hands, waving a greeting. The distant sound of birdsong rang from the forest behind the chapel. Slanting bars of golden sunlight angled across the well-manicured lawn, lighting the arcing rows of white crosses with a near-supernatural yellow glow. The blue shadows of the crosses stretched fully twenty feet and more across the dark, emerald-green grass.

"It's hard to imagine now, it's so pretty, but there was a battle here a long time ago," Alan said, his voice as distant and dreamy as the look in his eyes.

He reached out and took Sally by the hand as they walked out behind the chapel. For someone only twelve years old, Sally showed a remarkable level of maturity. Maybe it was because of what she'd had to deal with already in her short life. She didn't fidget as Alan, whom she called "Grampy," stood there for a long time, staring at the woods that bordered the cemetery.

"American soldiers who fought here and who sleep in unknown graves."

Alan flinched as he repeated the inscription on the memorial. He had visited here enough times over the years so every word on every plaque was seared into his soul, but like a litany, he repeated these words softly to himself every time he was here.

Until this trip, he had always come alone. This was the first time he had brought Sally or anyone else with him. He had his reasons for being here with her, and they may have accounted for the tears in his eyes as much if not more than the memorial to the American

Marines and Army soldiers who had died here more than ninety years ago.

"Can we go back to the hotel soon?" Sally asked as she cast a worried glance at the darkening sky above the trees. "I'm kinda afraid of the dark." When she looked up at Alan and saw the tears gathering in his eyes, she asked, "Why are you crying, Grampy?"

"It's just . . ." Alan sniffed as he wiped away his tears with the cuff of his jacket. Even though the day had been warm, the evening brought a chill. He shivered. "A lot of men—on both sides—died here needlessly."

"Is that why you're so sad?"

"Partly, yes," he answered.

"Did you know anyone who died here?"

For a long time, Alan didn't answer her as he scanned the darkening woods. The shadows under the trees were as black as a wash of ink, but even so, he thought he could see figures flitting about in the deepest shadows. With twilight, maybe they would come out.

"Yes, I did," he replied. "Back then, it wasn't beautiful like this. A lot of the trees were blasted by artillery shells, stripped of their leaves and branches, just stumps, and there were craters and trenches and foxholes and barbed wire . . . death and destruction everywhere you looked."

"And fighting," Sally said with a far-off luster in her eyes. "Why were they fighting, Grampy?"

Alan started to answer but caught himself and sighed. "For the same reason men have always fought, Sweetie . . . because some of them had what the others wanted."

Sally nodded and turned to follow his gaze out past the curving rows of crosses to the trees.

"It was terrible . . . absolutely terrible," Alan whispered with a shudder. "Truly, it was hell on earth."

He was grateful Sally couldn't see what was in his mind. As he stared across the cemetery to the woods, he superimposed over the view the churned-up mud, the chaos, the carnage that had surrounded him and the men in his unit of the AEF, the Sixth Brigade of the US Marines. He could still feel and hear and smell the war—the sticky mud, the reeking bodies that had been blown apart and left to rot, the smoke and exhaust that burned eyes and throats and lungs.

"It's hard to imagine this is even the same place," he said, but as he looked over the treetops to the slumped hill in the distance, he knew *exactly* where he was.

Back then, during the battle, that hill had been called Hill 193. Only much later, once the war was over and his wounds healed completely, did he learn the hill's real name—Belleau Torcy Hill. It was less than a mile away from the forest, and even with the sun setting and Sally's desire to get back to their hotel, he knew they had to go there.

Today.

"Grampy . . . ?" Sally said, her voice edged with real fear as she pointed off to one side. "Is there—? I thought I saw something in the woods over there." She sucked in a shallow breath, which clicked audibly in her throat. The glow of the setting sun colored her face, giving her skin an uncharacteristically healthy glow. "Are there ghosts here?"

"No, Sweetie. There are no ghosts. You don't have anything to worry about. Trust me."

Sally nodded, but when Alan looked in the direction she had indicated, he also saw something flitting in and out of sight. However, he knew what—or who—

it was. They were the reason he and Sally had come here.

"We called it going 'over the top,'" Alan said in a voice heavy with melancholy. Sally's grip on his hand tightened, but she was captivated by his mood and remained silent. Just like the words on the memorials, what had happened here in the summer of 1918 was seared into his heart and mind.

"We'd line up in the trenches, the stinking, muddy water halfway up to our knees, soaking our feet. The dead were lying all around us, and when the commander blew his whistle, we would clamber up over the top and run straight into the enemy machine-gun fire. Once we were in the forest, we couldn't see where they were until they started cutting us down with machine guns."

Staring blankly at the forest as he spoke, it didn't strike him at all odd that the darker it got, the keener his eyesight became. The figures moving about in the woods appeared more clear now. He wanted to tell Sally more about them and why they were here, but he wasn't ready to. Not yet. She had to understand about the war and what had happened to him, first.

As dusk came, the last few stragglers were leaving the cemetery. The gates closed at five o'clock, but Alan was prepared. He had parked the rental car far down the road, and he and Sally had walked up to the cemetery late in the afternoon.

"There were explosions everywhere . . . bullets whistling over our heads . . . men groaning as they fell, and screaming and crying as they died." He shivered as he looked at Sally, tears blurring his vision. "We were trying to get to that hill over there." He pointed toward Hill 193. "But I never made it." Kneeling down in front of her, he held Sally by both arms and looked deeply into her eyes. "Here in the woods is where I died."

For a moment, Sally's eyes widened with shock. A tiny exhalation escaped her as she stared back at him, and an expression of worry washed over her face. Alan knew she loved him as much as he loved her, and he knew she had to understand that she could trust him with her life because that was exactly what he was going to demand.

"The fighting lasted for three full weeks," he went on. "It was the first time, really, that Americans experienced the kind of trench warfare the French and English had been fighting for four years." He took a deep breath to steady his nerves. "It was a terrible slaughter on both sides, and as we pushed toward that hill, a bullet hit me. Here."

Reaching up to his neck, he hooked the collar of his shirt with his forefinger and pulled it down to reveal a thick tangle of white scar tissue on his throat. It looked like a miniature range of snow-covered mountains that wound from behind his left ear to just below his Adam's apple.

"What do you mean you *died*, Grampy? You're still alive."

She looked at him, her eyes glistening wetly in the gathering darkness. He hated himself for scaring her like this, but she had to know. She had to understand.

"No, Sweetie," he said, lowering his voice even though he knew those figures lurking in the woods could hear him clearly, no matter how softly he spoke. "I died that day more than ninety years ago. And I would have stayed dead if not for . . . them."

Saying that, he nodded toward the woods where the figures appeared to be moving slowly forward, becoming more discernible in the gathering twilight. Their silhouettes stood out in sharp relief against the black backdrop of the forest, but even so, it was difficult to focus on any one figure for more than a second or two. They flitted and vanished out of sight, only to reappear as soon as he looked away.

"They're here to help . . . I hope," Alan said, and he gave Sally a bracing shake. "Come with me."

With that, he stood up and, hand in hand, they walked down the gentle slope toward the woods.

"Pardonnez moi, monsieur," a voice suddenly called out from behind.

Alan looked over his shoulder and saw the cemetery guide standing in the doorway at the back of the chapel. He was waving his arm at them.

"We are closing soon," he called, his voice thick with his French accent.

Alan turned away and started walking more briskly toward the fringe of forest.

"Monseiur, arretez, s'il vous plait!"

"Grampy. He sounds mad. Will we get arrested?" Sally asked.

But Alan didn't answer her or the guide as he strode across the neatly trimmed grass toward the woods and the figures waiting for them there.

"I never knew what hit me," he said breathlessly as he practically dragged Sally along with him. Memories of what had happened that day were coming back with frightening intensity. "One second I was running. The next— Nothing . . . Darkness . . . And terrible pain. I have a vague memory of looking up at the sky. It was thick with gun smoke and shrapnel, and I saw flying things that looked like dragons and griffins, not airplanes. I thought I must be imagining it. When I tried to call out for a medic, my throat felt like it was on fire. The only sound I could make was a thick bubbling sound whenever I took a breath. And then . . . then I saw . . . someone."

They were halfway between the chapel and the forest now when Alan stopped short. Kneeling down again, he shuddered as he hugged Sally tightly to his chest and sobbed.

"I was sure I was dead," he said. "I knew I must be because even though I could see our own soldiers and medics rushing around the field, checking the dead and wounded, this person leaning over me—if it even *was* a person—certainly wasn't a soldier or medic . . . It was—"

His hand was shaking as he pointed to the woods where now more than a dozen figures were flitting back and forth in the shadows. He never got a good look at any one of them, but he could feel them watching both of them.

"It was one of . . . *them.*"

Sally's eyes widened as she looked from her grampy to the woods.

"I thought the one leaning over me was an angel who'd come to carry me off to heaven," Alan continued. "He had long, flowing white hair that framed his pale face, and his eyes . . . his eyes were large ovals, and the light in them was . . . was indescribable. I rolled my head to one side and saw several others, moving about the battlefield as if . . . as if they were medics, checking on the dead and wounded. And then this one picked me up. It was like my body didn't weigh a thing. I was as light as a feather to him. And he carried me off the battlefield."

"Where did he take you?" Sally asked, her eyes wide with equal amounts of fascination and fear.

Alan was silent for a moment as he stared into the distance. He wasn't sure how many of them were there in the woods now because he was remembering what he had seen that day more than ninety years ago.

"He took me into the woods. As we went, I saw more and more of them . . . hundreds, and then thousands—an entire army. Their weapons gleamed even in the deepest shadows under the trees, and they had banners and pennants, but I was in too much pain to see or think clearly."

He paused for a moment and looked at the figures in the darkening woods. Resting one hand on her shoulder, he looked down at Sally. Her gaze darted back and forth as she scanned the trees, and then looked back at him.

"There was an army of them, moving through the forest," he said. "They didn't look like they were heading off to war. I had the impression they were coming back from a battle of their own, but I couldn't tell if they had won or lost. Our own soldiers were running right through their ranks as if they couldn't even see them or me. I was the only one who could see them." Alan paused as an icy shiver ran up his back. "But you can see them now, can't you, Sweetie?"

Biting her lower lip and making a funny sound in the back of her throat, Sally nodded. She reached up and grabbed his hand. Her grip was cold in his, so he gently rubbed her hand to warm it.

"Their hair and clothes look all silvery and misty," Sally said. She was silent for a moment as she craned her head forward, studying the elusive figures. "But you're right. They're not ghosts, and they're not scary."

"No, they're not," Alan said breathlessly as a strong sense of relief washed over him. "And they wouldn't let you see them if they weren't willing to help."

Alan's knees popped as he stood up and started walking again toward the forest with Sally close beside him.

"They have different names," he said, "depending on which country—which *human* country they're in. The English have my favorite name for them. They call them 'the Fair Folk.'"

"Do you mean fairies?" Sally said.

"Yes. That's another name for them—fairies and elves, and some people call the land they live in the 'Land of Faery.' There are so many names for them, and they live in so many places, but most cultures agree that where they live is called 'under the hill.' That's where they took me to be healed. Under the hill."

"So you didn't really *die*," Sally said. "You were just hurt real bad." Sally looked at Alan with a mixture of confusion and fear and . . . was that hope he saw in her eyes? He certainly hoped so.

"They were checking all of the men who had been wounded and killed that day, going from person to person, and then they picked me up and carried me off with them." His voice caught, and the memory filled him with deep melancholy. "They took me under the hill where they healed me."

"And you—?" Sally started to say, but they were close to the forest now, less than ten feet away, and Alan drew to a halt. He cast a quick glance over his shoulder, expecting to see the guide rushing down the hill to escort them to the exit, but the man was nowhere to be seen. Alan was sure the fair folk were using their "glamour" to hide him and Sally as well as themselves from the man.

"If that's true," Sally said, "if this all happened almost a hundred years ago, that means you must be—"

"I was born in 1886, in St. Louis, Missouri," Alan said, "so that makes me one hundred and nineteen years old."

"Are you kidding?" Sally asked, giving him a sly, skeptical look. "No one lives that long."

"Well, you see . . . when I left them, when I came out from under the hill after they healed me, I realized I had been there for many, many years."

"Why did they save you and not all those other men who were hurt?" Sally asked. Her face was as pale as paper in the gathering gloom. Her eyes shone like two sparkling stars.

"I don't know," Alan said. "I asked them many times, but I never got a straight answer from any of them. They don't really explain themselves. It had something to do with what they called my 'birthright,' but no one ever explained that to me. As far as I could tell, I had been there only one night . . . maybe a day and a night . . . so you can imagine my surprise when I got out and discovered that forty years had gone by in the real world. The incredible thing was, I hadn't aged more than a day."

"Like Rip van Winkle," Sally said, "except he was asleep for only twenty years. And he got all old and stuff."

"That's right. Like Rip van Winkle. I don't really know how else to explain it. I guess it's . . . magic."

Alan and Sally were silent as they stared at the figures in the woods who seemed to have stopped moving, but even so, Alan found it difficult to look at any one of them for very long. In the blink of an eye, a figure would fade out of sight and then reappear someplace else. Their eyes glowed in the deepening gloom. Their hair, like fine-spun silver threads, wafted like gossamer on the slightest breeze. After a long silence, one of the figures raised a hand as if in greeting and beckoned Alan and Sally forward.

Sally held back, her hand squeezing her grampy's hand tightly.

"Is that why you've come back here?" she asked, her voice laced with fear. "Is it time for you to die, and you're going with them?"

Alan looked at her, emotion catching in his throat making it impossible to speak.

"I don't want you to die, Grampy. I love you," she said.

Tears spilled down her cheeks, glistening like quicksilver in the darkness as she clung to him. Her pale face, floating in the deepening darkness like a tiny moon, seemed almost as translucent and insubstantial as the faces of the figures in the woods.

"No. I'm not going to die," Alan said, gently touching her cheek with his fingertips and feeling the coolness of her skin. "Not for a very long time, anyway, but I wanted you to—"

His heart was breaking as he considered what he was about to tell her, but he had no choice. Pulling her close to him, he was terribly conscious of her frail, trembling body.

"You know the . . . the blood disease you have . . ." he said, almost choking on every word.

"Uh-huh," Sally said with a sharp nod. In an instant, her eyes seemed to cloud up, and her expression froze.

"And you know what the doctors have done . . . or tried to do."

The tears in his eyes made everything appear dim and hazy. Even the tiniest hint of light from the night sky shattered into a dazzling rainbow of brilliant colors. The forest was absolutely silent with not even a hint of breeze or birdsong.

"They're all trying to make me get better," Sally

said, but even as she said it, Alan could hear the note of resignation in her voice. She knew—even if not consciously—that there was no hope left.

"The doctors have done everything they can," Alan said. "And now I want to see if these . . . if my friends can help you."

Sally looked at him with a startled expression on her face.

"You mean you want *me* to go with them?"

Alan nodded slowly, and as he did so, he took her hand as if to guide her forward into the woods. A soft, murmuring sound that sounded vaguely like voices came from the darkness.

"How long will I be gone?" Sally asked, her eyes widening with fear and confusion.

"It will only be for one night," Alan said mildly.

"But I don't want to leave you, Grampy," she said, crying now, her whole body trembling. "What if it's like when you went under the hill? What if I'm away for forty years?"

"You'll get better," Alan said, and even as he said it, he tried his best to believe he was telling her the truth. "No matter how long you're with them, it's better than . . . better than . . ." but he stopped himself, unable to finish the thought.

Sally looked from her grampy to the motionless figures in the woods. The low sound of voices continued as one of the figures closest to them shifted forward and held a frail, white hand out to them . . . to *her*.

Sally looked up at Alan, tears streaming down her face.

"But if I go . . . if I stay with them for forty years . . . you won't live that long. You won't be here when I come back."

The desperate pleading in her voice pierced his

heart. It tore him up to think that he was looking at his precious great-great-granddaughter for the last time.

"Why can't you come with me, Grampy?" she wailed. "You said they're your friends. You come, too. We'll both be gone together."

"I'm sorry, Sweetie," Alan said, shaking his head, "but it just doesn't work that way. I didn't know until just now if they'd even let you go with them, but I see now that they will."

"What about Mommy and Daddy . . . and Charlie, my goldfish? What if they're all gone, too, when I come back?"

"It can't be helped," Alan said. "Last week, the doctors told your folks and me that there was nothing more they could do. If you don't go now, you won't live more than six months."

"But I'd rather live six months with you than forty years or the whole rest of my life without you, Grampy! *Please!* . . . *Please* don't make me *go!*"

Even as she said this, the figure closest to them stepped out of the forest and reached out to take Sally's hand. The instant their hands touched, she fell silent. The fear on her face melted away as she turned and looked at the figure.

Before leaving, the figure regarded Alan with a look of unfathomable sadness and compassion in his silvery eyes. Without thinking, Alan stood up straight, squared his shoulders, and stiffened his arm as he gave a snappy military salute. Like a soldier from one war recognizing a soldier from another, the figure clenched his right hand into a fist, raised it to his chest, and then solemnly bowed his head.

"You'll wait for me, won't you?" Sally called out as she stared moving off into the woods, still holding onto the hand of the mysterious figure.

"You know what I've always said, Sweetie. I'm going to live forever or else die trying."

"Please," Sally called out. "Please wait for me, Grampy. I'll come back."

With every word, her voice grew fainter and fainter until it was lost beneath the low sighing of the wind in the leaves. Numbed by sorrow, Alan stood where he was and sobbed, but he also was filled with a fresh sense of hope as the shadows blended into the darkness that now embraced the forest.

He had to believe that the fair folk who had tended him that day on the Belleau Woods battlefield in 1918 would save his great-great-granddaughter's life now. And he hoped that, when she emerged from under the hill, no matter if it was days or months or even forty years from now, it would be a better world to which she returned. In spite of whatever wars, seen and unseen, were being fought, it would have to be a better world because she would be in it.

THE BLOOD OF THE PEOPLE

by Fiona Patton

THE NIGHT WAS dark despite the half moon's struggle to light the sky from behind a ragged bank of cloud. Crouched on a high, ragged spur of lava rock on the westernmost point of Kuai Island, Kaloa Apone-pi'i stared down at the still waters of Kupua Bay. Far below, he could just make out the legion of pale, shimmering creatures—lapu, the restless, hungry spirits of the dead—rising and falling as inexorably as the tide as they pressed against the fine latticework of olena vine the people had woven that day to hold them beneath the waves. By dawn, much of it would be shredded by the lapu's constant worrying, but it would still be enough to keep most of them in check. Those that broke free were the quarry of Kaloa and his fellow Kahuna-moha'i, the warrior-priests trained to fight the lapu and protect the people of Kuai.

A single wisp of cloud broke free and, as one, the lapu turned their blank faces toward the shrouded moon. Heart pounding in his chest, Kaloa fought the urge to pull back into the relative safety of the hibiscus trees behind him. He knew the lapu could not see him so far up, but they could still feel his living spirit—his mana—and they hungered for it. They always hungered for it.

The scars across his face, both old and new, burned as he remembered his father's words the day he had become Kahuna-moha'i.

"The strongest of all mana is housed in the blood made sacred as it flows through each region of the body in turn. The arms and hands are sacred to the day; the legs and feet to the night; arms for working, legs for running. The chest and groin are sacred to the future and the face is sacred to the past, to the ancestors who see themselves in the features of their descendants. When shed in ritual, it is that blood that draws and binds the lapu."

Touching one finger to the newest wound across his cheek, Kaloa turned his gaze to the moon, watching it as the lapu watched it, and knowing as they did that, as soon as it lost its battle against the clouds, it would be time to begin the dead's battle against the living, the battle called by the blood of their descendants.

Deep within his mind, he could sense the others who waited with him: pragmatic Kama Moana, crouched on a steep, rocky cliff on the southernmost spit of land that jutted into the lapu's ocean territory. It was the farthest and most difficult path to take, yet she never faltered. It was rumored that she could see in the dark, but every time he asked her, she would only smile at him, her pale eyes wide and luminescent, as enigmatic as the sharks her family claimed as ancestors.

His younger brother, Mali Apone-pi'i, restless and

unpredictable, waited to the north. Kaloa could almost see him crouched in a stand of wauke trees, tossing a handful of kukui nuts into the air over and over, and reading the ever-changing pattern of omens in their movements to pass the time. Mali, strong and talented, but born too soon and taking too much of their mother's mana to power his own first breath. Some on Kuai believed that his birth signaled the coming of the final days when the lapu would grow strong enough to steal the spirits of their children as they were born. Their father, brokenhearted by their mother's death, had believed it, too, and had thrown himself from the place where Mali now waited each night.

Their leader and teacher, Hinohi Maka'aina of the owl family, the oldest of the island's Kahuna-moha'i, waited to the east, tending the trap they had readied for the lapu, sprinkling the walls of a deep cavern with water and earth mixed with the blood of the people.

And finally, to the west, Kaloa himself, head of the royal mo'o family of Pi'i-ka-lalau who had fought the lapu for the lives of Kuai, century after century. Generations of warrior-chieftains standing as he now stood, staring down at those who had made their own stand against the lapu and, one by one, had joined their ranks in death. If the lapu were not defeated by the time of his own death, he would join them, too, waiting to steal the lives of his own children in his turn.

A light, mist-filled rain began to fall, and he raised his face to the droplets, tasting the morning in their midst. It would be cool and clear tomorrow. A good time for harvesting the ripening kalo plants. Life went on even in the midst of battle. Even in the midst of seemingly insurmountable death. Life went on. But for how long?

The story of their struggle against their own ancestors was an ancient one told each year during Kaula—the Days of Storms—when the people gathered in the Pu'uhonua—the highest cave on Kuai—for protection against the rains that could wash them into the sea. Kaloa could remember sitting, wrapped in kapa blankets, safe in his mother's arms, while his father and the other Kahuna-moha'i stood guard at the cave entrance, barring the lapu's passage with ki leaf nets tied with kea limu, the rare white seaweed. Seated by the central fire, his scarred face a mask of lines that grew deeper with each passing year, Hinohi would tell the story once again.

"Hundreds of generations ago," he would begin, "the people of Kuai worshiped the Mo'o God Pi'i-ka-lalau, whose breath kept the waters of the ocean fresh and clean. Pi'i-ka-lalau protected the people, fathering many of the royal line who ruled in his name. But one dark day Pi'i-ka-lalau was attacked by his greatest enemy, his own brother, Pi'i-ua-awa. They fought for over a century, churning up the bottom of the sea and sending terrible storms toward each other, but—finally—Pi'i-ka-lalau was defeated and Pi'i-ua-awa devoured his heart, entrapping his spirit in an underwater spring.

"Pi'i-ua-awa then demanded the worship of his brother's people, promising them great power and wealth in return, but Pi'i-ka-lalau's spirit sent their Chieftain, Queen Kiha Apone-pi'i, a vision warning her that his brother ate the flesh of his own children, and so the people refused. In his rage, Pi'i-ua-awa visited a terrible curse upon them. Climbing upon his brother's half-eaten body, he breathed a great poisonous breath into the ocean toward Kuai. The waters turned a pale, murky green that withered the sea plants, and the people began to starve. But Pi'i-ka-lalau sent a new vision to Queen Kiha which taught her to throw the morning's pure surf mixed with the blood of her line onto the waves to sweeten the waters. And so the plants returned to life and health.

"Then Pi'i-ua-awa breathed into the ocean once again, and it turned a sickly yellow. It repelled the fish, and the people starved once more. But Pi'i-ka-lalau sent yet another vision to Queen Kiha teaching her to throw handfuls of alae salt and blood upon the waves, and once again the waters freshened and the fish returned.

"And so Pi'i-ua-awa breathed upon the ocean one last time, and a line of milky white foam crept in to poison the most sacred of all waters, those below the leinas where the dead leaped into the sea to begin their journey to the underworld. The dead became trapped much as Pi'i-ka-lalau was trapped, and this time it was they who starved and their starvation drove them mad. They came upon land to wrest the mana they needed from the living and so became the lapu, the terrible spirits of Pi'i-ua-awa's curse. And as the people joined their ancestors in death, one by one, they became part of Pi'i-ua-awa's army of lapu, driven to destroy their own children in his service.

"No one knows why Pi'i-ka-lalau's spirit finally failed the people then. Some believe that his spirit was also poisoned by his brother's final breath and became lapu as well. Others fear it might have been destroyed. But whatever may have become of their god, the people of Kuai refused to despair. When no vision came, Queen Kiha turned to her Kahuna—the priests of craft and magic—for new weapons to fight this terrible army. While the Kahuna-akaku searched in dream and in trance for Pi'i-ua-awa's imprisoned spirit, the Kahuna-pili taught the people to weave the nets that held the lapu under the waves, and the Kahuna-la'au ground the mixture of olena and kea limu that protected their doorways. The Kahuna-kilo read the moon signs and star signs that determined when the lapu would attack, and finally the Kahuna-moha'i—those who sacrifice—went out each night to lure the lapu into the trap that the Kahuna-pohaku had carved in the deepest caverns below our feet.

"And so we fight and search to this day. It is said that if Pi'i-ka-lalau can finally break free to overcome his brother the curse will be lifted, but it is also said that the fight will only go on so long as all the children of Kuai are born alive. If ever a child is born who joins the lapu before its very first breath, so will all the children of Kuai be born from that moment on, and then all will be lost. So we must always fight and search and hope until one or the other takes place."

Hinohi would fall silent then, and the people would hold their children tight, listening for the high, keening cries of the lapu as they tore at the blood-strengthened wards which held the rest of their numbers imprisoned below. Kaloa would close his eyes, imagining the dark, dripping caverns—underwater by this time—burning with the pale, milky-white glow of Pi'i-ua-awa's poisonous breath; the same milky-white glow which illuminated the waters below him now, night after night.

High above, the net of clouds finally passed completely over the moon and a fireball soared into the star-lit sky from the Kahuna-kilo's watchtower at the mouth of the Pu'uhonua. He felt Mali and Kama ready themselves. Standing, he stepped to the very edge of the cliff and held his arms wide. His living mana surrounded him in a pale, silvery light, the wind shifted, and suddenly he heard the faintest keening on the breeze. The lapu had caught his scent.

Far below, on the deserted black-sand beach, he saw small, dark figures trailing olena vines rise up from the glowering surf. They stood a moment, looking up at him, and he could almost see their cold, shimmering eyes staring into his. The figures glided silently into the trees beyond and Kaloa waited for the space of a heartbeat, before touching the protecting ki leaf tied at his throat, then turning to plunge into the forest himself.

He moved swiftly through the trees, not running, not yet, because that would bring the lapu down on him that much faster, but quickly enough. The path led him deeper into the forest, then began to descend in a series of winding turns. Behind him, he could feel the lapu moving inexorably closer. The air around him turned cold, and the scars on his face began to burn as the image of the ghostly creatures gliding through the trees without disturbing so much as a wauke leaf caused the fear to pump the mana into his veins until his entire body sizzled with it. It made him feel both light-headed and invincible, but Hinohi had warned him many times against giving in to either sensation.

"Never lose your fear of them, but also never let that fear control your actions. The lapu can steal your life in an instant, and one hesitation, one misstep, one rash act of suicidal bravery is all it takes, and your strength will become theirs to use against your people. So run, Kaloa, only run."

Passing the first of the hanging ipu'olelo gourds that told him he was nearing the trap, he quickened his pace and, as the leaves of the hibiscus trees began to tremble, he ran.

A bone-chilling breeze swept over him, dragging at

his limbs like a heavy undertow, mist rose up to obscure his vision, a hideous smell made him gag, and then he saw them: a dozen ghostly figures flickering in and out of sight, their misty features twisted beyond recognition. They reached out their clutching fingers toward him. Their mouths drawn open in a ghastly rictus from the madness brought on by their hunger and fear sent him almost flying into the clearing below the caverns. As he broke from the trees, the others burst into view.

Mali had half a dozen lapu snapping and screaming at his heels. The scars across his own face stood out like angry white snakes, but, as his eyes tracked to Kaloa, he veered deliberately to one side to allow his chief to take the lead. Kama did the same and, together, the three of them raced for a narrow cavern, glowing with fiery symbols at the edge of the clearing. The entrance was tight, barely wide enough for them to pass through, but they hurled themselves inside without pause. Kaloa felt the jagged rock scrape across his biceps, felt a freezing cold wind pass through his hair, and then he was inside the dripping darkness and whirling about to keep the lapu in sight. Mali and Kama rocked to a halt beside him. For the space of a single heartbeat he saw Hinohi raise his arms, then the trap was sprung, and the lapu were suddenly outlined in a terrible red fire. They began to scream, adding their voices to those already trapped inside.

Mali slapped his hands over his ears, hearing as always the tormented voices of their parents all around him. Kama caught him up in her arms, holding him tightly against her chest as Hinohi began to throw handfuls of blood-caked earth against the walls, binding the lapu tighter and tighter while Kaloa stood in plain view to keep them from breaking off the attack until the trap was completely sealed. The lapu fought and screamed, their vaporous limbs writhing like vines, desperate to escape, but, as the clouds covered the moon once more, Hinohi made one final gesture and the struggling lapu slammed into the walls at the back of the cavern, their suddenly corporeal forms hardening into solid rock.

In the now silent cavern, the four Kahuna-moha'i sank to the floor, exhausted, while outside, all that could be heard was the distant lapping of the waves against the shore and a single night bird signaling the all clear.

The entire village was waiting for them when they returned, standing as silent and grim as the lapu on the starlit beach. As they passed the ipu'olelo gourds that warded the central common, Kaloa's wife, Nalani, stepped forward, a haunted expression in her dark eyes.

"Lilia has joined the lapu, husband," she said woodenly. "Her birthing troubles began just after you left for the leinas. Her child . . ." she paused, closing her eyes briefly before continuing, "was born dead."

A terrible rushing noise like the sound of the surf crashing against the rocks at Kau-ula roared in on him. Kaloa felt himself sway as everything about him seemed suddenly far away. He barely heard Nalani speak again.

"And I am also with child."

Dawn found him standing on the highest rocks above the Pu'uhonua, staring out at the sunlit waters of Kupua Bay. No movement betrayed the presence of the lapu, but he knew they were there, hovering in uneasy sleep just below the surface. Waiting for the times that were now upon them. Lifting his gaze to the eastern horizon, he glared into the rising sun until it blazed across his vision.

After Nalani's pronouncement no one had spoken again for a long time, the wind feathering through the wauke trees the only sound to be heard. Finally, Mali had sunk to his knees, his eyes wide and staring.

"It's just as Papi said, then," he whispered, speaking the words they were all thinking. "The final days of Kuai."

Murmuring broke out across the common, and Kaloa found himself clenching and unclenching his fists in helpless rage. The image of the lapu rising from the waves filled his mind with despair and would not be banished. Generations of his family had fought the lapu; fought and prayed and sacrificed their lives with the hope that one day Pi'i-ka-lalau would escape his confinement and break his brother's curse upon the people. Generation after generation lost now with no more to follow. Shaking his head slowly back and forth like a wounded boar, he squeezed his eyes tightly shut, but the image of the lapu stood out like a beacon. Finally he opened his eyes once more, staring around him as if seeing his people for the first time.

"No," he said. "No."

Nalani stepped forward. "Husband . . ." she began, but he waved her away.

"No. This will not be the final days of Kuai. I will not have it so."

"Lilia's child . . ."

"Will be mourned."

"But . . ."

"No." Taking her in his arms, he held her as tightly

as his mother had held him in the cavern of the Pu'u-honua. "Our child will be born alive," he said. "We will break the curse."

All eyes turned to him then, and he could feel a new spark of hope begin to grow within them once more.

"How?" Hinohi asked.

"We will find Pi'i-ka-lalau; we will free him, we will follow him into battle, and we will kill Pi'i-ua-awa."

"Again, my chief, how?"

Staring at the ipu'olelo gourds swaying backward and forward in the wind, Kaloa bared his teeth in a grimace reminiscent of the lapu.

"With the blood of the people."

Now, turning his gaze to the west, he looked down at the hive of activity on the beach below him.

Once released, his plan had spewed from his lips like a freshwater spring. Loe, the oldest of the Kahuna-pili, was the first to understand, but the others had quickly followed. Now they directed the people who had once woven the great nets of olena vine to a new labor while the Kahuna-kalai—the boat builders—took their hatchets into the forests in search of the tallest and straightest koa trees on the island and the Kahuna-la'au began to harvest the kea limu in far greater numbers. Every single person had a task to perform—down to the smallest children who collected handfuls of unripened lele fruit with which Hinohi would weaken the bindings on the lapu.

After this aspect of Kaloa's plan had come to light, Mali had sought out his brother in private, his expression concerned.

"You mean to cease the trapping, then?" he asked.

Kaloa nodded. "Everyone is to have a hand in this,"

he said. "Even the lapu. It will return them to themselves and bring them peace at last."

Mali's face twisted in pain. "I pray that you're right, for their sake as much as for ours, brother, but it will be very dangerous to let them walk the island unchecked. It will strengthen them."

"Good. We need them strong."

"But the people?"

"The people will move to the Pu'uhonua."

"For how long?"

Kaloa's eyes tracked to where Nalani and the other Kahuna-ana were busy preparing Lilia and her child for burial. "Six months," he answered. "In six months Kuai's new chief will be born. We have that long to ensure the future."

"In six months it will be Kau-ula."

"Yes," Kaloa agreed. "One way or another."

The months passed swiftly. Kaloa's plan had given the people a new sense of purpose, and those not actively engaged in harvesting or fishing labored to bring it into being with an almost feverish intensity. By the time the skies darkened with the approach of Kau-ula, fifteen great double-hulled war canoes lined the western shore. Each one carried a full complement of figures woven from wauke branches and olena vines, decorated with feathers, shells, and flowers, and holding broad-bladed paddles and long, sharp-edge spears in their hands. As Kaloa moved among them, he marveled at how skillfully they'd been wrought before laying a hand lovingly on the small, one-man outrigger canoe he'd fashioned for himself. When Kau-ula came, they would be ready.

The first Day of Storms dawned cold and wet, the waves of Kupua Bay already driving up the beach to slap against the kapa ropes that held the war canoes in place. Standing ankle-deep in water, Mali and Kama argued furiously with Kaloa.

"We should come with you!" the younger man insisted, shouting to be heard over the rising wind.

Kaloa shook his head emphatically. "We've already been through this! The Kahuna-moha'i must stay behind to protect the people!"

"You are Kahuna-moha'i!" Kama shouted in reply, but broke off when Hinohi placed his hand on her shoulder.

"No," he answered. "Today, he is Kaloa Aponepi'i, Chieftain of Kuai, and descendant of the great mo'o god Pi'i-ka-lalau, and tonight he will lead the people against Pi'i-ua-awa and break the curse." Turning, he bowed to Kaloa. "Come, my chief, it is time to bring the final days into being."

Kaloa nodded curtly. Turning, he gestured and, one by one, the people came forward, each one carrying an ipu'olelo gourd filled with blood-caked earth strung on a piece of woven pili grass. As they hung them about the necks of the figures in the canoes, the fresh wounds across their cheeks glowed with a silvery light. And after Hinohi had finally bullied Mali and Kama into following suit only Nalani remained. Her normally fluid movements made awkward by the extent of her pregnancy, she came forward to hold her gourd out to Kaloa.

"The blood of our child flows through my body," she said. "Mingled with your own, it will protect you and bring you back to us."

When Kaloa made to speak, she placed two fingers against his lips. "You will come back to us, my husband," she said, a martial light gleaming in her eyes, "or you will not go forth at all."

Accepting the gourd, he smiled gently. "I will come back to you," he promised.

That night, crouched on the high, ragged spur of lava rock on the westernmost point of the island, Kaloa pressed the gourd against his chest as he felt for the others who waited with him: Mali and Kama standing guard before the doorway of the Pu'uhonua, Hinohi crouched before the central fire beginning the ancient story of Pi'i-ua-awa, Nalani, the birthing pains that would see their child born to the people of Kuai, or to the lapu, already begun, and finally the people and the lapu themselves, each as desperate as the other for his success this night.

Peering over the edge of the lava spur, he blinked the driving rain from his eyes as he stared down at the raging waters of Kupua Bay. By now the flooding would have reached the lower caverns, bringing the lapu together once again on either side of Hinohi's binding wards. This year, however, they would find those wards weakened to the point of breaking. The discovery would fuel their hunger and, with the added strength gained in the last six months, it would not be long before they tore the wards apart like so many olena vines.

As the storm grew in strength, Kaloa stood and moved out to the very brink of the leina. The air around him crackled with unreleased mana and he found himself holding his breath. He made himself breathe out slowly and deliberately. It would not be long now.

When it happened, the explosion of power that erupted out from the cavern hit him like a tidal wave. It threw him into the trees, filling his mouth with the taste of blood as his teeth snapped together, clipping his tongue. All around him, the shrieking of the lapu rose up, blotting out the sounds of sea and wind as they came together in a raging mass of hunger. He felt rather than saw the Kahuna-kilo's fireball shoot into the sky and, struggling to his feet, he pulled his knife, raising it high into the air.

"The blood of the people is sacred to the ancestors who see themselves in the features of their descendants!" he shouted into the storm. "When shed in ritual, it draws and binds the lapu! *All* the lapu!"

With a single motion he brought his knife slashing down across his cheek, then catching up a fingerful of blood-caked earth from the gourd about his neck, he smeared it into the wound.

The response was immediate. A freezing-cold mist shot up to wrap about his legs like pili grass, the overpowering smell of death sucked the breath from his lungs, and the lapu, stronger and more frightening than they'd ever been before, came streaking toward him like a swarm of ethereal insects, lips pulled back from their teeth in a parody of hideous laughter, their screaming filling him with a mind-numbing terror that threatened to send him tumbling into madness.

Dropping all pretense of bravery, he turned and fled.

Hurtling down the path, heedless of the wind and rain, he raced for the western shore. Sharp-edged leaves and branches scratched against his face and arms, and low lying vines entangled his legs, causing him to stumble over and over again, but he ran on. The lapu were close behind him, their clawed hands catching at his hair and clothes, their icy-cold breath freezing on the back of his neck. A single scraping touch across his cheek where the blood still flowed made him cry out and then he erupted from the trees onto the black-sand beach beyond. The line of war canoes loomed up before him and he put on an extra burst of speed as he plunged between their ranks.

The lapu came flying after him, and then with a new explosion of power, they slammed into the trap the people had set for them. The wards housed within the ipu'o-lelo gourds strained but held as the blood of the people bound the lapu into their new form, infusing the olena vine figures with a ghastly parody of life as they struggled to break free. The force of their battle snapped the kapa lines holding the war canoes in place and shot them forward into the waves.

Kaloa didn't bother to look back. Leaping for the outrigger, he broke its own kapa line and thrust it into the water. The waves fought him, bucking and jerking the small craft out from under his control, but he bore down, and when he finally dared to turn his head, he saw the armada of lapu sweeping down on him, vine-wrapped hands wielding the paddles with an eerie precision he'd never thought possible. They were already gaining on him and, as they broke free of Kupua Bay, the waves rose up in a fresh torrent, driving them even closer. His own craft nearly went under, but at the last moment the outrigger righted itself and drove on.

The sky grew black, the howling of the wind and rain merging with the screaming of the lapu close behind him. It seemed as if he'd fled from them forever, rising up and slamming down into the waves for his entire life, their desperate hunger for his living spirit dragging at the paddle in his hands, crying out to him to give in to them and rest. He felt the mana leaching from his fingers, but just as the paddle began to slip away, he sensed another's hunger rise up across the storm, swatting the lapu's desire away like so many flies. As great and terrible as a volcanic eruption and as familiar as his own breath, it sucked him forward with the power of a massive whirlpool. The outrigger shot into its swirling depths, dragging the armada of lapu behind and, as the ipu'olelo gourds shattered under the force of it, the entrapped spirit of Pi'i-ka-lalau exploded from his prison, released by the blood of his people. Pi'i-ua-awa rose up at once to meet him and the violence of their impact sent Kaloa hurtling through the air, over waves and cliffs and trees to crash down onto the sodden ground before the lapu's empty cavern. His own gourd shattered beneath him, the shards driving into his chest. For a moment all he could see and hear was the fury of Pi'i-ka-lalau and his brother, and then everything went quiet and he saw Nalani.

Her birthing pains had reached their climax, her face and body taut and strained, but, as he drew closer, her eyes snapped open to stare into his. They reached for each other, and as their fingers touched, he felt her living mana and that of their child pulsing with one strong and steady beat beneath him. Slowly, very slowly, the spirits of mother and baby separated, then as their newborn son began to cry, Nalani released him. Kaloa watched the Kahuna-ho'ohanau wash the boy with water taken from the morning's pure, clean surf, then turned as a new sensation drew him inexorably away from his family.

He ran.

Passing his crumpled body without so much as a glance, he raced up the path toward the western leina, then leaped out into the air. For a single instant he was flying, and then he hit the still-raging surf without a ripple. Far below in the inky darkness he saw the shimmering silver line of Pi'i-ka-lalau's children, most still clutching the ghostly remains of their ipu'olelo gourds, as they made their way toward the underworld. Taking up his own gourd still glowing faintly with the mana of his wife and son, he joined his ancestors at last.

BROTHERS IN ARMS

by Tim Waggoner

"**D**O YOU YIELD?"

The voice echoed from within a hollow stone throat, then passed through an unmoving stone mouth. It was a human voice, but rough and without easily discernible emotion—at least to those unused to dealing with a Stoneguard Warrior. But to the being lying helpless on the ground—chin sheared away, cracks and fissures spiderwebbed across the rocky surface of his chest, arms and legs snapped off like so much kindling—the voice communicated a wealth of emotion. For he, too, was one of the Stoneguard.

The voice repeated the question, stressing each word individually this time.

"Do . . . you . . . yield?"

The being lying on the ground didn't answer. His throat had been crushed and was incapable of producing sound. The defeated warrior felt no pain from his numerous injuries, severe as they were. If he had been flesh and blood, he would be dead by now.

The Stoneguard Warrior stepped forward until he

straddled the dismembered torso of his fallen opponent. He lifted gray, thick-fingered stone hands above a head wrought to resemble a skull with jutting demon horns. "Answer me, my brother, or my voice will be the last sound you ever hear in this world." Within the hollow eye sockets of the stone skull burned twin pinpoints of crimson flame.

The fallen one tried to point to his throat, hoping to indicate that he was currently incapable of communicating by speech. But then he remembered: he'd lost both his arms.

"Have it your way." The Stoneguard Warrior interlaced his fingers, tightened his grip, and brought his joined hands down toward his brother's stone chest.

The horse-drawn wagon juddered across the uneven ground, making Coran's kidneys ache. He drew back on the reins to slow the team, but it didn't help. If anything, the slower pace made the wagon shake even worse.

"I can see why this place is called the Treeless Plain," said the woman sitting next to Coran. "The ground here is so hard and lumpy, it's a wonder that even scrub grass grows."

Coran didn't turn to look at his companion. "Is this your first time here?"

"Yes." A pause. "In truth, this is my first journey since I obtained the rank of Underwizard."

"Ah." Through they'd been traveling together for the better part of two weeks, this was the first time Elleka had admitted how inexperienced she was. Coran had suspected as much, given her age. He doubted she'd reached her twentieth summer yet. She'd have been far too young to come here before. The last time Coran himself had been here was seven years ago. Elleka would've been thirteen then, perhaps younger. Still an acolyte studying in the Halls of Arcane Wisdom, and not a soldier in the front lines ˙ of battle.

Elleka was a petite woman with blonde hair arranged in a complex pattern of braids favored by both male and female mages. She was garbed in a simple brown traveler's cloak of coarse woven cloth, the hood drawn up to conceal her braids. She looked human enough, save for her amber-colored eyes and a sprinkling of silver scales around her eyes. On most mages, such scales looked like snakeskin or perhaps some disease of the flesh. But on Elleka they helped accentuate her large yellow eyes. She was beautiful as well as young, but Coran felt no attraction toward her. Not only were mages and ordinary humans forbidden to mate, the fact that she wasn't quite human made her seem less like a woman to him and more like some kind of alien creature.

You're a fine one to talk, Coran Yrggson. You're not altogether human yourself.

Coran glanced sideways at Elleka. More human than *her,* he thought.

Mages—both Overwizards and Underwizards— were the servants of the Magelords themselves, and went out into the world to do their particular lord's bidding. Though he didn't know it for a fact, Coran had heard it rumored that the last ritual a person went through before assuming the mantle of Wizard was to be touched by a Magelord. This touch imbued them with a small portion of the Magelord's inhuman essence, thereby trebling their magical strength. But as far as Coran was concerned, giving up part of one's humanity was a high price to pay for power.

And what of you? What price did you pay for your power?

Coran thought of the cargo they carried in their covered wagon—the only cargo besides food and water for themselves and their horses—and shuddered.

Coran wasn't that much older than Elleka, only ten years or so, but he *felt* much older. He had short brown hair and a beard to match, and while his features were on the plain side, he was not considered unhandsome by women. Perhaps it had something do with the weary sorrow that perpetually clouded his gaze. It made women pity him, want to take care of him, mother him, heal him. He sometimes took advantage of such women, but most of the time he ignored their interest. Some wounds were just too deep to heal.

Like Elleka, Coran wore a traveler's cloak, though he kept his hood down. The two of them were supposed to look like husband and wife merchants on a trading trip from the Southern Kingdom to the Northern. Thus, their simple clothes, plain covered wagon, and unimpressive horses. It all seemed a bit *too* calculated to Coran, and he wondered if Balasi would be fooled. He supposed it didn't matter if Balasi fell for the ruse or not. Just so long as his brother came out of hiding to investigate.

Coran gazed out across the hard, uneven gray plain toward the Daggerfrost Mountains to the north. The tallest of the grim, forbidding gray peaks were capped with snow, and Coran thought it was a good thing that winter was still several months away, or they'd never have made it this far. When he'd last been here, this plain had been covered with thousands of tents, wagons, horses, cookfires, and—of course—soldiers, all of them waiting in uneasy truce while their superiors attempted to negotiate a final and lasting peace. Emphasis on *attempted*.

Coran was surprised at how peaceful the land

looked now. There was no sign of the blood that had been spilled on this ground, of the thousands of men and women from both kingdoms that had breathed their last here. This should be a place where the ghosts of the angry dead marched in legion, seeking redress for the foolish way their lives had been wasted. Seeking vengeance against Coran, for if he hadn't failed to stop Balasi seven years ago, they all would still be alive today. Now that he was here, he expected to feel the full weight of his guilt settle upon him, bear him to the ground, and crush him beneath its awful weight. But other than a distant muted sadness, he felt only the breeze whispering across the rocky plain and the gentle warmth of the sun on his face. He looked up at the sky, half-expecting to see the ghostly images of a thousand dead warriors gazing down accusingly at him. But he saw only blue sky dotted with gray-white clouds, and the mountain range rising up on the horizon. It seemed almost as if the world had moved on, forgotten the devastating battle that had once taken place here. But Diran hadn't forgotten. And neither, it seemed, had Balasi.

"What does it feel like?" Elleka asked. "To return here after all these years?"

The sounds of the wagon wheels creaking as they turned on their axles, and the hooves of the four quarter horses clopping on the hard ground as they pulled their load without complaint . . . these sounds fell away, to be replaced in Coran's mind by the clang of metal as sword struck sword, the twang of bowstrings being released, the thunder of hooves as cavalry advanced, the high-pitched tones of signal horns being sounded, and of course, the omnipresent screams of the wounded and dying.

Coran turned and gave his companion a weary smile. "What makes you think I ever truly left?"

Elleka cleared her throat. "Yes, well . . . I was, of course, too young to have fought in the war, but I can imagine what it must have been like."

Coran stared off into the distance for some time before replying.

"No, you can't."

"Aren't they beautiful?"

"I think they're hideous."

Balasi laughed and shook his head. "Perhaps they are at that, little brother, but then they have been crafted for warfare, have they not?"

Coran had to allow that Balasi had a point, though he'd never admit it to his brother. The two of them stood inside a large tent that had been pitched on the grasslands of Moora, in the heart of the Southern Kingdom. Within the tent a small glowstone hung from a strip of leather tied to one of the supports. The glowstone's light was dim and feeble; instead of dispelling the gloom within the tent, it seemed to accentuate it, deepen it, gather it in dark pools of inky blackness that seemed somehow more than the mere absence of light. It seemed somehow almost alive.

The shadows created by the glowstone's weak light made the two large figures lying on the wooden dais before them seem even more sinister. They were taller than a human, ten feet at least and perhaps a bit more. They were broad-shouldered and thick-limbed, with rippling muscles formed of stone and blunt fingers that looked more like the head of a hammer than digits. They wore no clothes, but since they had been created to only approximate human form, they had no genitals to conceal for modesty's sake, and no matter the weather, how dry, wet, hot or cold it became, they wouldn't feel it. But worst of all—at least as far as Coran was concerned—were their faces. Hairless, wrought to resemble demonic skulls with empty eye sockets, fanged teeth, and ram's horns jutting forth from the temples. They were dark gray from toe to horntip, the color of the specially enchanted stone from which they had been made. Neither golem was outfitted with a weapon, for each was a weapon in its own right. Carved into the chest of each golem was the symbol of the Magelord Marsyas: an upraised fist within a circle of flame.

"Just think," Balasi said. "Come tomorrow, when the battle is joined, we will animate these two golems. They will serve us as suits of armor and even as weapons." Balasi stepped up to the dais and reached out to touch one of the statue's blunt-fingered hands. "Can you imagine how much force this hand can strike with?"

Balasi's own hand could strike with quite a bit of force, as Coran had learned growing up with him. He was shorter than Coran, but his shoulders were broader, his chest wider, and while he appeared stocky, Coran knew from experience that his brother's meat was all muscle. Balasi's hair had the same brown shade as Coran's, but he wore it longer, and his beard was thicker and fuller. Though they were both adults, Coran thought that of the two of them it was Balasi who most looked like a man, while Coran still looked too much like a boy.

"I don't have to imagine," Coran said. "I've had the same training as you, don't forget." But, unlike Balasi, who was as enthused as a child soon to receive a long-desired plaything, Coran wasn't excited by the thought of the destruction the golems were capable of causing. He was afraid of it. Afraid of being in control of such power—or of being controlled by it.

"There's no reason for worry, brother," Balasi said. "The golems will do only what we command them to."

Before Coran could stop his older brother, Balasi leaped up onto the dais and rolled over onto one of the golems. As soon as his flesh came into contact with the stone, both forms blurred and merged, and then Balasi was gone. A moment passed, and the golem Balasi had entered sat up. Its demon-skull head swiveled on a neck made from rock to look at Coran. Tiny crimson fires burned deep within the skull's dark eye hollows, a sign that Balasi's spirit was inside the golem, granting it life and mobility. Together, man and golem had become a Stoneguard Warrior.

The golem's right hand shot forth and stone fingers fastened around Coran's neck. At first the grip was so tight that Coran couldn't breathe, but then Balasi opened his hand and released his younger brother.

The crimson fires within the golem's sockets flickered and danced with merriment. "See?" The voice that echoed from the demon-skull's open mouth was low and grating, and without any hint of emotion. "Nothing to worry about. I'm in total control."

Coran forced a smile as he rubbed his sore neck muscles.

That's precisely what I'm afraid of, he thought.

"Are you certain we're on the correct route?" Elleka asked for the third time that morning. "You'd think there would be signs that this was a path frequented by trading caravans."

Coran suppressed a sigh. The young Underwizard had a tendency to be a bit of a worrier. Once, he'd been that way himself, but instead of making him more tolerant of her fussing, it actually made him more impatient with her.

"The hard ground, remember? The land is almost solid rock here. While it's not easy going, it's the most direct route between the Two Kingdoms. Skirts westward around the foothills of the mountains. Trust me, this is the right place."

They continued on in silence for a time before Coran spoke again.

"There was no reason to bring the golem. I won't use it." *Can't use it,* he amended mentally, but he didn't know Elleka well enough to tell her that. He doubted he'd ever know anyone that well. "I made that clear to the Overwizards before I agreed to accompany you on this journey."

Despite the enchantments that allowed the wagon to bear the golem's weight without collapsing—and which helped lighten the load for the horses pulling it—the going had been slow these last few weeks, and it seemed even slower today. Coran wondered if the enchantments were beginning to weaken and, if so, if Elleka could refresh them.

"My masters hoped you might change your mind during the trip," Elleka said. "But even if you don't, hopefully it won't matter. Perhaps you'll be able to make your brother see reason without resorting to violence. If not, there are . . . other resources available to us."

"Chief among them your skill at spellcraft," Coran said.

Elleka hesitated before replying. "My magical abilities might prove useful, yes. My masters—"

"Don't play games with me. I know the Overwizards gave you orders to stop Balasi by whatever means necessary. I'm one of those means, but if I fail, you'll surely use your magic against him. What will you do? Cast a spell that will force the separation of his human and golem bodies? Or will you simply cause his stone form to crumble away to nothing, thereby ensuring he'll no longer be a threat to anyone in the future?"

The Underwizard didn't answer, but then she didn't need to. Coran was confident that he'd guessed the truth.

"Look at it this way," Elleka said, tone neutral but expression grim. "If you can convince your brother to surrender voluntarily, then nothing need happen to him."

"That," Coran said, "will no doubt prove to be the biggest *if* of my life." *And Balasi's, too.*

Half an hour later they came upon a scattered collection of splintered wood. Amidst the debris were rotting corpses that had been picked over by scavengers. Some of the bodies were human, and some were equine. Some had been crushed or pounded to a pulp, and it was impossible to say what species they belonged to.

Coran reined the horses to a stop, then pulled the wooden lever to set the wagon's brake. While he did so, Elleka stared at the corpses splayed upon the ground.

"Did . . . did Balasi . . . ?"

"I expect so," Coran said in a toneless voice. "After all, that's why we've come here, isn't it?" He climbed down from the driver's seat and scanned their surroundings for any indication that Balasi might be lying in wait somewhere nearby. But even though they were but a half mile at most from the mountain known as Firstpoint, the ground here—while corrugated and rough—possessed no outcroppings large enough to conceal Balasi, especially if he were still inside his golem form.

Elleka climbed down from the wagon and joined Coran on the ground. Coran had made no move to help her, partially because he was too busy keeping watch for his brother, but also because it was a breach of protocol for a human—even an Augment such as Coran—to initiate physical contact with a mage.

Elleka continued staring at the dead bodies amidst the wreckage that was all that remained of the trading caravan's wagons. "It looks as if they were struck by an avalanche."

It was difficult to tell, given the current state of the caravan, but judging by the amount of splintered wood, the number of intact wheels, and especially the number of corpses, Coran felt confident there had been at least three wagons in the caravan, perhaps four.

"An avalanche," Coran murmured. "That's as good a way to describe it as any, I suppose." He sighed. "Balasi always was more aggressive than I. Our father was a soldier—human, not Augment—who fought for Lord Marsyas. He died at the Battle of Serpent-Tooth Ridge when Balasi and I were both children. We became determined to follow in his footsteps and become warriors, but where I wanted to do so to honor our father's sacrifice, Balasi wanted only the glory and adventure that he believed battle would bring." He turned to look at Elleka. "You can't imagine how many times we played warrior in the woods near our cabin as we grew up. Balasi always made me be one of Jirkar's warriors, of course." He smiled sadly and shook his head. "It all seemed so innocent then."

Coran turned his gaze toward the mountain a half mile to the north. Elleka looked in the same direction.

"Is that it?" she asked.

Coran nodded. "That's Advent Mountain."

Elleka squinted. "I don't see the tower."

Stone crumbling, clouds of gray dust rising into the

air, and above all, the screams of the men and women trapped inside the tower as it collapsed upon them. . . .

"That's because it's not there anymore," Coran said softly.

Silence fell between them for a time while they stared at the mountain, Coran glanced sideways at Elleka. *She's probably trying to imagine the tower's fall,* he thought. Coran wished he could forget it.

"How much do you know about being a Stoneguard Warrior?" he asked the Underwizard.

"I'm acquainted with the physical construction of the golems, as well as the myriad of complex enchantments that allow—"

Coran held up a hand to stop her. "No, I'm speaking of *being* a golem . . . of inhabiting and operating a stone body."

Elleka's silence answered for her.

"It's a very strange experience. There is a sensation of strength and power that's almost intoxicating. You feel as if you are capable of anything, that you are almost a god. And yet . . . there are limitations. While you can see and hear, you cannot smell, cannot taste, cannot feel the objects you touch. Since there is no need to breathe, not even to speak, you do not draw air into your lungs. Indeed, golems don't possess lungs or internal organs of any sort. They are simply stone all the way through. If you remain inside a golem body for too long, you can become . . . cut off from the experience of being human. Even forget what it's like to *be* human." He gazed with sorrow upon the twisted, mutilated corpses of the merchants and their steeds. "That's what happened to Balasi."

"And what of you?" Elleka asked. "What effect did becoming a Stoneguard Warrior have on you?"

Coran hesitated before answering, and when he finally did so, it was in a soft, quiet voice. "You're a mage. You know there's always a price for power."

Elleka reached up with her left hand and lightly stroked the silver scales near her eye. Coran wondered if she was aware of doing so.

He went on. "Sometimes that price isn't magical. Sometimes it calls for one to sacrifice a bit of his mind . . . or soul."

"I'm impressed. I didn't know my brother was a poet."

Coran and Elleka turned in surprise toward the harsh, grating voice and saw a large stone figure shove aside a pile of rocks and pull itself out of the ground. Coran thought of spiders that laired within the earth and leaped out to snatch passing prey. He understood then how Balasi had managed to surprise the trading caravan—he'd dug himself a hiding place.

Eyes blazing crimson, Balasi emerged from his pit and came striding toward them. Though the golem's skull face was incapable of expression, Coran could hear the smile in its voice when Balasi said, "What's wrong, brother? Aren't you happy to see me?"

Battle raged less than fifty yards from them, but Coran and Balasi remained with the wagons, as they'd been ordered. It was eight months after their baptism of fire on the grasslands of Moora, and the war against the north wasn't going well. The forces of the Mage-lord Jirkan had penetrated into the south as far Three Forks River, only ninety miles from the stronghold of his father—and mortal enemy—Magelord Marsyas. Jirkar's army had captured the riverport city of Ghrell, one of the most important centers of trade in Akantha. Marsyas have given orders for his army to recapture Ghrell, no matter the cost. They fought in cramped city streets, standing on cobblestones, the fresh smell of riverwater rich in the air. The human soldiers fought hand to hand, while Augments used their mystical abilities to deadly effect, sometimes against their opposite number on the other side, but often against any mortals unlucky enough to get in their way.

As the battle wore on, Balasi smacked his fist into his palm. "Damnation, but I can't stand just watching! We should be out there fighting!"

Coran wasn't upset to be hanging back. In fact, he hoped they wouldn't be called to battle at all this day, but he couldn't tell his brother that. There was no way Balasi could understand.

"We have our orders," Coran said.

"Orders from a man, not from an Augment," Balasi said in a voice close to a growl.

Though Coran knew Commander Arkash was out there in the thick of the fighting, he nevertheless cast a quick glance around to make sure the man, or one of his subordinates, wasn't close enough to overhear Balasi's words. "Augments are no better or worse than humans. Just different."

Balasi snorted. "So different that humans are afraid of us, afraid of our power. Why else would Arkash order us to hold back?"

Coran knew it was because there were far fewer Augments than human warriors in Marsyas' armies, and that they were spread throughout the various divisions. Coran and Balasi were the only two Stoneguard Warriors in Arkash's command, and the soldier wasn't about to deploy them unless it was absolutely necessary. Not because he feared them, but because he wanted to conserve them, not risk their becoming damaged until he had no choice. Balasi was well aware of this, of course, but Coran reminding him wouldn't do much to calm him. Balasi was caught in the throes of battle fever now. He needed to be inside his golem form, needed to be stomping across the battlefield on stone feet, slamming rock-hard fists into fragile flesh and bone protected by only slightly less fragile armor. Balasi needed this the same way some people needed strong drink or intoxicating drugs. And only shedding the blood of the Magelord's enemies would satisfy his all-consuming craving.

The peal of a horn cut through the sounds of battle—three short blasts, followed by two long. Arkash had sent the signal for his two Stoneguard Warriors to join the fray.

"At last!" Balasi grinned and hopped onto the open wagon where his golem body lay prone and still. Its eyes were dark hollows, empty of crimson fire.

Coran made no move toward the wagon containing his golem. He knew he should, but he couldn't force his feet to move. He turned to Balasi, though he wasn't sure why. Perhaps to ask for his brother's encouragement—or forgiveness. But Balasi had already merged with his golem. Crimson fire blazed forth within its eye sockets, and the golem sat up.

"Time to go to work, my brother." The voice that emerged from the golem's mouth was harsh and grating, like two large rough stones grinding together. Without waiting for Coran to reply, Balasi climbed out of the wagon, the wooden vehicle creaking alarmingly beneath his weight, and then strode off toward the mass of battling soldiers. The ground trembled slightly with each of Balasi's footfalls, and he released a battle cry that sounded like a monstrous roar. More than a few combatants on both sides paled when they saw the massive skull-headed, demon-horned golem approach.

Coran turned toward his wagon and looked at the golem lying prone in its bed. His golem looked exactly the same as Balasi's, save for a few scratches and knicks the Overwizards hadn't gotten around to repairing yet. These marks corresponded to scars on Coran's body—scars that no magic could erase. To enter the golem and take command of it, to *become* it, all Coran had to do was climb atop the stone figure and merge his body with its. The golems were constructed by the Overwizards for a specific Augment, and attuned to them so that no one, not even another Stoneguard Warrior, even Balasi, could enter and control Coran's golem. The only one in all the world who could make use of the great weapon lying motionless in the wagon bed was Coran—and he was too terrified to move.

Beads of sweat formed on his skin, and his heart pounded rapidly in his chest, blood surging through his veins so fast that it sounded as if the ocean roared in his ears. He felt a cold crawling sickness deep in the pit of his stomach, and his vision became edged with gray, as if he might pass out any moment. Coran had never been comfortable joining with his golem, though he had done so dozens of times before. But each time the fear had grown steadily worse, until now he couldn't bring himself to take a step toward the wagon, let alone merge with the stone figure within.

It wasn't that the joining hurt. During the merging all sensations save sight and sound were cut off, so it was impossible to feel pain. Physical pain, at least. But the act of allowing one's entire body, one's very *self,* to become encased in a stone figure was like being buried alive. Coran had suffered from a fear of enclosed places since childhood, but it had never proved a great impediment to him—until he'd undergone the

mandatory testing Magelord Marsyas required of all
youth in his kingdom. The Overwizards had discovered that he—along with his brother—had the potential to survive the dangerous process of Augmentation
that transformed a human into a mystically powerful
warrior. Coran might've been all right if the Overwizards had transformed him into a Wolfclaw or a Basi-
lisk, but no. They'd decided both he and Balasi were
most suited to serve the Magelord as Stoneguard
Warriors.

But Coran couldn't do it, not again! He couldn't
bring himself to enter that prison of cold stone. He
turned away from the wagon and faced the battle to
see how Balasi was faring. But before he could track
his brother's progress, a silver glint from above caught
his attention. He looked up just in time to see a
Swordfalcon swooping down toward him. The silver-
winged avian held a razor-sharp black-diamond sword
in each clawed hand. The enchanted weapons were
capable of cutting through stone like butter—including
the living stone that made up a golem's body. She
wore a silver helm wrought to resemble a falcon's
head, and though the eyes that gazed out were human,
they glittered with the cold calculation of a bird of
prey preparing to strike. She wore an ether-mail vest,
the magical armor paper-thin but strong enough to
withstand the blow of even a Stoneguard Warrior.
Over the armor she wore a tabard emblazoned with
the cerulean-eyed symbol of Magelord Jirkan.

It seemed the Swordfalcon had decided to slay
Coran before he had a chance to merge with his
golem, thereby ensuring one less Augment would fight
this day for Marsyas' side. As swiftly as the bird-
woman came, Coran knew that even if he could bring
himself to enter his golem form, he'd never reach it

before the Swordfalcon cut him down. He was a dead man.

But then Coran became aware of the cobblestones shaking beneath his feet, and, moving far more swiftly than seemed possible for such a large, ungainly creature as a golem, Balasi came toward him. When he was close enough, Balasi reached out and grabbed the Swordfalcon by her ankles. The Stoneguard Warrior planted his feet solidly against the ground and yanked backward with all his might. The Swordfalcon screamed as her leg bones shattered and muscles and ligaments tore. The woman released her grip on her black-diamond swords, and the mystically sharp blades spun through the air—barely missing Coran—and sliced into the cobblestone street, sliding smoothly into the ground as if it were liquid instead of solid, until only their hilts remained visible.

Before the Swordfalcon could recover from the surprise of Balasi's attack and begin to fight back, he took hold of one of her silver wings at the juncture where it emerged from her shoulder and ripped it out. The woman's previous scream was nothing compared to the high-pitched shriek that she released now. Blood spurted from her wounded shoulder and splashed onto Balasi's chest, obscuring the symbol of Marsyas engraved there. Balasi flung the torn wing away and it soared overtop the roof of a nearby tannery. He then took a grip on the other wing.

"No!" Coran shouted. But Balasi ignored his brother's protest and blood gushed from a second wound in the Swordfalcon's back. The woman was no longer screaming. She now hung limply in Balasi's grip, whimpering softly as her lifeblood pattered to the street.

Balasi looked at Diran, the red fire in his eye sockets growing smaller and dimmer, the golem equivalent of a scowl. "What's wrong, brother? Losing your stomach for battle?"

Coran struggled to find his voice. "Battle is one thing. Slaughter is another."

Balasi laughed, the sound booming forth from the golem's stone throat. "Don't be naïve. War is killing, pure and simple." He closed a massive hand over the Swordfalcon's helmet and squeezed. Metal crumpled and flesh and bone were reduced to a pulp. Balasi dropped the woman's twitching, headless corpse to the cobblestones and wiped the gore form his hand onto his chest, further obscuring the symbol of Marsyas. Coran watched bits of helmet, skull, and gray matter slide off his brother's body and fall with soft wet smacks onto the blood-slick street.

"Enough talk," Balasi said. "Enter your golem and join me." He started to turn and head back toward the thick of the fighting, but he stopped when Coran said, "I can't."

Balasi turned back around to face his brother. "What do you mean *you can't*?"

Coran looked up at his brother with eyes suddenly moist with tears. He opened his mouth to try to explain, but no words came out.

Balasi stared down at his brother, eyes of crimson fire blazing, his emotions unreadable on the skeletal features of his stone face.

"Coward," he snarled at last, then turned and stomped back toward the battle.

Coran fell to his knees and sobbed, his golem form lying in its wagon, lifeless and useless, as the fight raged on without him.

"Direcat got your tongue, brother?"

Coran stared at Balasi. His golem body had changed

a great deal since Coran had last seen him. The living stone was light gray instead of a healthy dark, and it was shot through with cracks and fissures. It was so dry that tiny pebbles broke off as he moved and pattered to the ground like hail. The golem was missing fingers on both hands, and its right horn was gone, broken off sometime during the last seven years. But worst of all were the brown stains covering the golem's hands, arms, and chest. The stains resembled rust, but Coran knew what they really were—blood.

"You've looked better, Balasi." Coran was surprised by how calm he sounded.

"The enchantments that animate and maintain the stone body have grown weak," Elleka said. The Underwizard's voice held a slight quaver, but she didn't shrink back as Balasi drew closer. He stopped five yards away from Elleka and Coran—close enough to attack but still far enough away that he could flee if necessary.

"Who is your companion, Coran? Do I have a sister-in-law now?"

"I am the Underwizard Elleka, sent by the Hall of Arcane Wisdom on behalf of Magelord Marsyas himself." Her words were meant to be official, but she didn't sound very self-assured speaking them. Coran imagined it was difficult to maintain one's confidence when surrounded by the dismembered and crushed victims of a golem attack.

Elleka continued. "Balasi Yrggson, in the name of the Southern Kingdom, I command you to separate from your golem form and turn yourself over to us immediately."

The Stoneguard Warrior looked at Elleka for several moments, crimson eyes flickering enigmatically. But then finally he put his hands on his hips, threw back his demon-skull head, and let out a booming laugh. The action was so sudden, and the posture so *human*, that Coran was startled.

"For what reason?" Balasi asked.

Coran detected an edge of anger in his brother's golem voice, something an ordinary human—even an Underwizard—wouldn't notice. He wished Elleka would stop talking and give him a chance to speak to Balasi brother to brother, one Stoneguard Warrior to another. But she was his superior on this trip, and thus he remained silent as she went on.

Elleka gestured at the splintered wood and ravaged corpses surrounding them. "For attacking the trading caravans that pass through here, for—" she swallowed, "—murdering all these people, and dozens more like them." Her face went pale, her words ending in a whisper. Coran guessed that the full implications of what she was doing had struck her: she was speaking to the creature that had committed these atrocities, that had used his stone hands to mangle and crush the twisted, broken bodies scattered around them.

"It's not murder if one kills during the course of battle," Balasi said. "The trade routes between north and south were closed by order of Marsyas. I am simply enforcing his wishes, as any good soldier would."

Coran could no longer remain silent. "The war is over, Balasi. Peace was declared seven years ago."

Balasi's demon-skull head swiveled toward Coran, and his crimson-flame eyes flared as they gazed upon his brother. Coran almost thought he could feel the heat emanating from the golem's eye sockets.

"The peace negotiations failed," Balasi said.

"The initial talks, yes. After Firstpoint Tower came down, there were nine more months of fighting." And those nine months had been more savage and deadly—

and exacted a higher toll—than all the fifty-three years of combat that had preceded them. "But then talks began again, and this time they were successful. Peace now reigns throughout the Two Kingdoms. An uneasy, fragile peace, perhaps," Coran admitted, "but peace nonetheless."

"You lie." Balasi spoke these two words coldly, and even Coran couldn't detect the least hint of emotion in them.

Elleka spoke once more. "So you see, if there is no war, if trade between the Two Kingdoms is no longer forbidden, then what you have done is indeed commit murder, numerous times over. But as bad as that is, it's still not your worst offense. As Coran said, the peace is an uneasy one, and your actions threaten to reignite hostilities between our peoples. Both Magelord Marsyas and Magelord Jirkar wish to avoid that happening. The Two Kingdoms are still struggling to recover from the ravages of the war. Neither can afford to return to those dark days of conflict."

Balasi looked back and forth between Elleka and Coran before speaking once more. "Even if I believe that the war is over—which I don't—how can the actions of one warrior defending one trade route set off a new war? Every man likes to think himself important, and while I *am* an Augment, I am still only one man, and this is only one place."

"It's the Land Barons," Coran said. "Both Northern and Southern. Marsyas and Jirkar were weakened by their decades-long conflict, for all magic—no matter how great or small—comes from them. They both expended a great deal of their personal power during the war. The Land Barons have grown in confidence since then and now wield greater influence over the kingdoms than ever. The Southern Barons blame the destruction of the trade caravans on the north, and the Northern Barons believe the south is responsible. So in this case, the actions of one man can indeed spark a war." *Just as the action of one man prolonged the last war,* Coran thought bitterly.

"I care not for politics," Balasi said. "I am a warrior. I live only to fight."

"The war is over," Elleka insisted. "You no longer have any reason to fight."

Balasi ignored her words and returned his attention to Coran. "How did you know it was me, brother? I was certain you believed me long dead."

"About a year ago you attacked a caravan coming from the north. I'm sure you thought you killed everyone, but a single member—a young boy of twelve—survived. Despite his injuries, he managed to make it back to the nearest northern settlement, where he told the tale of a giant of stone destroying his parents' caravan. The boy died soon after, but the story spread until at last it reached Jirkar's ears. He sent a message to Marsyas, and Marsyas dispatched us. The Magelord used his magic to confirm your identity, but he needn't have wasted his power. I knew it had to be you. Who else could it be? Now you tell me something, brother. Have you remained inside your golem form all these years? Have you never left it?"

Balasi didn't answer.

"I see." It was as Coran had feared. "You're not in your right mind, Balasi. Cut off from almost all human sensation for seven years . . . isolated from all human contact. It's no wonder that you chose to believe the war is still going on, why you decided you needed to continue enforcing the old trade embargo. But there is no war, my brother. You are no longer a warrior but a man who has refused to stop fighting.

Please—in the name of our father—separate from the golem and leave this place with us. It takes a strong warrior to know when to lay down his weapon and walk away, Balasi. That's what I'm asking you to do now."

Ever since Elleka and he had departed the Hall of Arcane Wisdom, Coran had mentally rehearsed what he would say to Balasi once they found him. But now his words sounded hollow and ineffectual to his own ears, and he feared that he had failed to reach his brother.

"Who are *you* to lecture me about what it means to be a warrior?" Balasi said, crimson eyes blazing in fury. "Tell me, brother, what have you done with yourself since last we saw one another? How have you honored our father's memory?"

"For the last seven years I have made my living as a fisherman. I have a cottage on the edge of Crystalmere Lake, and I own a small boat. I live alone, but it's a peaceful life and it suits me well enough. You would be welcome to join me there, if you wish."

"And do what? Catch fish so others can fill their bellies and grow fat?" Balasi said. "Father would be ashamed of you."

"And you think our father would be proud of you, continuing to fight a war that ended almost a decade ago?"

Out of the corner of his eyes, Coran saw Elleka take a step closer to Balasi and raise her hands. The air around Elleka's hands blurred as she began summoning forth mystic energy. A crackling sound filled the air, as if a raging fire had been lit, but there was no light, no heat. Only the strange shimmering around the Underwizard's hands.

Balasi made no move toward Elleka, and at first it

appeared that he wasn't going to defend himself. Coran wondered if, despite his brother's words, he was tired of his one-man war and wanted Elleka to destroy him. But then Balasi lifed his right foot and slammed it down onto the rocky ground. Coran braced himself as a sound like thunder split the air and a jagged crack opened in the ground, running swiftly from Balasi's foot toward Elleka. The Underwizard struggled to maintain her footing as the crack widened beneath her, but the vibrations from Balasi's attack were too violent and she fell onto her side. Her left elbow hit the ground with a solid crack, and Elleka grimaced in pain. But despite being knocked off her feet and likely breaking her elbow, she maintained her concentration, and instead of winking out, the shimmering around her hands grew stronger.

Balasi lumbered toward Elleka, obviously intending to prevent her from completing the spell she was attempting to cast. Coran knew from too many battle-field experiences that his brother struck swiftly and without mercy. If Balasi reached Elleka, the Underwizard would die, pure and simple.

Coran ran toward Elleka. He was closer to her than Balasi, and a human form was far lighter and more maneuverable than that of a golem, and thus Coran reached the Underwizard first. She'd managed to pull herself into a sitting position, and the shimmering around her hands was now so intense that Coran could no longer see the hands themselves. She chanted furiously in the ancient tongue of the Magelords as she drew upon the power that Marsyas had implanted in her, shaped it, and prepared to hurl it at Balasi. Elleka's voice rose in volume and pitch, and Coran sensed she was close to completing her spell.

As he reached her, he leaned down, made a fist,

and struck her jaw as hard as he could. Elleka's head snapped back, her eyes rolled white, and she slumped to the ground, unconscious. The shimmering around her hands was gone, and the air held the singed-hair and sulfur scent of magic power that had been gathered but remained unchanneled. But the smell quickly faded as the magic energy dissipated.

Coran looked up just as Balasi reached them. He stepped between the unconscious Underwizard and his brother, knowing there was nothing he could do to stop Balasi if he truly wished to kill Elleka, but knowing that he nevertheless had to try.

Balasi stopped and looked down at his brother, flicking red eyes unreadable.

"What's wrong, little brother? Do you think me incapable of handling one underwizard?"

"I wasn't trying to save *you*," Coran said. "I was trying to save *her*."

Balasi gazed down upon Elleka's motionless form and chuckled, the sound reminding Coran of bone-dice rattling around in a stone cup. "If that's how you protect your friends these days, I'd hate to see how you treat your enemies."

Balasi took another half step forward, and for an instant Coran thought his brother was going to knock him aside and slay Elleka. But then Balasi stopped and cast his crimson-flame gaze toward the covered wagon Coran and Elleka had arrived in.

"What's in the wagon, Coran?"

"What do you think?" Coran answered with more bravado than he felt.

Though Balasi displayed no reaction, Coran had the sense that if his stone features were capable of smiling, they would've done so now.

"Is your golem in there, little brother? Did the

Overwizards send it along in the hope that you'd overcome your cowardice and use it against me? Why don't you go slip into it, and then the two of us can spar for a bit. It's been a long time since I've had an opponent that could match my strength."

"Not *your* strength," Coran said. "Your golem's."

Balasi shrugged, the gesture looking stiff and awkward as the golem body performed it. "What's the difference? So how about it? You going to indulge your big brother one last time?"

A chill ran down Coran's spine at the thought of merging with his golem after all these years, and cold sweat began to roll down his face. "You've been inside your golem for far too long, Balasi." Though Coran tried, he couldn't keep his voice from shaking. "The experience has rendered you insane."

"I'll take that as a no."

Before Coran could react, Balasi—moving with startling speed for a creature so large—swung the back of his hand toward Coran's face. Coran felt an impact, saw a flash of bright light, and then knew only darkness.

When Coran awoke the only reason he knew he wasn't dead was that his head hurt so damn much. He struggled to pull himself into a sitting position, and once he did, he nearly fell back over, so dizzy was he. But he managed to stay upright and took slow, even, deep breaths until his head cleared somewhat.

He tried to recall what had happened. He remembered riding in a wagon for a long time . . . remembered a woman with braided brown hair . . . Ermalyn? Elsperth? Elleka! That was it! But what had he been doing riding with her? Where . . .

And then his full memory came rushing back, as if

some sort of hastily erected dam in his mind had
broken.

Balasi!

He looked around for any sign of his older brother,
but he saw none. He also didn't see Elleka. Coran
understood at once what had happened—after knocking Coran out, Balasi had picked up Elleka and carried her off. Not to harm her; he could easily have
done that while both Coran and she remained unconscious. Balasi had taken her to taunt Coran, to lure
him to come after his older brother.

Coran rose to his feet. His knees were weak and
wobbled beneath his weight, but they held—barely.
Coran took several lurching steps, but then the world
seemed to suddenly spin around him, and he fell to
the ground once more. As he lay on the hard, cold
rock, Coran knew he was in no condition to go after
Balasi. Not if he continued to rely solely on his human
form. He turned his head, wincing at the pain the
simple motion caused, and looked at the wagon. It
was still intact, but the covering had been torn away to
reveal the massive stone figure lying in the wagon bed.

The message was clear: Balasi didn't want Coran to
come after him as a human. He wanted his little
brother to come to him as a Stoneguard Warrior.

"No," Coran whispered. But then he thought of his
poor brother, his mind trapped within a stone prison
that had driven him mad. He thought of Elleka, an
innocent woman who would surely die at Balasi's
hands if Coran failed to do what his brother wanted.
But how could Coran bring himself to go near his
golem form, let alone merge with it once again? The
thought of being encased within living stone, cut off
from the world of physical sensation, made him feel
as if he might vomit any second. But if he didn't do

it, Elleka was as good as dead—and Balasi would be lost forever.

Trembling, Coran once more rose to his feet, and this time he starting shuffling toward the wagon.

Coran stood atop Advent Mountain in the northen-most climes of Akantha, looking down upon a vast rocky plain covered with a sea of tents that seemed to stretch from one horizon to the other.

"How many do you think there are?" Coran asked.

Balasi answered without turning to look at him. "Ten thousand at least, perhaps as many as fifteen."

Coran shook his head in wonderment. "I never thought this day would come. Did you?"

The sky was a clear bright blue dotted with full white clouds drifting lazily above the world. Coran had always loved looking at clouds. They were beyond the petty affairs of mortals and immortals alike. Clouds were free and pure, unspoiled by the conflicts of the tiny, inconsequential beings that crawled about on the ground below. But then again, perhaps not completely unspoiled, for tendrils of smoke rose into the sky from hundreds of cook fires scattered across the plain.

Balasi didn't answer, and Coran didn't press him. After the battle of Ghrell, they'd hardly spoken to one another—and in the months since, Coran hadn't once merged with his golem.

They gazed down upon the tents in silence for a time. Roughly half of the tents were crimson, the other cerulean. None were very large, for these were not the tents of commanders or Augments, but of fighting men and women. The lowest ranked among them, common foot soldiers known as Firsters because they were the first into battle and most often the first to die as well, had no tents at all. They had to sit on the ground, huddled together as close to the cook fires as their low status permitted. There were supply wagons, horses, oxen, tents for blacksmiths and farriers. Flags and banners flew from poles erected across the plain. Some indicated the presence of special divisions or told from what region of the Two Kingdoms a particular company hailed. But the two most common standards were the crimson eye of the Magelord Marsyas and the cerulean fist of his son and enemy Jirkar. Two armies, gathered upon a single plain, but these forces weren't assembled for combat . . . at least, not yet. They had assembled to wait while their commanders met, talked, and laid the foundations for what—after fifty-three years of constant warfare between the two Magelords—might hopefully become a lasting peace. Or at least a cessation of hostilities while the Magelords themselves met to resolve their decades-old conflict.

Coran glanced over his shoulder at the graystone tower that rose from the top of the hill. This was Advent Mountain, the ancient site where the Magelords—all fifty of them—had first arrived in Akantha long millennia ago from whatever alien world had birthed them. This was the only truly neutral ground left in Akantha, and here Magelords, or more often their representatives, met within Firstpoint Tower to negotiate trade agreements and resolve disputes . . . such as fifty-three years of war between father and son. High-ranking Overwizards from both sides were meeting in the upper levels of the tower at this very moment, just as they had for the last three days. But whether they had made any progress or not, no one knew.

The Augments—the elite forces of the Magelords—

had spent the last three days housed in the lower levels of the tower, while the negotiations took place above their heads. All were present: Jirkar's Swordfalcons, Dreadbones, and Ebon Reavers, as well as Marsyas' Wolfclaws, Baslisks, and Stoneguard Warriors. Despite Coran's . . . problem, he was still technically a member of the Stoneguard, and thus had been permitted to join the other Augments on Advent Mountain. Coran suspected this was a decision that his brother did not agree with.

The arcane power that had altered the Augments' bodies and made them into deadly warriors also gave them a tendency to be high-strung. And they had a difficult time being in such close proximity to other Augments, whether friend or foe. To avoid getting into fights—and risk disrupting the peace negotiations—individual Augments would occasionally leave the tower and spend some time outside, as Coran and Balasi were doing now.

Balasi squinted in the light, and Coran noticed that he kept his gaze focused on the ground whenever he could. Balasi hadn't wanted to come outside—Coran had practically been forced to drag his brother out into the fresh air and sunshine.

"I have a confession to make, Balasi."

"Oh?" The word dripped with scorn. Ever since Coran's failure at the Battle of Ghrell, Balasi had shown nothing but contempt for his younger brother.

"I wanted you to accompany me out here for a different reason than merely taking in the view. I'm . . . worried about you, brother."

"*You?* Worried about *me?*" Balasi laughed. "You'd make a fine jester, Coran."

Coran ignored the gibe and went on. "Over the last several months you've become increasingly ill-tempered and belligerent. What's more, you shun open spaces and your eyes can't seen to tolerate even the mildest light. And though you try to hide it, I've noticed how you keep sneaking glances back at the tower, almost as if you cannot wait to go back inside."

"I take it back. You're not a jester—you're a fool, and a cowardly one at that." Balasi turned to go, but Coran took hold of his brother's arm to stop him. Balasi broke free of Coran's grip at once and whirled around to face him, hands bunched into fists. Coran thought Balasi would attack him, but he held his ground. Balasi continued glaring at Coran, but he relaxed his hands and some of the tension drained out of his body, if not all.

"I fear that your time as a Stoneguard Warrior has had the opposite effect on you than it did on me," Coran said. "Where I cannot stand to merge with my golem form, you have difficulty being away from yours. Don't bother to deny it."

Balasi didn't say anything right away, but then he lowered his head and slowly nodded. "You're right, Coran. When I'm a golem, I'm strong, invincible. Nothing can touch me . . . I'm the greatest warrior that ever lived. But when I'm *this*—" Balasi thumped his hand against his chest, "—I'm small and weak. I *hate* it! If I could, I'd remain inside my golem form forever."

Coran put his hand on his brother's shoulders. Balasi's condition was worse than he'd feared.

"Of the two of us, brother, your condition is by far the worse. For once the war is over, there will be no further use for Augments. Like any other warrior, we shall have to put our weapons away and try to forge new lives for ourselves. Lives without our golems."

Balasi looked up and stared at Coran, eyes wide,

and Coran realized that his brother had never given any thought to this matter. Indeed, it had most likely never even occurred to him.

"I . . . suppose you are right, brother," Balasi said softly. Then he glanced toward the tower. "Assuming the peace talks are successful."

Coran give his brother's shoulders a reassuring squeeze. "They appear to have gone well so far. Why shouldn't they continue to do so?"

Balasi kept looking at the tower, one corner of his mouth lifting in a half smile.

"Why, indeed?"

Elleka was aware of the throbbing in her jaw before anything else. She considered returning to the dark depths where she'd been, where pain was nothing more than a half-forgotten memory. But then she felt the ground tremble beneath her and she heard a rough voice shouting "Do . . . you . . . yield?" Then, much softer, "Answer me, my brother, or my voice will be the last sound you ever hear in this world." A pause. No reply came. "Have it your way."

Elleka opened her eyes and sat up in time to see a demon hewn from living stone bring its fists down upon the chest of another demon, lying cracked and broken on the ground. She felt the impact in her bones, almost as if she were the one that had been struck. The damaged golem flew apart in a shower of rock dust and stone fragments, and Elleka raised a forearm to shield her eyes from the debris. When she heard the last patter of falling stone, she slowly lowered her arm.

The victorious golem stood over the shattered remains of its foe. Little was left intact beside the demon-skull head, and that was now missing both horns and its lower jaw. Still a skull, but demoniac no more. Within the dark hollows of its eyes pinpoints of crimson fire still flickered, but weakly, like candle flames that had nearly burned down to the ends of their wicks.

The surviving golem stood looking down at the remains of its enemy. Its body was criss-crossed with cracks and fissures, and it was missing a good part of its left shoulder. But it still had both horns, and its color was a healthy dark gray.

"Coran," she whispered.

The intact golem turned to look at her. The crimson fire in its eyes blazed so fiercely that it seemed as if the stone skull could barely contain it.

"Yes," Coran said simply.

Elleka rose to her feet and rubbed her sore and swollen jaw. She took in her surroundings and saw a great mound of rubble formed of large stone blocks, many of them still intact.

"That was Firstpoint Tower, wasn't it?" Elleka said. She heard heavy footfalls as Coran walked over to join her.

"It was. It fell on the eve of the fourth day of peace talks. Each side blamed the other for the collapse, and the war resumed. No official cause was found—not that anyone investigated thoroughly after the resumption of hostilities. But I knew what had happened. Balasi had brought the tower down in order to prevent peace so that he could continue to fight as a Stoneguard Warrior. And it was I who had accidentally given him the idea."

Though Coran's golem voice sounded little different than Balasi's, she'd gotten to know Coran well enough over the last few weeks to detect the sadness in his rough, measured tones.

"I thought that Balasi had been caught in the tower's collapse and destroyed. It wasn't until the messenger from the Hall of Arcane Wisdom contacted me that I realized that Balasi had somehow survived. Perhaps he had been buried beneath the remains of the tower, and it had taken him a long time to dig free. Or perhaps once the tower came down he realized what he had done and fled into hiding, until his madness took complete hold of him and he began attacking trade caravans."

Coran turned and glanced back at his brother's jawless head. "I suppose we'll never know for sure now."

Elleka was still struggling to fully understand what had taken place. "You struck me unconscious to prevent me from destroying your brother . . . or him from destroying me. But then Balasi carried me up Firstpoint Mountain to the ruins of Firstpoint Tower, and you were forced to use your golem to save me. Thank you."

Coran turned to look once more at his brother's decapitated head.

"I couldn't save Balasi, though."

She wanted to comfort Coran, but as she reached out to touch his arm, she drew back. Despite all her mystic training, Elleka couldn't get used to thinking of this . . . *monster* as Coran, and she couldn't bring herself to touch the cold, hard stone of his golem body.

"I don't think anyone could have saved him at this point," she said softly.

Just then the crimson flame smoldering deep within Balasi's eye sockets began to dim until it was gone, leaving behind only two dark, empty holes.

"He's dead," Elleka declared.

Coran stomped over to his brother's head, bent

down, picked it up, and straightened once more. He held the head up to his own stone face and examined it closely. Elleka walked over to join him.

"Perhaps," Coran said. "Or perhaps that's what he wishes us to think. Extinguishing eyefire is no more difficult for a Stoneguard Warrior than it is for ordinary humans to close their eyes."

"I can tell you if Balasi's spirit is still present. A simple spell will allow me to detect—"

Coran cut her off. "No. If Balasi is dead, then so be it. But if he only *wishes* that we believe him to be dead, then we shall honor that wish. Despite what he did these last several years, he was once a great warrior . . . and a good brother. He deserves our respect."

Coran considered his brother's golem skull for a few moments longer. Then, as if reaching a decision, he stomped over to the pile of rubble that was all that remained of Firstpoint Tower. Coran had to pick his way carefully because of his size and weight, but eventually he managed to reach the top of the mound of debris. Carefully, almost tenderly, he placed his brother's skull atop the broken stone slabs and splintered wooden timbers. Coran then made his way back to Elleka, moving with just as much care as before.

"A monument to his memory?" she asked.

"If Balasi *is* alive and one day chooses to open his eyes again, at least he'll have a good view from up there."

Elleka gazed at the bright blue sky, thick white clouds, and the rocky plains spreading out beneath.

"A good view, indeed," she said.

Without another word, Underwizard and Stoneguard Warrior turned their backs to Balasi's head and began the long trek back down the mountain. As they descended, Elleka said, "What will you do now that our task is done?"

"Once we get back to the wagon, I'll separate from my golem body and, gods willing, never enter it again. We'll take it back to the Hall of Arcane Wisdom where the Overwizards can do what they like with it. After that, I'm going to return home, get into my boat, row into the middle of the lake, toss in my fishing line, and doze in the warmth of the afternoon sun while a gentle breeze blows across the water."

After they'd gone some ways down Firstpoint Mountain, Coran said, "Do you remember a few days ago, when you told me that you could imagine what war was like, and I said you couldn't?"

"Yes."

"Well, after today, you *do* know what's it like . . . a least a little."

Elleka thought on this for a moment. "Yes, I suppose I do."

They continued making their way down in silence after that.

Resting on the debris at the top of the mountain like some ancient stone sentinel, Balasi watched the two of them descend, eyes flickering with crimson fire, mind aflame with images of a war that—for him— would never end.

UNNATURAL

by Alan Dean Foster

THE LONGER HE stared at the battlefield map floating just above the massive wooden table in front of him, the tighter grew the knot that had formed in General Jaquard's stomach. He was not distracted from his study by the distant baying of stabled wyverns, the howling of massed gryphons, and the familiar, reassuring crackle of evening cooking and cleaning spells. Wholly absorbed in the most recently revised field map, he desperately looked for surcease where there was none. Lying snug on his head and low on his brow, the golden wreath of rank glowed an unsettling red, reflecting his apprehension.

There was no denying the reality. The entire city was encircled and cut off. Desperate attempts by the defenders to break through the Misarian lines had been repeatedly rebuffed by the besiegers. A relief column sent in haste from the capital had failed to break through. Propelled by anxiety and desperation, it had been ambushed by the enemy's fast wendigo cavalry and cut to pieces by lightning and wind.

Though Tesselar was the harbor through which the majority of the kingdom's goods passed, the disaster at Modrun Pass would force the government to think twice before attempting to relieve its garrison a second time. This had profound implications.

Foremost of which was the inescapable realization that the defenders of Tesselar were, essentially, now on their own. The responsibility for saving the city and, therefore, possibly the entire kingdom from the invading Misarians now fell on his shoulders. These were broad, strong, but—at the moment—tired.

What could he do? Each day, the incantations that protected the citadel's walls weakened beneath the assault of relentless hexes cast forth by the attackers. Yesterday the South Gate had nearly splintered under a surprise late-night assault by a force of Misarian woodwraiths. Only the alertness of a certain Major Bolcapp in rushing up a squad of engineer forest sprites to rebond the wood fibers had prevented a potential disaster. For his speed and skill in responding to the unexpected attack, Bolcapp had been promoted to light colonel. Posthumously, unfortunately. While directing the defense and repair of the gate, he had taken a choke curse above his protective body charm and had suffocated.

With the South Gate reinforced, the city remained safe. The surprise attack was but one more indication of the skill and stealthiness of the Misarian invaders. There was no telling what cunning enchantment they might invoke next, what unimaginable force their general sorceral staff might pull from the depths of military conjuration. Despite this, Jaquard did not feel overwhelmed. He was as adept at strategy as any senior officer the kingdom's College of Martial Magic had ever graduated, and individually skilled as well. But he felt very alone.

Gryphons. If only he had more gryphons. More than ever, they were Tesselar's lifeline to the outside. Supply ships could not get through because of the Misarians' effective sea serpent and water sprite blockade of the harbor. Somehow, the city had to be relieved. Somehow, the siege had to be broken. It was clear now that after Modrun the government would be wholly occupied with marshaling its forces for the expected defense of the capital. He and his garrison were on their own.

It was at that moment that the bellspell attached to the door that led to his rooms appeared. It jangled apologetically next to his ear. Brushing it away, he turned irritably toward the entry. It was after hours. Conscious of their commander's troubled state of mind, advisers and junior officers would know that at this time he would either be deep in thought or asleep and not to be disturbed. He muttered under his breath. An interruption this late likely meant another serious loss somewhere along the city wall. Waving a hand in the direction of the fireplace, he murmured an indifferent numinous word. The subdued flames within immediately responded, adding their additional light to the illumination from the drifting glowbulbs.

"Come in," he barked, "if you must."

He recognized the captain. Petrone, his name was. Jaquard prided himself on knowing the names of every one of his junior as well as the senior officers. Petrone was a third-degree adept. To be promoted to a senior level, you had to be at least a seventh-degree. The man was old for a captain. That might reflect on his ambition as much as any ostensible lack of skill.

While Petrone was old for a captain, the officer who accompanied him looked young even for a junior lieutenant. Jaquard sighed internally. Were the kingdom's forces spread so thin that the College had been reduced to sending out ungraduated adepts? This—this *boy* ought to be at home with his parents, helping out with chores or reading books. Not preparing to sacrifice himself on the altar of national defense. He looked hardly old enough to know how to cast a warming spell to heat his rations.

A standard, perfunctory glance at the lean lad's kit washed the empathy from the general's thoughts. The flickering light in the room further crevassed his frown.

"Soldier, where's your weapon?"

Automatically, the young officer glanced down in the direction of his empty holster. He swallowed hard. "I—I must have left it in my room, sir. I thought that since Captain Petrone and I were coming here, I didn't . . ."

"Didn't need your wand?" Jaquard slapped his own holster. The heavy, powerful rod nestled snugly within responded by emitting an iris-shrinking blast of vertical light. "You're defending a city under siege, whose attackers are inordinately clever and forever plotting. A soldier fighting under such circumstances should never be without his wand. Especially," he added sternly, "an officer."

"Yes, sir. I'm sorry, sir." The lieutenant nervously shifted the beige cloth bag he was dragging from his left hand to his right.

Petrone stepped forward. Memories of supper and remnants of gravy flecked his beard, but Jaquard said nothing. In difficult circumstances, certain aspects of professional comportment had to be overlooked. Defending a city from looting and rapine allowed for different rules than when one was on parade.

"It's my fault, General. And I'm the one who insisted on coming here at this awkward hour." The old officer lowered his head slightly. "I thought it of vital importance that you see what this youngster has developed."

"Developed?" Jaquard was twice surprised. First, at hearing that the late-night interruption was on behalf not of the captain but of his protégé, and, second, that such a callow-faced lieutenant might have something to contribute beyond stammer and shyness.

Petrone looked up at his commanding officer. Years seemed to drop away from him. "A matter of defense, sir. I was greatly skeptical when I first heard about it from other junior officers who had been witness to the progress. I was skeptical when I queried this young soldier about it." There was a flash in his eyes of something Jaquard had not seen in his troops for many days now. Hope. "I was skeptical, General, until I saw it for myself."

Petrone's demurral did nothing to reduce Jaquard's impatience. "Saw what, Captain?"

The old officer stepped aside. "Show him, Lieutenant Kemal."

Stepping forward, the lieutenant started to dump his heavy sack onto the stout wooden table, but hesitated. "General, sir, is it . . . ?"

"Go ahead," Jaquard told him irritably. "Do whatever it is you have come to do." Turning his head, he glared meaningfully at Petrone. "This had better not be a waste of my time. I'd say that it took you a considerable number of years to make captain. I wouldn't want for you to have to start over again." He shifted his penetrating gaze to the nervous but busy lieutenant. "Either of you." Petrone offered a wan but slightly defiant nod in return.

In the light from the huge stone fireplace and the hovering glowbulbs, the young officer dumped a singular object out on the table. At first Jaquard thought, quite naturally, that it was some kind of modified wand. It had the right general shape. But it was unusually large, nearly half his height, and festooned with additions he did not recognize. Though milled from honest wormwood, the handgrip, for example, bulged alarmingly at one end. Other odd protrusions were as unrecognizable as their purpose. Most of the wand, interestingly, appeared to consist of an iron tube.

"A two-handed wand," he commented as the lieutenant carefully laid other items out on the table. Perhaps he had been too hasty in reprimanding the younger officer. "Powerful I would assume, though not suited for close-quarter work."

Still arranging his adjunctives, the lieutenant spoke without looking up. "Begging your pardon, General, sir, but it's not a wand."

"Not a wand." Jaquard's frown returned. He studied the metal tube. "A pixie-duster, then."

"Not a pixie-duster." Was that a hint of a smile creasing Petrone's bewhiskered visage? "Sir."

"Well, then, what the many devils regrettably not fighting on our side is it? Besides a potential waste of my time, soldier."

"I hope not that, General." The lieutenant picked it up. It did indeed require two hands to support. "It represents an interest of mine that has afflicted me since I was very young, but I've only just managed to make one work properly. It represents . . ."

"A new way of looking at the world," Petrone could not resist putting in. "Perhaps even a new way of thinking about it."

What was all this nonsense? Philosophy? The Kingdom's Council was beridden with philosophers—none of whom could cast a fighting spell worth a lick. He said as much, utilizing language that would have seen him swiftly excused from court.

"I call it a 'stun,' " the lieutenant said. "Because that's what it does."

"Ah." Jaquard relaxed, just a little. "It's a designated wand, then. For casting a stun spell."

Forgetting for a moment who he was talking to, the lieutenant looked exasperated. "No, sir, it's not a wand of any kind. It's something else. It's . . ." He paused, finished rather lamely, ". . . a 'stun.' "

"Show him," Petrone suggested hurriedly. Even in the dim light, he could see the color in the general's face darkening.

Nodding, Lieutenant Kemal set to work. First he dumped a small amount of a powder Jaquard did not recognize into a tiny pan positioned near the rear of the metal tube. The powder neither flashed nor smelled of even the simplest charm. From a small cloth bag, the lieutenant removed a thumb-sized ball of metal. That, at least, was immediately familiar to the general, whose sense of arcane smell was well trained and highly sensitive. The ball was made of lead. He was not impressed. When it came to utilization for military incantations, lead was a notoriously ineffectual metal.

Tilting back the metal-and-wood contraption, the lieutenant proceeded to drop the lead ball into the metal tube. He followed it with a packet of ordinary, unenchanted cloth, ramming both deep into the tube with a long, thin piece of metal. This concluded, he stood cradling the tube in both arms, an air of readiness surrounding him. To the perceptive Jaquard, this glowed a very faint blue.

Petrone stepped forward. "We need a target, General."

"A target?" Jaquard's doubt was plain to see. "For that thing?" When neither junior officer responded, he shrugged and turned, gesturing absently at a sturdy wooden chair resting near the far wall. He was running out of patience for what increasingly appeared to be an elaborate farce. If it was not more, not a good deal more, the ranks of the defenders of Tesselar would be reduced by two officers.

"Defend the chair," Petrone requested.

This really had gone far enough, Jaquard felt. But having already sat through the first two acts of the play, he decided he might as well stay for the conclusion. Drawing the potent service wand from his own holster, he aimed it at the inoffensive chair. The wand was gilded and embedded with filigreed electrum, a gift from an admiring council upon his last promotion. For all its embellishment, in the hands of a twelfth-degree adept like himself, it was frighteningly powerful.

"Horfon descrine immutablius!" he rumbled authoritatively.

A thin shaft of purple light lanced from the tip of the wand to strike the chair, which was immediately enveloped in a globe of amethyst radiance. The glowing sphere was bright and perfect and impenetrable. It would take an equal force, focused hard and exclusively, to so much as dimple it. The Horfon was the strongest singular defensive spell Jaquard knew. On the city wall, it had once saved him from an enemy slashing a corkscrew summons that had felled half a dozen brave but lesser soldiers around him and left a foot-deep hole in the stone surface itself.

Petrone nodded at the lieutenant and stepped back. "Show him, Kemal."

Holding it in both hands, the lieutenant raised the

tube and pointed the narrow end at the distant chair. Jaquard waited for the murmur of an incantation. It did not come. Instead, the young man pulled back on a small piece of metal that protruded from the underside of the tube. Another piece of metal on the top flicked downward, very fast. Powder ignited. Ignited, a stunned Jaquard observed, without so much as a whisper from either junior officer. There was a brief, bright flash of light and smoke. It was followed by a tremendous bang that echoed off the stone walls of the chamber. This despite the lieutenant not having voiced so much as a hint of a thunder spell.

It all happened so fast. The light and the smoke were followed by the lieutenant taking a forced step to the rear as the end of the tube kicked up and backward. That was the sum of it. As theater, it was certainly impressive. But as a device, beyond its ability to startle it appeared to have no practical use. Recovering his poise, Jaquard said as much.

Petrone was decidedly smiling now. Jaquard did not like it when others got the joke and he did not. "Is that all it does?" he muttered uncertainly.

Petrone gestured. "Let us check the chair, General."

Dubiously, Jaquard followed the captain across the room. The purple sphere of the Horfon still surrounded it, refulgent and intense as ever. It took the general a moment before the impossibility of what he was seeing registered fully on his brain.

In the back of the heavy wooden chair was a hole big enough to push a finger through. Leaning close, he saw that the edges of the hole were ragged and torn as if by a powerful piercing curse. Beyond, the stone wall was scored where the metal ball had struck it after passing completely through the chair. The Horfon continued to hover in place, apparently intact. It had been penetrated as if it consisted of nothing but air and words.

Petrone was clearly enjoying his superior's reaction. "Imagine, General Jaquard, if this chair was the chest of a Misarian soldier."

"It's not possible." Straightening, a disbelieving Jaquard turned to look first at the captain, then at the lieutenant. "This contravenes every known law of nature!"

"Did I not say it represents a new way of looking at the world?" Petrone murmured.

Striding over to confront the lieutenant, Jaquard extended both hands and asked, as deferentially as any supplicant before a spelling physician, "May I?"

His expression a mixture of pride and bashfulness, Kemal handed over the stun. It was heavier than Jaquard expected, but not unbearably so. He studied it carefully.

"How does it work?" he asked without taking his eyes off the device.

The lieutenant proceeded to explain. "The powder is a special mixture of my own devising. Its components are quite commonly found in the ground and require little in the way of preparation. Nothing like a hammerspell or levitation necromancing." Leaning forward, he pointed. "When this small held stone and this piece of metal come together, the powder is ignited and . . ."

"Just a minute." Jaquard looked up. "Let me make sure I am understanding this. The powder is ignited by bringing together a rock and a piece of metal? No incantation of any kind is involved? Not even the most basic fire spell?"

His shyness compelling him to glance downward, Kemal replied. "That's correct, sir."

A disbelieving Jaquard turned to Petrone. "The fire spell was perhaps the first basic incantation discovered by our primitive ancestors. Yet the device creates fire by bringing together pieces of wholly inert rock and metal? How can this be?"

Proud but honest, the captain replied straightforwardly. "I have no idea, sir. When I first saw a demonstration of the process, I was as incredulous as yourself."

"Fire without a fire incantation. Such a thing has never been imagined," Jaquard murmured. He looked up sharply. "If it is not born of conjuration, it cannot be countered by conjuration."

"That is my way of thinking also, General," the lieutenant told him, nodding.

Turning, Jaquard gestured in the direction of the shattered chair. "What propels the ball with such force?"

Letting the general continue to hold the stun, the lieutenant proceeded to explain. "The entire force of the sudden fire is trapped within the tube. This force drives the ball forward and with great velocity out the only opening. In the absence of a directional spell, the length and straightness of the tube alone decide its course."

"Astounding." A glint appeared in the general's eyes. "Can you make more than one of these?"

The lieutenant glanced at the captain, who smiled back. "I don't see why not, sir," the younger man declared. "With the help of skilled hands, the process of manufacture should be greatly accelerated."

"The powder," Jaquard pressed on. "Where does it come from?"

"That's the interesting thing, sir. Ample supplies of most ingredients are present within the grounds of the city itself. The only other critical component is readily available on at least two of the islands in the inner harbor." He hesitated, then added, "It is the residue of the seabirds that nest there."

"The residue of . . ." Now it was the general's turn to break out into a wide grin. "Are you telling me that one of the vital components of this deadly magic you have devised is bird shit?"

"It's not magic, sir," Petrone corrected him tactfully. "It's something else. We don't have a name for it yet." He looked at his protégé and smiled. "That is, Lieutenant Kemal does not have a name for it yet."

All trace of Jaquard's lethargy had vanished. He was once more a determined, fervent soldier of the kingdom, eager to do battle. And what a battle it was going to be, he mused, envisioning the effect on the confident Misarians when ball after ball of despised and debased, ordinary, unenchanted lead smashed through their strongest incantations to deal death and injury. They would not understand what was happening to them. Not understanding, they would panic, turn, and flee, to be driven from the kingdom's shores forever.

Handing the unnatural weapon back to its maker, he reached down to the table to pick up one of the metal balls that had spilled from the cloth bag. Holding it up to a glowbulb, which drifted closer at his beckoning, he rolled the metal sphere back and forth between powerful thumb and weathered forefinger.

"This killing sphere, this innocent inert bit of meager lead: what do you call it? A stun-ball?"

"Well," Lieutenant Kemal murmured, "when I first got everything to work, the force of its strike reminded me of a charging bull. So I thought to call it a bull. But it's so much smaller than a bull I felt it necessary to add a diminutive. I call it a bullette.

" 'Bullette.' And not a spell to be sensed anywhere about it. The Misarian misanthropes won't know what hit them. Their sorceral strategists will strive to emplace thaumaturgic defenses only to find themselves devastated by ordinary lead. Ordinary lead and," he added with an unmistakable hint of glee, "bird shit!" Putting down the innocent-seeming sphere, he turned back to the two waiting officers.

"Whatever you need, requisition it from stores and supplies. I'll sign the necessary orders. Work as fast as you can." He looked sharply at the lieutenant. "How quickly can you produce these stuns and bullettes?"

"It will take some time, sir," the lieutenant told him. "To fashion this one, by myself, required several years."

Some of Jaquard's initial enthusiasm faded. "We don't have several years, lieutenant."

"I know, sir. The enemy must be kept at bay while we make a start with the necessary manufacture. Realizing this, I set my mind to devise possible means by which we may delay and even drive them, at least temporarily, away."

"Another miracle," Jaquard muttered. He raised a hand. "Excuse me, gentlemen. Another way of thinking." He gazed hard at the lieutenant. "What did you have in mind, *Captain* Kemal?"

The lieutenant took the instant promotion in stride. "I'll need," he told his expectant commanding officer evenly, "a gryphon. And some men to help me collect more ingredients. A *lot* more ingredients. And several metal cylinders of the kind that are commonly used to store fresh milk."

In spite of what he had just witnessed, the general could not keep from repeating, "*Milk* containers?"

The new captain stared back at him. Suddenly, he

did not look so young. "I'm going to try and make
something a little bigger than a stun."

Several days later Jaquard and his senior staff were
watching from the highest tower of the city walls as
the lieutenant and his double escort sped toward the
blockading Misarian fleet. Major Petrone was present
as well. The appearance of a squadron of gryphons
heading toward them would have sparked an immediate response from the enemy, in force. A triplet of
gryphons, without any escorting pixies or other aerial
manifestations, was presumed to consist of scouts who
would stay high and not attempt to cast any spells.
Any surprise incantations launched from altitude
would, in any case, easily be countered by the fleet's
alert defenses. Save for conjuring a few flaming salamanders in their general direction, the trio was ignored. In any event, the sortie from the city soared
too high for the keening, combusting salamanders to
reach. Failing to hit any targets, they fell backward
to land in the sea. There they promptly flamed out,
hissing softly.

A personal magnifying spell hovering in front of
him, General Jaquard watched as the three gryphons
tilted their wings and banked sharply to the right. Riding wand on the middle gryphon, behind its pilot, Captain Kemal could be seen to lean out of his harness
and drop something. It was a fairly large object and
shaped like a teardrop. Observing this, Colonel Aspar-
eal theorized aloud that it might be a crying spell designed to put out of action the sailors on one of the
blockading ships, though what such a temporarily inca-
pacitating incantation could hope to accomplish in the
long run the good colonel could not imagine.

The gryphons banked sharply away. The teardrop

shape struck not a ship but the resting, finned serpent to which it was harnessed. There was a tremendous explosion. Jaquard found the startled cries of his experienced senior staff most gratifying, though he was hard-pressed, even though he had some idea of what was coming, to hold back his own astonishment.

When the smoke cleared, both ship and serpent were as before—except that the serpent was now missing its great, fanged, seaweed-fringed head. As the massive serpentine, decapitated body sank beneath the waves, there was panic among the sailors on the ship. Deprived of its motive force, the vessel found itself suddenly at the mercy of the currents that ran outside the entrance to the harbor. It promptly slammed into the blockading vessel next to it before those aboard could rouse their own harnessed serpent to pull it out of the way.

A second teardrop fell from the middle gryphon. This time its target was one of the largest ships in the blockading fleet. To their credit, the vessel's defenders were ready. A golden cloud appeared above the ship, passionate and beautiful. No gryphon, no dragon, no fire-spell could penetrate it. Beneath, the defenders threw up a curtain of dismay designed to shunt any incoming enchantment harmlessly off to one side.

The heavy teardrop shape went right through the center of the golden cloud as if it was no more than a cloud, ignored the curtain of dismay as though it represented nothing more than the distraught thoughts of the officers who had sent it forth, and struck the ship. A second explosion ripped through the air. By now it seemed as if half the besieged population of Tesselar had gathered atop the harbor walls. Some of them were jumping up and down and thrusting hands and fists in the air. A hole well and truly spelled (no, not spelled, Jaquard had to remind himself) in its hull, the Misarian ship began to sink rapidly. Distraught sailors could be seen leaping off its deck and sides. Desperate officers tried to repair the hole with several patching spells. But because the perforation had not been caused by a spell, their efforts proved futile.

A sea-based squadron of gryphons was already launching from the Misarian flagship, but by now Captain Kemal and his triumphant escort were winging back to the city. Soon they would be safely within its outer defensive spells. Observing their approach, Jaquard realized that not only was it going to be possible to defend Tesselar, today represented a significant shift in the balance of power. The kingdom would be saved. The equation had been changed. Thanks to the discoveries of a persistent, different-thinking junior lieutenant, warfare would never be the same again. *Nothing* would ever be the same again. If the powers-that-be so desired it, the Kingdom of Brevantis would become a force the likes of which the world had never seen. Or would at least until other lands and kingdoms independently made the same discoveries as the resourceful Captain Kemal. A way of doing things that was other-than-magic had been revealed. Undoubtedly, it would be exploited in ways a simple career soldier like himself could not foresee.

Though this invention would allow the salvation of his city and his country, General Jaquard was surprised to discover that his feelings about it were, at best, mixed.

BLOOD IN THE WATER

by Tanya Huff

"**M**ISTER TRYNT! Get that anchor line on the lateen moved aft!"

"Aye, sir!"

With the line moved and more of the sail engaged, Captain Harl shaded his eyes and searched for the shadow against the horizon that meant land. Cut off from the mainland by the Catline Strait, the island of Barravista had always depended on the sea—on the fish that silvered the water over the coastal shoals, on the ships that brought in the food the rocky, wind-swept soil couldn't produce. When the war had threatened to cut them off, when privateers backed by the enemy's treasury had swept in from the south stripping schooners and caravels bare, Queen Isabella had called in Admirl Buryl and commanded him to take control of the sea lanes. "*. . . hold against all Navareen aggression. I will not have the edges of my empire starved into surrender.*"

So the admiral had pulled the *Dawn Arrow* out of the battle in the gulf, loaded its hold with grain and wine and oil, and sent it to Barravista. After the *Arrow*'s heavy catapult had sent the third privateer to the bottom in flames, the rest had cut their losses and headed south for easier pickings. Unfortunately, the admiral had decided to maintain the show of force and Harl continued to ply the merchanter's route, the only danger the monotony of an easy passage.

"Land ho!"

The cry from the crow's nest jerked him out of his reverie.

"Tighten up those lines; let's put some wind in those sails! I want to clear that headland by . . ."

Impact threw him against the helmsman. He swore and grabbed for a ratline, hauling himself back up onto his feet.

"Heading?"

"We're dead on course, sir." The helmsman hauled the wheel around. "It's no reef."

"Debris?" There'd been enough merchant ships taken down in these waters to add the hazard of floating timbers to the trip.

"Nothing on the surface, sir!" the bow lookout called. She hooked her legs around the bowsprit and leaned out over the water. "And nothing just be . . ."

"Serpent!"

"In these seas?" Harl snarled as he turned toward the call. "Don't be . . ."

Its head was already a tall man's height above the waves and still rising. Glistening green and gold and blue, the color of sunlight on the sea, it blinked onyx eyes and tasted the air with a forked tongue. The only sound was the lap of water on wood and the hum of the wind in the lines as the crew stood frozen in shock. The great serpents were rare even in the south and never seen this far north.

It rose above the starboard rail.

Almost up the lowest spar.

"Archers!" The Weapons Master's voice shattered the silence and jerked the crew into action.

Harl clamped his teeth shut on commands of his own. They were already running full out and had no hope of outdistancing the serpent even should he find more wind.

"Fire at will!"

As the serpent continued to rise, a rain of arrows bounced off iridescent scales and fell into the sea.

"Aim for the eyes!"

But the eyes had risen past the upper spar, the folds and ridges of the creature's muzzle making it an impossible shot from below. As Harl watched in horror, the great head dove forward between the masts and arced down over the port side. Between one heartbeat and the next, a belt of flesh constricted around the ship.

"Blades!"

The belt tightened, unmarked by weapons. Ends of broken lines whipped around the masts. A body tumbled shrieking from torn rigging to the water. The upper rail splintered.

"All hands!" Harl bellowed pulling his long knife and charging forward. "Use your points! In behind the lap!"

They drew blood then—but not enough. It had barely splashed against the deck when the deck boards shattered. Curses and prayer came mixed from the sailors chancing the sea and the monster within it rather than be caught in the dangerous mess of wreckage.

As the masts toppled and the weight of the sails pulled the halves apart, Captain Harl went down with his ship, still driving his knife between the serpent's scales. Finally, lungs screaming for air, he kicked toward the surface.

Felt sharp teeth close around his waist.

"So there's a sea serpent in the Catlaine Strait destroying ships and then devouring the crews."

"Yes, sir. One of my people was on the *Sea Shepard*. Given his report, I believe the *Lord Ryden* and the *Dawn Arrow* suffered the same fate."

Admiral Buryl peered out from under heavy brows at his head of Naval Intelligence. "If this serpent is devouring the crews, how did your man escape?"

"My people are very fast swimmers when motivated, sir."

"No doubt," muttered the admiral's aide. "Your people excel at getting away."

Gaison NcTran ignored her and, with an effort, kept from rubbing the stump of his left arm. His people gathered intelligence; they didn't fight battles they had no hope of winning. Nor did they die trying to save lives already lost.

"The moment we knew the *Arrow* was lost, I would have put one of your people on the *Ryden*. We wouldn't have lost the *Shepard* if we'd had word earlier."

He turned to the nearer of the two captains who'd accompanied the admiral to the briefing. "Our assumption was that the privateers had returned more heavily armed. Until we had confirmation this wasn't so, my people were better deployed elsewhere. Our numbers are limited, and we need to go where we can be best used."

"You need to be used where you're most needed!"

They locked eyes. The captain looked away first.

Unlike the admiral's aide, who had all the prejudices of a fisher family toward shapeshifters who were not only their competition in the boats but had the unfair advantage of becoming seals in the water, the captain spoke from distress at loss of ships, of life.

"And you're sure, NcTran, you're sure this serpent is being used by the enemy?"

"As sure as I can be, sir." Gaison turned his attention back to the admiral. "They hate the cold and the Catlaine Strait is never warm. Even in the south, they rarely bother with ships because the food value isn't worth the effort expended. And, more tellingly, the Navareen fishing fleets have left the Empire Banks."

"They're paying the serpent in fish?"

The Navareen were paying the serpent the way all those who brought a tactical advantage to war were paid—it had been deeded its own estate, sole access to one of the richest fishing areas in the West Sea. But as that essentially meant they were paying it in fish, Gaison nodded. "Yes, sir."

"Wonderful." Admiral Buryl sighed and stared down at the map table. "It's not enough we're fighting them on the sea, now we have to fight them under it as well. Can you talk to it?"

"It, sir?"

"The serpent, man, the serpent! If it was convinced to fight for the Navareen, maybe you can convince it to change sides."

"Unfortunately, Admiral, even if we had something to offer it . . ." And there was no need to add that they didn't. ". . . none of my people speak serpent. The Navareen have to have paid for the services of a Mer."

"A Mer?"

"It's the only way they could make the deal, sir."

Buryl sighed. "They must really want to win this war if they're willing to dump that much of their treasury into the sea. All right, we can't talk to it and we can't outrun it. Can we go around it? Stay in water too shallow for it, maybe."

"Unfortunately, there's no way to get to Barravista without crossing deep water. Miles of deep water," he added, turning enough to the side that he could trace a large area out on the map with his remaining hand. "The serpent could be anywhere in this area."

"Wonderful. What's left?"

Gaison shrugged. "We destroy it, sir."

"Of course we do. How?"

"The Mer . . ."

"Too expensive." The second captain, the Admiralty's member on council, raised her hand, cutting him off. "Even if the council would allow the expenditure, this war's left bugger all in the treasury. You'll have to think of something else."

Buryl reached out and picked the wooden ship representing the *Dawn Arrow* off the table. "Think of it soon, NcTran, or we lose Barravista. Make stopping this serpent your first concern."

"Sir, my regular duties . . ."

"Can be handled by your second. The queen refuses to lose that island, which makes it our job to hang onto it. Go. And I don't want this to get out," he continued, his voice stopping Gaison with his hand on the door. "People find out Navareen's sent a sea serpent into our waters and we'll have panic in every village up and down the coast. Every idiot who lives by the sea will be assuming the serpent's come for them. No offense."

All of Gaison's people lived by the sea. "None taken, sir."

No point in being offended at an accurate observation.

"Gaison!"

Closing the admiral's door behind him, he turned to see Jeordi NcMarin, his Second and a cousin on his mother's side, hurrying along the corridor, a sheaf of paper in one hand.

"We had a bird from outpost seven." Jeordi thrust the paper toward him. "Mirag made landfall day before yesterday. She says there's a new design being built in the Navareen shipyards. Shallow draft, lean and fast. She thinks they're planning a run up the coast."

Gaison nodded, ignoring the paper. "Makes sense. What with our attention on deep water right now. What about the second bird confirming?"

"Not yet. Weather's been unsettled. It may have run into trouble."

"It may have been shot and eaten," Gaison snorted. "Wouldn't be the first time. Take the report into Admiral Buryl."

"Me?" Jeordi's dark eyes widened.

"He's got me dealing with the trouble in the Catlaine Strait." No need to be more specific, not within the Admiralty wing.

"Dealing? How?"

"Damned if I know."

When the war with Navareen escalated from a border conflict into out-and-out conquest, Queen Isabella had conscripted all the mages within her borders into her service. Since four of the six were already in her service and the fifth had just celebrated his 107th birthday, while the sixth had barely passed his 17th, this made very little impact on either the mages or the nation.

They'd been given the top floor of the palace's old south range and told to direct their studies toward winning the war. Their only contribution to date had been a spell that delayed the ignition of fireballs until the impact with the target shattered the glass ball containing the spell. When it worked, when the cork remained in the ball and the catapult operators hit the target, the results were impressive—but only the glassblowers were completely happy with it.

The way Gaison saw it, enlisting the wizards might not help, but considering what they were facing, it couldn't hurt.

"Preposterous." The middle-aged woman peered at him from under an impressive tangle of bright red hair. "Sea serpents don't come this far north."

Gaison sighed and tried again. "This one's working for the Navareen. They've sent it north into our shipping lanes to cut off Barravista. It's attacking our ships from below."

"Well, of course it's attacking from below. It would hardly be attacking from above, now would it? You're one of the seal people, aren't you? Got your skin put away safe, do you? Have you been to a council meeting? This palace is a den of thieves, you know that, right? I imagine you'd be lost if it was stolen, wouldn't you? Couldn't change then, could you?"

"What do you want *us* to do about this serpent?" asked another wizard while Gaison still reeled under the spate of questions from the first.

He turned away from the redhead faster than was strictly polite. "I need to destroy it, and I was hoping you might have some ideas."

"As a general rule, when the great serpents begin hunting in shipping lanes, it's easier to move the shipping than the serpent." The youngest wizard looked up from the massive book in front of him and Gaison caught a glimpse of an illustration of a ship split in two—very much like what had been reported happening in the Caitlaine Strait. "Is that possible?"

"Not this time. Her Majesty doesn't want to lose Barravista."

"I imagine Barravista doesn't want to be lost, does it?" snorted the redhead.

"No. But neither," Gaison added pointedly, "do we want to lose more ships or more lives. They're going down with all hands, and I have orders to stop it. It seems the only way to stop it is to destroy the serpent."

"The only way? The only way?" A wizard wrapped tightly about with strips of blue cloth rolled her eyes. "Isn't that just like the army."

"Navy."

She ignored him. "The only way is destruction! Typical. Honestly. It takes your arm, you take its life."

"What?' He glanced down at his pinned sleeve then up at the wizard. "I lost the arm in the last war. The serpent had nothing to do with it."

The redhead snorted again. "So you say."

Nodding and grumbling, four of the six wizards returned to what they'd been doing when he arrived. The fifth continued snoring and the sixth squared his shoulders.

"I'll see what I can do," the youngest wizard said. "I had an uncle on the *Dawn Arrow*."

Gaison had almost reached the shipyard when he realized the wizards had given him an answer.

* * *

"What do you mean we don't have to destroy it?" Admiral Buryl growled.

"It's the ultimate solution, sir, but until we can work out how, what we really need to do is get ships through to Barravista and home again."

"You're trying my patience, NcTran."

"Sorry, sir." Gaison straightened involuntarily, as though he were back on board ship being chewed out by the mate. "If the great serpents don't normally attack shipping because there's so little food return for the effort they put out, what we need to do is draw the serpent away from the ship with food that won't require much of an effort. Decoy food."

"Decoy food?"

"Yes, sir. When the serpent is spotted, half a dozen of my people will hit the water and lure it away from the ship. They'll lose it in the shallows off the west end of Barravista, follow the shoals around to the harbor, and pick up the ship for the trip back where they'll do the same thing."

Heavy brows drew in. "You can order your people to be sea serpent food?"

"Decoy sea serpent food, sir. I'm pulling six of my best off intelligence work. After all, we excel at getting away." He glanced over at the admiral's aide, who colored.

Buryl stared at the map, at the blocks of wood that represented three ships lost with all hands, at the outline of the island cut off from desperately needed supplies. "They're *sure* they'll be fast enough?"

That was the question, wasn't it? Gaison rubbed at the stump of his left arm. "Unfortunately, there's only one way to find out."

"There's another problem. Your report mentioned that the lookout didn't see the serpent until it surfaced for the attack. That's too late to decoy it away."

"It is well camouflaged, sir, but I think I have a solution. It doesn't go deep because it doesn't like the cold, and so it tends to stay just under the surface where there's some warmth from the sun. . . ."

"Wait."

Gaison fell silent while the admiral gathered his thoughts.

"If it can swim that shallow," Buryl asked after a moment, "how can your people lose it in the shoals?"

"Shallow's not the same as just under the surface, sir. Something that big needs a lot of water around it."

"Yes, well, you'd know," the admiral grunted, his gaze flicking over the other man's bulk. "Carry on, then."

"The lookouts couldn't see the serpent because of their angle . . ." He sketched it in the air. ". . . and the reflection of light on the water, but if we brought in some aerial support . . ."

"What did you have in mind, NcTran?"

"We borrow a couple of Hawk-eyes from the army."

The waves remained ever changing, no section of the sea the same twice, but Donal NcAylo was positive they were nearly at the point the *Dawn Arrow* had gone down. "Anything yet?"

"No. Nothing. There was nothing half a second ago and there's nothing now." Somehow, the Hawk-eye managed to glare even through her feathered blindfold. "When I see something, you'll be the first . . ."

"What?" he demanded in the pause.

"I see something."

Donal stepped away from the scout and peered up at her hawk—a black speck growing larger as it broke off its search pattern and dove toward the sea.

"It's the serpent." The Hawk-eye cocked her head. "Damn, that thing's huge."

"Starboard side, people! Let's move!" He slipped out of his breeches as his team joined him. "Remember we're going to draw it as deep as we can. The cold water will slow it down."

"Big snakes don't like the cold," his brother Eryc muttered as he stripped.

"That's not what I'd call a big snake," a cousin snorted, glancing at his crotch as she tossed her clothes onto the pile.

"Keep your attention on the job," Donal reminded them. "Maintain formation as long as possible; we want it to think it can get us all in one mouthful." Scooping up his skin, he went over the rail, aware of his team hitting the water behind him even as he changed to seal-shape.

A quick surface to check position—no mistaking Eryc, he was a big man and a bigger seal—then a deep breath and, digging at the sea with his flippers, Donal led his team toward the serpent.

When he heard the hawk scream a warning, he rose just far enough to fill his lungs then, nostrils clamped shut, he slid down into the trough of a wave and dove. Felt the others dive behind him. Felt currents shift and eddy as death changed course.

Donal tipped the whole formation deeper—left flippers up, right down, powerful tails beating against the sea—and felt the water begin to cool. The serpent followed.

So far, so good.

*　　*　　*

"Well, it's not stupid, I'll say that much for it, but it *is* hungry, so the plan worked." Donal accepted the mug of sweet tea with thanks and all but gulped it down. "Worked better on the way there than the way back though, Gaison. If Kytlin hadn't rolled back and slammed it in the eye, Eryk's rear flippers would have been a mouthful shorter."

"She damage it?"

The younger man shook his head. "Startled it is all, threw it off its stroke. Fortunately, we know these waters and it doesn't, so we worked the currents and got clear." He held out his empty mug.

Gaison took it, refilled it, then walked over to the window. He could see the tops of masts in the harbor, smell the salt, hear the gulls, and wanted nothing more than to swim away and leave the serpent for someone else to deal with. "Can you do it again?" he asked without turning.

"What, now?"

"We've had information that Navareen is planning to send two ships out and around to attack Barravista from the west." Gaison turned then, his hand falling to stroke the sealskin lying on the end of his desk. "Her Majesty is sending two of the new warships out to defend the island."

Donal's dark eyes narrowed. "They'll be stationed there? With full war crews?"

"Yes."

"That'll mean . . ."

"Supply ships will have to run more frequently, yes." He waited while Donal thought it through, weighing the condition of his team against need.

"Will the army let us keep the Hawk-eye?"

"The army has volunteered another two pairs."

"Really?"

"No." Donal's expression forced out the first smile Gaison had managed in weeks. "But the admiral convinced the queen that we needed the air support, so the army had no choice." Then he sobered. "I'm putting together another two teams, but it'll take time to pull people from the water and replace them with . . ."

"The young and the old," Donal filled in the pause.

"Younger and older," Gaison corrected, praying the war wouldn't last long enough to make Donal's words true. "Next time you're in, you'll get leave, but this time . . ."

He scooped up the bag that held his sealskin and stood. "Duty calls."

Eyrk's luck ran out on the return trip. They lost two members of the second team the trip after that. The next trip ran clean. The next they lost another two and Donal lost a back flipper when he turned to help a cousin caught but not dead. The serpent had slid farther up onto the shoals than it ever had before. It *wasn't* stupid. It was learning and it was losing interest in the decoys. The last team practically had to feed themselves to it to get it to follow. The only good news was that with the serpent in the strait the sharks stayed away, even when there was blood in the water.

Gaison finished his report for the admiral and worked the stiffness out of his hand. The ships were safe, but at what cost? His people, their numbers never large, were dwindling. His family mourned. They were not the only family mourning, of course. This war with Navareen was being fought, and men and women were dying in places other than the Strait of Catlaine, but there were damned few among his people not family by blood or marriage, so every death swept past them all like an icy current.

The serpent had to be destroyed.

Unfortunately, all the information he'd been able to gather suggested the serpent couldn't be destroyed. They had no way to attack it underwater and it only surfaced when it attacked a ship. Conventional weapons were useless until it was close enough to drive blades up under its scales, and by then it was far too close for blades to matter.

It had no natural predators, and poison enough to kill it would destroy everything else living in the strait. Gaison had even asked the herbalist about poisoning himself and then diving into the sea to poison the serpent. She'd shaken her head and said, *"If this creature is as large as you tell me, you could not swallow enough poison to kill it. Seven, maybe eight of your people, yes, provided it got you all down before it noticed how nasty you tasted."*

Seven or eight to save the rest. They hadn't come to that yet, but they might. . . .

A tentative knock brought him back to his office. He waited for Jeordi to open the door, remembered Jeordi had gone to the strait, and barked, "What is it?"

A thin, almost familiar young man stuck his head into the room. It looked as though bits of his hair had been burned away. "Commander NcTran?"

No one used his rank as a title. "What it is?" he asked again, beckoning the young man in.

"I think I know how we can destroy the serpent."

Gaison frowned as he shoved back his chair and stood. "You're the sixth wizard."

"Alaster Grant."

Of course he had a name. And, apparently, a solution.

"It's a variation on the time delay spell we set up for the catapults. We tuck it into a heavy load, something that'll sink fast, and, at the same depth as the serpent swims, it'll explode."

"Explosions underwater?"

"Yes. It's the depth that sets the spell that blows the charge."

"What if the serpent changes depth?"

"Each spell can be set before it's fired."

"The explosions will disorient it," Gaison allowed. "Might give the ships time to get clear."

Alaster straightened thin shoulders. "Pack the load with nails. It may do more than disorient it."

Gaison grinned and grabbed the young wizard's arm. The scorch marks on his robe matched his hair. "I like the way you think. Come on."

"No! I couldn't find anyone to get you! I'm not supposed to be out of the workshop!"

"Workshop be damned, lad. You're going to sea."

"I'd feel better about this if we could take a few practice shots," the Weapons Master on the *Dark Dancer* grunted, glaring at the wizard once again bending over the rail.

Jeordi shrugged, tugging the heavy fleece robe tighter around his shoulders. He was too old to stand in a northeast wind wearing nothing but breeches. "Alaster says the spells are hard to set, and this . . ." A nod toward the row of eight depth charges. "This is all we have."

"Better be enough or your lot'll be freezing your tails off in the water."

"We'll be warmer in sealskins," Jeordi told him.

"And the colder the water gets, the better our odds of outswimming the serpent."

The Weapons Master turned his scowl on the four men huddled around the Hawk-eye, their bulk shielding her from the worst of the wind. "No women in this group."

"No." Just younger and older men. Young and old men soon enough if the serpent wasn't stopped.

"Are we there yet?" Alaster moaned, staggering back, wiping his mouth.

Before either Jeordi or the Weapons Master could answer, the Hawk-eye stiffened and cried, "Serpent!"

Jeordi grinned. "That would be a yes."

Firing coordinates came from the bird struggling to maintain position in the chill wind, to the Hawk-eye, to the Weapons Master. There was no need to reset the first spell; unsuspecting, the serpent cruised at its usual depth.

The explosion to larboard was muffled but near enough to the surface that a geyser of water shot up tying sea to sky.

"It didn't like that!" the Hawk-eye called, as someone cheered from the forecastle. "It's turned. New coordinates—left about twenty degrees, maybe three meters deeper."

Brow furrowed, Alaster laid his hands on the charge.

The second shot drove it deeper still. The third . . .

"I can't tell for sure . . ." the Hawk-eye cocked her head as her bird barely skimmed the tops of the waves, ". . . but I think it took damage!"

The fourth went off close enough to the ship that there was a series of small thuds below the waterline and the fifth blew another geyser.

Then a long silence as half the crew of the *Dark*

Dancer watched the bird, wheeling against low gray cloud, and half the crew watched the Hawk-eye.

"I can't see it," she said at last.

"Is it dead?" the captain called from her place by the helm.

"I don't think so. But it's gone!"

"What if it comes back before we get clear of the strait?" Jeordi asked under the cheers.

The Weapons Master shrugged. "Then we hit it again."

"And on the return trip?"

They looked together at the three remaining charges and then went to rescue Alaster from the enthusiastic congratulations of the crew.

Injured or cautious, the serpent stayed well away for the remainder of the voyage into Barravista. For the five days in port, Jeordi's team escorted the wizard from one celebration to another. Feted by sailors and locals both, Alaster was so overwhelmed by the attention that Jeordi was amused to note he actually welcomed their return to the *Dark Dancer*, even if it meant a return to hanging over the rail.

When the Hawk-eye spotted the serpent on the trip back to the mainland, everyone watched and waited, breath held, as Alaster laid shaking hands on the first charge and reset the spell.

"It's turning. Heading aft!"

The second charge arced over the stern, disappeared beneath the waves, and blew a column of water nearly the serpent's height into the sky.

"It's not coming any closer!"

"Hold that last charge!" the Weaponsmaster bellowed. "Keep it in reserve until that monster comes closer in!"

A day and a half later, they sailed into the harbor

with the last charge still loaded but unfired. The serpent had followed at a cautious distance to the edge of the deep water. Once or twice it lifted its head above the waves and fixed the ship in an onyx gaze as though trying to work out just how exactly its intended prey was connected to the noise and pressure and pain, but it came no closer.

The captain had sent a bird when they reached safety, and Gaison was waiting on the pier.

"Not dead, but definitely discouraged," Jeordi called as his commander came aboard. "Alaster's done it. The strait is ours again."

"Glad to hear it." Gaison gripped his cousin's shoulder, then turned his attention to the wizard. "The admiral wants you with him when he speaks to the queen. Her Majesty will be well pleased with what you've accomplished, Your Wisdom." He grinned as Alaster looked startled at the honorific. "I expect she'll want to reward you before you head back to Barravista."

"Back?"

"Well, I imagine Her Majesty will eventually order at least one of the other wizards shipboard, but for now, you're it."

"Me?"

"The *Sea Vixen* leaves tomorrow on the late tide."

Eyes wide, Alaster clutched at Gaison's sleeve. "But we've only one charge remaining!"

"Here."

"No. Well, yes, but here is all there is. I only had ingredients to make the eight before we left."

Gaison stared at the wizard, at Jeordi, and, just because he needed a few moments more to gather his thoughts, up into the rigging. "All right," he said at last. "I'll tell the admiral you need more time, and he

can delay the *Vixen* until she can be armed. While
you're building new charges, you'll put together a
workshop so that while you're at sea everything but
the final spell can be reconstructed, ready for your
return. How much time do you need?"

"Two of the elements are very rare . . ."

"You'll have access to all the manpower you need,"
Gaison told him. "How much time?"

"Six or seven months."

"What?"

"Five," Alaster squeaked, taking a step back. "Five,
if the army has retaken Harstone and reopened the
mines."

"Six or seven months!"

The army had not retaken Harstone.

Alaster ducked behind Jeordi as Admiral Buryl
stomped around his office growling curses under his
breath. The admiral had gone to sea at fifteen and he
had an extensive list of profanity to work through.
Finally, he wound down, took a deep breath and
glared at his head of Naval Intelligence. "Now what?"

Gaison glanced at his cousin. "My people go back
in the water, sir," he said.

"Will that even work?" the admiral demanded.
"Suppose the serpent thinks, 'Aha, those seals are in
the water again. There were no explosions when they
were in the water before so there'll be none now and
I can go after that ship.' You said it was already losing
interest in the decoys."

"Yes, but I don't think it thinks like that." Gaison
half shrugged as the admiral's brows rose dramatically.
His job was to know, not to think, and to find out if
he didn't know. Unfortunately, in this situation they
had theories but no facts.

"It was hanging back on the return trip," Jeordi

offered. "Maybe that last charge might discourage it permanently."

"Maybe. Might," the admiral grunted. "I can't risk crews on a maybe or a might. The only way to permanently discourage that monster is to destroy it."

"If the serpent would swallow a charge . . ." Alaster began, flushed and fell silent as the other three turned to stare.

"Go on," Gaison prodded.

The youngest wizard looked as though he wanted to run, but he cleared his throat and finally managed to keep talking. "Well, if it would swallow a charge, it's possible that at a certain depth, when the spell went off, its physiognomy would react violently."

"Its what?"

"Its, um . . . its physical construction."

"How violently?"

"Ka boom. Where the ka refers to the charge blowing and the boom to the serpent."

"How possible?"

Alaster cleared his throat again. "Fairly."

"Would you risk your life on it?" Admiral Burl demanded.

After a long moment, Alaster nodded.

"If we could get it to open its mouth," Gaison began.

"It would be easy enough to slap it in before the spell went off," Jeordi finished.

"Easy," the admiral snorted. But he didn't argue. "I assume this puts your people back in the water, NcTran." He drummed his fingers against his desk. "One question. If it's lost interest in the decoys, how do your people get it to open its mouth?"

Gaison rubbed the stump of his left arm. "We make it an offer too good to ignore."

*   *   *

"I can't believe Admiral Buryl agreed to let you do this," Jeordi muttered, head sunk deep within the high collar of his robe. "Setting yourself up as bait is completely insane. You're in no kind of shape to be doing this."

"If I was in shape," Gaison reminded him, "this wouldn't work. And besides, it's not like I'll be swimming alone—there'll be others in the water."

"And a sea serpent!"

Feet braced against the movement of the deck, Gaison ignored his cousin's protest the way he'd been ignoring his protests ever since he'd floated the plan. He'd always been among the larger of his people and the last decade of relative inaction had helped to pack on more bulk. The serpent would not only see a large, meaty seal, it'd see a large meaty seal missing half a front flipper. Food that had no chance of getting away.

"What if it sees the charge?"

"What? With me there to snack on? I doubt it."

"All right, what if you can't get clear? What if it takes you as well as the charge? What if Alastar's wrong and there's just ka, not ka boom?"

"Then it looks like you get my job." When no response was immediately forthcoming, Gaison clapped the younger man on the shoulder. "Look at the bright side; we're almost in sight of land with no sign of the serpent."

And right on cue, from the crow's nest: "Land ho!"

Jeordi peered toward the low smudge of gray on the horizon. "Do you think it's gone?"

"Serpent! Starboard side!"

Gaison tightened his grip as the Hawk-eye tightened her bird's pattern. "Actually, no."

"This is insane," Jeordi repeated when Gaison dropped his robe.

Gaison ignored him as Alaster handed over a slightly scaled down charge hammocked in a length of net.

"It's set to go about six meters down," the wizard told him, pointedly not looking toward his stump. "You need to . . . it's just . . . I mean . . . Good luck."

"Thank you." Sealskin in his hand, net in his teeth, he waited until the others were all in the water and moving into position before he followed.

He missed the sea when he wasn't in it, and he wasn't in it much these days. When this was over, one way or another, he'd spend more time in the water. Net still clenched in his teeth, charge dangling below him, Gaison pushed himself forward and down with his tail, right flipper sculling back hard to keep him swimming in a straight line.

He could feel the serpent drawing closer and every instinct screamed at him to turn and swim for his life. Down as far as he needed to be—below the serpent but above the depth to set the spell—he paused, hanging in the water, the charge hanging down by his tail, his single front flipper driving him around in a flailing aimless circle.

Sharks would find the preformance irresistible. What large predator could resist prey already maimed?

Maimed, undeniably, but he'd had years to practice and adapt. When he finally came around to see the serpent diving for him, mouth gaping, he stopped his spin, flipped back and, releasing the net, slapped the charge right into the serpent's mouth. If he also emptied his bladder, no one needed to know.

The charge clanged off a row of serrated teeth and bounced down the creature's throat. Gaison knew that for a fact because he was staring right down that throat. Then two lithe forms slammed into him from below, driving him toward the surface. One of the longer teeth dug into his side as he twisted to clear the upper jaw. He rose in a haze of blood as the serpent continued down, too big to change direction immediately.

Two more dark shapes darted past, wedge-shaped shadows in the deep and the serpent, cheated of a sure meal, followed.

Gaison knew it the moment Alaster's charge went off, knew it because with his two minders moving him toward the ship, he was free to twist his head back in time to see the great tail come whipping up toward the surface. He pushed the boy on his right hard away and rolled with the one on his left tight against his body. They fought turbulence sucking them under and down and had no idea how close they were to the ship until they slammed into it, his wound darkening the water with another cloud of blood.

Nostrils still clamped shut, he struggled to the surface pulling the stunned young seal with him. Heaving the limp body up onto his shoulders, he rolled it into the net and found himself rolled in turn by the second boy. By the time the sailors pulled them on board, the serpent had stopped writhing.

"I don't see it," the Hawk-eye announced.

Gaison shrugged out of his skin and stood, blood dripping to the deck as he counted his people. His two, one of them not happy but alive. One of the two who'd led the serpent deeper. Two short.

Barking from the larboard side drew everyone across the deck and the two uninjured seals went back into the water to help roll a bleeding body into the net and then roll in after it.

"This isn't a wound I can treat a on a seal," the

ship's medic protested, so they pulled Jeordi out of his skin and wrapped a leather belt lightly around the stump of his leg.

"The serpent?" he gasped.

Gaison shook his head and turned toward the wizard.

"There was no boom," Alastar said miserably. "There should have been a . . ."

The water on the larboard side of the ship suddenly erupted. Chunks of scaled meat slammed into the deck.

A moment later, there was only an oval of white foam bobbing on blue-green waves.

"I suspect that was your boom," Gaison said dryly, lifting the wizard back onto his feet.

Alaster stared down at the bloody mark where a fist-sized piece of meat had slammed into his chest. "Ow."

"You're lucky it wasn't a bigger piece."

"I know, but . . ." He lifted his head, eyes suddenly widening. "It worked."

Gaison nodded, suddenly very, very tired. "It worked."

The wizard frowned as he counted the hunks of meat. "But the serpent was huge. Enormous. This can't be all of it."

"The rest of it sank," the Hawk-eye told them, holding her arm out for her bird. "Three, maybe four big sections heading for the bottom."

"It's dead, then?"

"Idiot," Jeordi hissed through clenched teeth.

The cheering started then and continued into Barravista. This time, without an escort to run interference, Alaster lasted three days before he staggered back to the ship and hid out with the injured. Gaison sent a sloop out with birds to carry the message to the admiral and the queen.

A week later, after a heavily laden caravel came into port, the *Vixen* started home. Standing at the rail, watching the waves, Gaison realized that the serpent had gone down close enough to the *Dawn Arrow* that its body probably rotted on the seabed within sight of the first ship it had destroyed.

He couldn't help but feel that Captain Harl would enjoy the view.

IOWA UNDER SIEGE

by Mickey Zucker Reichert

AN AUTUMN BREEZE ruffled Kyle Holcomb's hair, luffing beneath the thick, sandy waves to tickle ears roughened by weather. He looked out over his fields: cornstalks battered and broken by the combine, starlings fluttering down to snatch remaining kernels from the tire-pocked earth, and surrounding tree lines awash in amber, scarlet, green, and lavender. This time of year he appreciated the animals he battled all summer. Even the deer became welcome visitors after the harvest. Every leftover kernel they ate meant one less volunteer corn stalk stealing nutrients from next year's crop of soybeans. Wisps of cloud shielded the sun just enough to keep the temperature from soaring, and Holcomb appreciated the cool serenity of this fall day. For now, it left his bare arms awash in gooseflesh. Hours later, he would not have the slimy discomfort of a T-shirt wringing sweat, hair clinging to the back of his neck, or the beet-red pain of a sunburned face.

Pulling on his weathered gloves, Holcomb ap-

proached his John Deere tractor, its cheery green fa-
çade faded and chipped beneath a layer of dust and
grime. He double-checked the plow's three-point
hitch, glancing over circular blades still clutching last
year's divots. Everything appeared ready. He trotted
to the front, put a foot on the step, and heaved his
bulk toward the driver's seat. In midair, he spotted a
stranger already sitting there.

Startled, Holcomb lost his grip and fell, jerking to
keep from slamming his chin against the foot plate.
He managed an awkward landing on the ground that
spared him any injuries. He squinted upward, looking
for the one who had surprised him. No one occupied
the tractor seat, just his grubby cap dangling from the
backrest. *What the hell?* Holcomb blinked, trying to
reform an image of the person he had glimpsed only
for a moment. *Female*, his mind told him, *small and
thin.* He conjured nothing more than that hazy
impression.

"Farmer?" The bell-like voice came from behind
Kyle Holcomb. He spun to face a small, sweet-faced
woman with fine features and long hair in a brilliant
shade of blue. He had seen teenagers with multicol-
ored hair before, every shade from bleached white to
hot pink, orange and purple, to Labrador retriever
black. All of them had looked silly—outrageous attempts to demand attention while, at the same time,
denouncing those who stared. This woman looked
older, perhaps his own age, in her early forties. And,
oddly, the color suited her perfectly. In fact, he had
not even noticed it the first time he had glimpsed her
on the tractor seat. If nothing else, he should have
remembered the hair.

Realizing he was gawking stupidly, Holcomb
glanced at his scratched, faded work boots and cleared
his throat. "Name's Kyle." He held out a hand.

The woman made a garbled sound, more like a sneeze, though she did not close her eyes or cover her mouth. No spit flew out. She ignored the proffered hand.

Holcomb blinked, arm sagging to his side, and found himself staring again. He had never seen a grown woman so delicately boned and petite. She seemed insubstantial, as if she might break if he touched her. Her eyes had a slight slant to them but lacked the epicanthic folds that usually accompanied such a feature, and the irises perfectly matched her hair. She wore a simple dress, brown in color, with an enormous real daisy at the waist attached by its own long stem rather than a belt. "Are you . . . all right?" he asked, feeling huge and ungainly in her presence.

The stranger looked herself over with delicate grace. "I'm fine. Why do you ask?" She added carefully, "Ky-el."

Holcomb liked the way she said his name; it sounded like music. "I just . . . you made that funny sound . . . and I couldn't tell . . ."

"Funny sound?" Her head cocked to one side as she considered, then laughed. "You mean . . ." She repeated the noise.

Holcomb nodded briskly. "Yes, that one."

"That's my name. I thought you wanted it when you gave me yours."

"Name?" Holcomb's stare grew even more intense, despite his best efforts. "What an odd—" He caught himself, not wanting to sound offensive. "I mean, I've never heard anything like it."

Her head bobbed like a marionette's, free and loose yet with clear grace. "Of course not. You've surely never met a sprite before."

Holcomb rubbed his gloved hands together, uncertain where to take the conversation. "A . . . sprite? Like . . . like the soda?"

Now it was her turn to look confused. "Soda? Is that what you call creatures of Faery?"

"Creatures of . . ." Holcomb rolled his eyes, laughing nervously. Suddenly, the whole thing made sense: the cerulean hair, the oddities of speech, the whimsical spirit that caused her to skip from place to place when she clearly belonged elsewhere. *She's crazy.* He had seen far too much of that lately. Chris Barnholdt had become outcast since he started babbling about some Jack-and-the-Beanstalk giant shouting gibberish in his pasture while the cows huddled in the barn. The Weingards had moved to the area from the city with their sweet little daughter and seemed reasonably normal until last year when the mother gave birth to a terror of a son. Devon, they named him, but the locals called him Demon. His bulbous head with its shock of red hair little resembled his parents or sibling, and eyes like charcoal seemed out of place amid his father's blue and his mother and sister's green. He had started walking at six months of age and never stopped moving, usually to shove someone down a staircase or against a hot stove with that otherworldly, screeching laughter.

Mind working quickly, Holcomb softened his tone, as if speaking to a toddler. "Ooooh. A creature of Faery, eh? Thaaat kind of sprite."

The woman studied Holcomb, head bobbing as she looked him over from head to toe. "What are you doing?"

Holcomb stepped toward her, reaching for an arm. "Taking you home, wherever that may be."

She dodged him with barely a motion. "You can't walk me home, Human. Only magical creatures can enter Faery."

"Right," Holcomb said, humoring her. "I'll just

have to walk you as near as I can." He reached for her arm again.

The self-proclaimed sprite placed both hands firmly on her tiny hips. "Kyle, you moron. You think I'm crazy, don't you?"

Trained not to offend, Holcomb found himself cowed by the directness of her question. "Well, now. Not exactly 'crazy,' ma'am. Just a little . . . confused."

She opened her mouth to protest, but Holcomb forestalled her with a raised hand. "Not that it's your fault or anything, ma'am. There's a lot of craziness going around these parts. I think something got in the water supply or the air blowing in from the Quaker Oats factory—"

The sprite did not wait for him to finish but raised both arms with a keening wail. The sound ripped through Holcomb, physically painless but mental agony. It set his teeth on edge, raised every hair on the back of his neck, and sent him pawing at his ears as if to rip them from his face. It reminded him of the dying scream of a rabbit but was more intense and desperate, more piercing and violent. The sound of twisting metal followed. The tractor jerked, then seemed to melt. Its chipped green paint flowed, distributing evenly over metal turned to softer material that closely resembled flesh. The headlights became eyes, the tires legs, and the plow a massive, club tail. The loader stretched into a wide and toothless grin.

Holcomb gasped, back-stepping wildly until he hit the power pole and fell on his butt. The tractor swung its front end toward him. The headlights glinted wickedly, and the loader curled into a snarl. It gathered its tires to spring.

Covering his face with a protective arm, Holcomb screamed. He braced himself for a tonnage of attack that never came. When he peeked around his arm, the tractor had returned to its natural form, its front wheels twisted as if making a tight turn, the color no longer spotty and chipped but evenly spread, so that it looked a sickly pea green all over. He scrambled to his feet, heart pounding wildly, glancing repeatedly from tractor to sprite. He wanted to speak, but nothing emerged from his gaping mouth.

The sprite's utter calm seemed a wicked counterpoint to Kyle Holcomb's panic. "We have tried to communicate in the past, but we chose our ambassadors poorly."

Holcomb found himself incapable of anything but gawking. He kept his attention mostly on the sprite, but his eyes strayed frequently to the tractor.

"The pixie thought she could get her point across with magic. The giant's English was, apparently, too ancient a dialect. The changeling . . ." The sprite waved her hand dismissively. ". . . well, what can one ever expect of changelings."

Holcomb's heart continued to hammer. He remembered Chris Barnholdt saying the giant's words reminded him of the Pink Floyd song "Several Species of Small Furry Animals Gathered Together in a Cave and Grooving with a Pict." Just suggesting that any musical group would give a song such a title made Barnholdt seem mad by itself, but Holcomb had been curious enough to look it up and find that such a song really existed. However, the tale of the giant was too fantastical even for him. He had worked cautiously around Barnholdt since that day; and, now, it seemed, he owed the other farmer an apology. "So," he finally managed through lips that felt rubbery. "You . . . speak English very good."

The sprite made a gesture toward the tree line. "It's

my job to color the leaves in autumn, so I spend more time around humans than most of the others. I hear them talking from the treetops." She shrugged. "Without realizing it, I learned the language."

Holcomb swallowed hard. He had finally recovered from the ordeal with the tractor, and he felt certain the whole encounter had to be a dream. Unobtrusively, he pinched himself several times, feeling only the pain. He did not awaken. "Why—why did you folks need to talk to us?" He concentrated on the colors around him, the feel of the breeze, the gurgling of his stomach over its scrambled eggs breakfast, details that did not exist in dreams.

"Well, we're immortals, you know."

Holcomb did not know, but he did not interrupt.

"Over the millennia, we've simply outgrown our space and we need a bit of yours."

"Of . . . mine?" Holcomb managed.

"About this much." The sprite's arms flashed outward, and lines of light erupted from them. They flew far beyond Holcomb's fields to encompass part of Muscatine County, all of Johnson, and some of Louisa.

Holcomb did not know how he knew the boundaries of the sprite's indicated territory; it went far beyond his line of sight. Yet, somehow, he could see it as clearly as a map. "That's a fair piece of Iowa." It seemed like a stupid thing to say, yet he could think of nothing better.

"The world of humans is huge. Surely, you won't miss a bit."

The sprite had a point. Most of the world would not care about this fragment of Iowa, mostly farmland sprinkled with towns and even a few small cities. "I would sorely miss it. And eighty or ninety thousand other humans as well. It's our home."

The sprite tipped her head, and the mass of blue hair slid sideways. "Plenty of room elsewhere for you in the human world. We're only taking a very small piece."

Holcomb found his gaze straying to the tractor again, its new coloring a reminder of what he had seen. If these creatures could turn machinery into living weapons, what chance did he have to stop them? He cleared his throat, hoping to make his point without antagonizing the sprite. "Ummm, a small piece, yes; but it is our home. We cannot just let you . . . take our property. Our houses. Our farms."

The sprite shook her hair back into position. "We are informing you humans of our plans as a courtesy. Whether or not you move willingly is your decision."

It was the gentlest threat Holcomb had ever heard, yet he sensed the menace behind it. "You're saying this is nonnegotiable?"

"It is."

"And if we don't leave?"

"We will remove you forcibly."

Holcomb wondered what exactly that would entail. *More changelings? Sharing our houses with elves?* Then, he glanced at the tractor and started to imagine the potential of such magic. He had once seen the devastation an SUV left after the driver used the gas pedal in lieu of the brake. It had smashed out the glass front of a pet store, bending beams, breaking shelves, and shattering merchandise, leaving a trail of squashed bunnies in its wake. He envisioned an army of minivans assaulting Iowa City, cars chasing children down the bloody streets, tanks stomping through Kalona, swinging their gun turrets like trunks. Tiny Tinkerbelles twined through the massacre, exhorting their larger companions as their wands set rooftops alight.

Giants lashed clubs at humans and animals or flung boulders that mowed down forests like bowling pins. A corps of gremlins, grinning and gibbering, swallowed down animals and fleeing humans in enormous, sharp-toothed bites.

His own imagination set Holcomb to trembling. He wanted to run, screaming, to alert all of Iowa to this terrible danger. Instead, he remained in place, willing himself to remain calm. No one would believe him. He would find himself imprisoned in a mental institution while the folk of Faery ran amok. "I . . ." he started and stopped. "Why . . . why now? You said you'd been around for thousands of years."

"Immortals rarely reproduce. After a few millennia, however, that small reproduction becomes significant enough to require more space."

It made sense to Holcomb. In the same few millennia, humans had brought their numbers from thousands to billions. "But isn't there somewhere else—"

"No," the sprite said, with her first show of impatience. "We have chosen here. Be gone by the morrow." She turned wispy.

"Wait!" Holcomb shouted.

The sprite's slender form became solid again. "What?"

"What exactly is 'the morrow'?"

The sprite smiled, rolled her pale eyes. "Tomorrow. Usually in the morning."

Holcomb wondered how many shocks his heart could take before bursting. "You want us all gone by tomorrow morning?"

"Please."

Please. Just like that. What a polite turn of phrase for "get out of your homes, or we'll kill you." "There's no way." Holcomb shook his head at the enormity of the task. First, he would have to convince someone in power of the truth of his allegations. Then, they would have to prepare for war or move everything they owned. *To where?* "We need more time."

"Fine. Three days, then," the sprite said dourly, with the air of one who has no intention of taking "no" for an answer. Before Holcomb could say another word, she disappeared.

Kyle Holcomb sank to the ground. And began to sob.

A half hour later, Kyle Holcomb sat in Chris Barnholdt's tiny kitchen, cupping his hands around a Farm & Fleet mug. He could feel the warmth of the cocoa seeping through the calluses on his palms and fingers but did not bother to take a sip. The scrambled eggs were still churning in his stomach, and anything on top of them might make him violently ill.

"So," Barnholdt said cautiously, as if afraid any word might send his neighbor skittering away in panic. ". . . what can I do for you, Kyle?"

Holcomb whispered into the steam rising from his mug. "I believe you."

"What?"

"I believe you. About the giant."

Barnholdt's weathered cheeks turned pinkish. "Oh, that old thing. I'd nearly forgotten."

It was a blatant lie. The folks around the rural route would never let him forget it. They started whispering the moment they saw him until he drew near enough to hear, then slipped into that same creepy style of speech that Holcomb had used when the sprite had first named herself a creature of Faery. They indulged him, and they pitied him. Now Holcomb felt guilty even though he had not done any of the talking. He had not stopped it either.

"No, Chris. I mean it. I know it really happened."

Barnholdt brought his own mug to his mouth, a chipped, flowered one deeply stained but clean. He could not have drunk for as long as he held it up there, or it would have burned his lips.

Holcomb closed his eyes, about to tell his story for the first time. He could think of no one less likely to laugh at him, yet he still worried for his neighbor's reaction. "Chris, I talked to a sprite today. And she told me it was true."

Barnholdt's eyes widened over his mug. Holcomb thought he might spit the contents all over the rickety table, but he did not. He simply stared, the mug still at his mouth.

Holcomb also waited in silence, worried Barnholdt might think he was being baited. They had known one another too long for that kind of meanness, had shared balers, rakes, and combines, along with smaller tools when the need arose. Though they lived two miles apart, they were one another's nearest neighbors. They were also both bachelors, Holcomb because he had never married and Barnholdt after his divorce. Finally, he broke the hush. "She had blue hair, Chris. Natural blue. And she said an army of magical creatures was going to take our land if we didn't hand it over peacefully."

Barnholdt finally lowered his mug. "Are you bullshitting me, Kyle? Because, if you're bullshitting me, I'm going to kick your ass right now."

Holcomb could understand his friend's consternation. "I'm not making this up, and it wasn't a dream. A goddamned blue-haired fairy came to my house and turned my tractor into a living thing. She also mentioned your giant."

Barnholdt continued to study Holcomb's face, as if waiting for the moment he would crack and admit his prank. "You know, if we hadn't been in the bar when I mentioned that giant, I'd be rotting in the loony bin right now. But I wasn't drinking when I saw that critter in the pasture."

"I know." Holcomb hoped he sounded suitably sincere.

"And I heard it using some bizzaro language—"

"—an ancient form of English," Holcomb finished, then added, "she said."

"Kyle." There was real vulnerability in Barnholdt's tone.

"Yeah?"

"Do you reckon we're both crazy?"

"Nope," Holcomb answered honestly. "But I do reckon anyone we tell this story to will think so." He amended, "Except maybe the Weingards. Turns out Devon's a changeling."

"Really?"

Holcomb thought back to exactly what the sprite had told him. "And, apparently, someone was approached by a pixie. But whoever that was isn't talking."

"That . . . would be me."

Holcomb's eyes widened. "Why didn't you mention it?"

"Would you of?"

"You talked about the giant."

"And look where it got me."

Barnholdt had an undeniable point. "Well . . ." Uncertain where to take the conversation, Holcomb let it hang as he considered. "I guess we can assume that whatever doorway these creatures use to come to us is either on your land or mine."

"I reckon so." Barnholdt took another sip of cocoa. "Blessed, aren't we?"

Holcomb's mind raced. Only half listening, he replied vaguely, "Yeah, blessed." Their next step seemed obvious on the surface. They needed to contact the governor or the president, someone with authority to reason with aliens and either dissuade them from war or fight them.

"It won't work, Kyle."

Jarred from his thoughts, Holcomb looked at his fellow farmer. "What?"

"I know what you're thinking, and it won't work."

Holcomb shivered. "You know what I'm thinking?"

"Did you happen to see the movie *National Treasure*?"

Holcomb shook his head. He rarely bothered to drive the thirty-five miles to Coralville, especially to watch a movie alone.

"Nicolas Cage and a buddy have to convince the powers that be that someone is going to steal the Declaration of Independence because it has an invisible treasure map on the back of it."

Holcomb considered the task, realizing that any agency contacted would believe the claim preposterous. They would get laughed out of the offices, if not locked up for their own safety. That got him thinking about their own predicament. *Who in his right mind would believe that creatures of Faery are coming to steal the better part of three counties in Iowa?* "You're saying there's no way Tom Vilsack is going to believe us."

Barnholdt lowered his mug again and leaned across it, the steam puffing into his face. "I'm saying our own mothers, God rest their souls, would cart our asses off to University Psychiatry in a minute."

It was the sanest single thing Kyle Holcomb had heard all day. "All right, then. What did Nicolas Cage and his buddy do?"

Barnholdt rubbed a finger along the mug, tracing

the flowers. "They had no choice but to handle the problem themselves."

Holcomb closed his eyes. He was more interested in controlling pests and weeds, improving his corn and soybean yields, than becoming a hero. "I was afraid you were going to say that. How did they do?"

Barnholdt cringed, his mouth a grimacing line. "Let's just say it worked out in the end."

Knowing Hollywood's propensity for gunplay and explosions, Holcomb thought it best not to ask for details.

The Weingards lived on a hill surrounded by forty acres of untillable sand. Painted white with pale blue trim, the house sat amid a sea of oak trees. Piles of raked leaves filled the areas between the trunks, most with ragged outlines and flattened tops that revealed children had leaped into them. A fluffy, off-white dog greeted Barnholdt's battered pickup in the circular driveway, tail waving merrily in greeting. The crisp aroma of barbecued meat filled the air, and Holcomb's mouth watered. He could not remember the last time he had cooked himself a decent meal; even his scrambled eggs came out lumpy. Barnholdt pulled the truck around, then cut the engine.

The family sat on a three-season porch, finishing their lunch and watching the farmers approach. Holcomb appreciated that the sprite had come to him on a Saturday. Otherwise, Mr. Weingard would be at work and Mrs. Weingard might not feel comfortable meeting with two large male farmers alone. Now, Holcomb opened his door and leaped out to find parents and children waving an eager greeting. He waved back and forced a smile as Barnholdt also climbed down from the truck.

Mr. Weingard opened the door, his daughter Emily hiding demurely behind him. Devon shoved past both and charged down the stairs, his tiny legs shockingly coordinated for a child of his age. He stormed a leaf pile, diving into it with a gusto that sent oak leaves spiraling in all directions. The father called enthusiastically, "Hi there, neighbors!"

"Howdy, Mike," Barnholdt said, clearly trying to sound cheerful. "Would it be all right if we talked with you and your wife for a bit?"

"Sure." Weingard held the screen door open, then addressed his daughter, "Emmy, why don't you and Devon finish destroying my morning's work while I talk to Mr. Barnholdt and Mr. Holcomb."

Emily smiled shyly. "Excuse me," she said politely, starting down the stairs to join her rambunctious brother.

Holcomb could not help smiling at the little blonde as she tripped quietly down the stairs in her pink shorts and plastic Dora sandals. A family did not seem part of his future, but he most missed the possibility when he thought about having a sweet daughter to call him "daddy." He would spend hours pushing her on a swing set made with his own hands, would let her gather eggs from her little, banty flock while he worked on the tractor. They would both laugh when he affectionately touched her nose, leaving a smudge of grease. Her mother would look on with a long grin stretching her face, shaking her head at their antics. He already knew he would name her Elizabeth, after the grandmother she would never meet.

The two farmers came up the stairs, work boots clomping hollowly against wood. Each stepped around Weingard, who still held the door open, to join Mrs. Weingard on the tidy, little porch. A picnic table took up most of the space. Mrs. Weingard had gathered the dirty dishes, but a plate of hot dogs in buns still sat in the middle of the table. She gestured toward them. "Please, help yourselves. I can get some plates."

"Don't trouble yourself, ma'am," Barnholdt said for both of them. Holcomb wished he had spoken first. He had had nothing to eat since breakfast. Now that his stomach had settled, the hot dogs, brown with black grill marks, looked nearly irresistible. "We have something important to talk to you about that will sound kind of off the wall."

Holcomb reluctantly took his gaze from the food to look squarely at Mrs. Weingard. "Cait, Mike, you're going to think I'm loony for saying this, but . . ." He tried to gauge the woman's reaction. "I know for a fact that Devon is a . . . a . . ."

Mrs. Weingard closed her eyes with a deep sigh. "What did he do this time?"

All friendliness left her husband's face. "A what? What are you about to call my son?"

Barnholdt stopped Holcomb with a gesture. "Mike, we have nothing against Devon. We're not trying to insult him or you. We just got hold of some information about him that might help explain a few things."

Mrs. Weingard took her husband's arm. "Let them talk, Mike. The doctors can't figure it out."

Weingard was a tall man, thinner than the two burly farmers, his hair nearly black and his eyes a pale blue. A mechanic, he had hands as crusty and calloused as theirs. His face flushed, and he spoke through gritted teeth. "What can they possibly know that hasn't already been considered?"

Mrs. Weingard apologized for her husband. "We've been through a lot with Devon. The doctor said his red hair could come from buried genes on both sides, though neither of us could think of any redheads—"

"Cait," Weingard hissed. "They don't need to know our—"

She continued as if he had not spoken. "—but two light-eyed people can't make a dark-eyed baby, so they tested Mike and—"

"Cait!" Weingard snapped. "This isn't something—"

Holcomb knew what had to come next. "He isn't the father."

"The *biological* father," Weingard said in a flat tone that betrayed his anger. "I *am* Devon's father."

Mrs. Weingard did not allow the exchange to derail her explanation. She clearly had waited a long time to unburden herself from this story. "But I knew I had never, would never cheat—"

"You're not the biological mother either," Barnholdt finished.

As the bombshell dropped, Holcomb seized the moment to grab a hot dog.

Finally, Mrs. Weingard lost her momentum. "How . . . how could you possibly . . . know? It seems our baby was switched at birth."

Barnholdt looked at Holcomb, clearly expecting him to explain. After all, he was the one to whom the sprite gave the information.

Caught squeezing a line of mustard onto his purloined hot dog, Holcomb glanced around the table. "He's a changeling."

"A what?" both Weingards said together.

"A changeling." Holcomb put down the mustard and clutched the hot dog in one beefy hand. Dirt rimed the lines of his palm. "As I understand it, magical creatures exchange a monster for a human baby."

Weingard slammed his fist on the table so hard it startled Holcomb. He dropped his hot dog, and it fell from the bun, smearing a yellow line across the table. "My son is not a monster!"

Barnholdt gave Holcomb a hard glare. "He didn't mean a monster, Mike, really. He just picked a poor word to describe a . . . a . . . mischievous . . . um . . . being."

The farmers had looked up changeling in the dictionary together, and Holcomb distinctly remembered the word "monster." He glanced at his hot dog, but it seemed uncouth, under the circumstances, to worry about food.

Mrs. Weingard grabbed her husband's arm so tightly that she bunched wrinkles into his shirt. "Mike, that would explain everything."

Silence followed her proclamation.

She continued, "The MRIs, the chromosome studies. Everything!"

When no one spoke for several moments, Holcomb quietly gathered his hot dog and bun. Taking a napkin, he started cleaning up the mess.

Weingard finally broke the hush. "But this is crazy, Cait. Can't you see that?"

"What I see, Michael Weingard, is answers to questions that previously had none."

Weingard threw up his hands. "*Crazy* answers, yes. Any difficult situation could be explained by the supernatural, but doesn't it make sense to exhaust all of the scientific possibilities first?"

Mrs. Weingard finally raised her voice. "Haven't we done that already? Medical science can't explain this, and we're not blood related to any other child born at Mercy Hospital around the same time as Devon."

Holcomb took a bite of the hot dog. The cold meat tasted of charcoal and wood, but it made his gut growl for more.

Weingard stared at his wife with catlike intensity. "So you're just going to believe that evil spirits stole our baby and replaced him with a monster?"

"With a . . . mischievous being," Mrs. Weingard corrected, using Barnholdt's softened description.

As if suddenly remembering they had an audience, Weingard turned his attention to Holcomb. "And how do you know this?"

Holcomb deliberately took another bite of the hot dog while he considered. He needed time to properly word his reply. But, the food ran out too soon, and he was forced to say the only thing he could. "A sprite told me."

"A sprite," Weingard repeated incredulously. "A sprite told you."

"Yes," Holcomb said, wiping his mouth on his sleeve. "I'm not crazy, Mike. I know what I saw and what I heard." An idea came to him and he spoke it before fully exploring it. "Now, you can help us out and possibly get your real son back. Or you can call us insane and lose him forever."

Every eye went to Holcomb. Even Barnholdt stared. They had never discussed the idea that they might recover the baby. The dictionary said nothing about what creatures of Faery do with the human babies they take in trade for their changelings. For all he knew, they might have killed and eaten it already. Adding more difficult chores to an already impossible task seemed utter madness. Yet he could think of nothing that had happened that day that would not already qualify.

Mrs. Weingard said softly, "Count me in."

Weingard looked stricken. "In what?"

"In whatever it takes to recover our natural-born son."

Two days of library and Internet research brought Kyle a pounding headache. He leaned back in the library's plush rolling chair and rubbed his temples.

He could find nothing definitive. Stories of fey creatures came from every part of the world. Each called them something different: elves, dwarves, fairies, pixies, nixies, naiads, dryads, ogres, bugbears. The list went on, seemingly without end. It was all conjecture, all stories, all explanations for reality that did not, at the time, have an understandable cause. The changeling stories haunted him. Most involved severely beating, drowning, or burning the changelings in the hope that their cries would bring back the devil, demon, or nixie to return the human child for her own. He hoped the Weingards would not resort to any of these methods, assuming they discovered the same sources he did.

Most of the stories seemed like explanations for congenital or environmental conditions that ancient peoples did not understand. Infants with large heads and coarse features might have connective tissue or chromosomal disorders. Autism, cerebral palsy, muscular dystrophy, cystic fibrosis. Surely, all of these syndromes existed throughout history, and people created stories to tease logic from the baffling. What better way to explain the loss of the perfect baby imagined by parents in-utero than that a hill dwarf had replaced it with one of her own?

It took force of will to look at these myths as truths, to thrust aside the mind-set of an ancient peasant seeking answers to find the reality of a sprite on his tractor. The tales contradicted one another, even within the same mythological context, even within the same source. And none of them placed the entrance to Faery in a farmer's field in Iowa. In fact, the stories all seemed older than America.

Holcomb lowered his head. He had read enough and gleaned very little. He only hoped the others' searches had proven more fruitful than his own.

*   *   *

They met at the tree line dividing the southern edge of Kyle Holcomb's land from Barnholdt's. The Weingards had chosen the location without explanation, and the two farmers waited anxiously for the couple. Dressed in his best-fitting Carhart overalls, clutching his favorite deer rifle, Holcomb crouched beside his fellow farmer. "Do you think they'll give us a chance to talk?"

Barnholdt lit a cigarette. "I reckon so. I mean, they tried to talk to us three or four times and didn't give an ultimatum till they dug up one who speaks our language." He stuck the cigarette between his lips.

Holcomb moved upwind. He hated the smell of smoke, and imagined it was what had driven Mrs. Barnholdt to divorce. "We don't know that for sure."

"What d'ya mean?" Smoke dribbled from Barnholdt's mouth with each syllable.

"Who knows what the others said or tried to say?"

"Yeah. But they didn't attack, did they?"

"No," Holcomb had to admit. "They didn't attack." Nervously, he checked the chamber and the safety.

Barnholdt took another puff. "What's that for?"

"The hunting rifle?"

"Yeah."

Holcomb gave his neighbor a look to which he had grown accustomed over the past several months. "Did you forget a magical creature that can turn tractors to life threatened us?"

Barnholdt blew out a plume of smoke. "So what's the gun gonna do, huh? Get turned to a snake and bite us?"

The other farmer had a good point, but Holcomb felt safer with it in his hands. The technology might catch the creatures of Faery off their guard and gain

him a few seconds in a brawl. With or without it, the
entire situation seemed hopeless. What chance did
four regular folks have against an entire army of fantastical creatures, with inhuman strength and magic at
their disposal? Again, he tried to imagine the methods
of their enemies, ignorance further enlarging the task.
There was no possible way to know what powers these
creatures might have. They might call down lightning
or fire from the sky, perhaps the sun or moon itself.
They could hurl mighty gouts of ice or rock. They
could fry a man's blood from the inside out. Perhaps
they had dragons with breath like a nuclear explosion
or magical bombs that could level all three of their
chosen Iowa counties with a word. "We should have
pleaded with the governor. Got him to call in the National Guard."

"Yeah, right." Barnholdt blew smoke out his nose
this time, the cigarette burning in his grip. "That
would've worked.

"We could have tried." Holcomb knew Barnholdt
was right but clung to the possibility from fear. *"We
could have tried."*

The appearance of the Weingards walking toward
them saved Barnholdt from a reply. He dropped his
cigarette and crushed it into the dirt. "They've got a
child with them."

Holcomb looked more closely, only then noticing
the small figure waddling at their side. "It's
Devon."

"That's odd. Why would they bring a child—?"

The answer came to both men at once, though Holcomb gave it voice, "They're going to try to exchange him."

"You think?"

"Don't you?"

Barnholdt bobbed his head as the trio drew within earshot. "But you think they told *him*?"

Devon pointed to a spot several yards to Holcomb's left, and the family veered toward it. "This way," Mr. Weingard said.

Holcomb studied the boy. Gel plastered his brilliant, red locks neatly to his head. He wore a clean, collared shirt, striped, and a pair of dark blue dress slacks. The impish twinkle that usually filled his dark eyes had gone out, replaced by a more mature light. The child had clearly changed. Caught staring, Holcomb smiled gently. "Hi, Devon."

To his surprise, the normally taciturn boy replied, "Hi, Mr. Holcomb."

Holcomb jerked his head to Mrs. Weingard, who smiled.

"When we did our research on-line, we discovered a common theme about changelings. If you boil water or beer in egg shells, it makes them talk."

Barnholdt recovered first. He gave the boy a genuine smile. "Hey, Devon. So you can talk now?"

"Actually, Mr. Barnholdt," Devon said in a voice like a rusty spigot, "I've been able to talk for a very long time."

Under ordinary circumstances, Holcomb might have laughed. *How long is a very long time to a one-year-old boy?* "I see," he said.

"And I know where the entrance is to Faery."

Holcomb's nostrils flared. Still clutching the rifle, he pointed to the same place Devon had indicated earlier.

Mr. Weingard nodded.

Holcomb wondered how much else the Weingards had found out about changelings. Perhaps they planned to beat or burn or drown the boy right here, where his original parents might take him back in ex-

change for the human baby. He bit his lip, hoping
Devon would not pay the biggest price for the sins of
Faery. The boy had his problems, but few in this world
deserved actual torture.

"Are you ready?" Devon asked.

Mr. Weingard looked around the group. Holcomb
nearly asked, "For what?"—but before he could,
Weingard gave his son a gesture.

Devon pursed his toddler lips and made a piercing
sound like nothing Holcomb had ever heard before.
It echoed across the open fields and seemed to stretch
to the horizon.

The sprite appeared suddenly from the indicated
spot in the tree line. Her long, blue hair fell in waves
to her waist. Her belt now consisted of woven, multi-
colored leaves. She looked the four adults over, then
stated, "You're still here."

"We have another day," Holcomb reminded her.

Mrs. Weingard added, "And we're not leaving without our baby."

"Your baby?" The sprite's pale gaze leaped around
the gathering to land on Devon. "Ah, of course. I
suppose it's only fair to trade you back your young
one."

"No," Mr. Weingard said with the same force his
fist had displayed on the table. "You don't understand. We aren't giving up Devon either."

The sprite stared, her canted eyes growing into the
shape and size of Brazil nuts. "You mean . . . you
want to keep . . . the changeling, too?"

"His name is Devon," Weingard said. "And he is
our son."

Holcomb could scarcely believe what was happening. He had once had control of the situation, only to
surrender it to a family whose personal strife appar-

ently drove them to suicide. He looked at the sprite, and a sudden understanding gripped him. These creatures of Faery were immortal. They could not die of age, but legend suggested they could be killed. Creatures accustomed to living for all eternity, who took millennia to substantially reproduce, would have to fear death more than any mortal. To kill one meant not a waste of decades but potentially of millions of years. His hand tightened on the rifle, and he raised it cautiously.

The sprite clearly took no notice. "You know this creature is a changeling, yet you still call him son?"

Tears filled Mrs. Weingard's eyes. "We do not just call him son. He *is* our son. We love him as much as any parent can ever love a child, and that love is never bounded. It is a forever love, without conditions. His biology, his past, his future, do not matter. Devon is our son. And so is the baby boy you exchanged for him."

Holcomb now understood why the creatures of Faery had given the humans so many chances. Fairies, elves, and pixies thought little of humans, whose short lives passed like moments to the immortals. To chase them off of property meant nothing, like poisoning mosquitoes for the comfort of a midnight party. It might only take the death of one creature of Faery to drive the point home. Humans could and would fight back. Was the life of even one immortal worth the battle? Holcomb took aim.

The sprite continued to glance wildly between the Weingards, including Devon. "And you, changeling? You wish to stay with these humans?"

The little boy cleared his throat and spoke in plain English. "They do love me, despite what I am and what I've done. They have sacrificed their joy and time for me, have done everything possible to make my life and my future happy despite my shortcomings, of which I have many."

Holcomb's hands shook. Such long words had emerged from the mouth of a toddler. A toddler who was not quite, perhaps not at all, human.

Devon continued, "Love of that intensity, of that caliber, is something a creature of Faery rarely experiences."

The rifle grew heavy in Holcomb's hands. He could fire at any time, but he needed to hear the end of the exchange first.

"You . . ." The sprite's face became a wrinkled mask of confusion. "If you stayed, you would become . . . mortal." She pronounced the last word with such distaste, it sounded like a curse. "Is that . . . what you want?"

Every eye went to Devon. Even Kyle Holcomb gave up his sighting to see the changeling's reaction.

"Better a life with the beauty and grandeur of a shooting star then an eternity of steady yearning for those golden moments only a mortal can experience. Without sorrow, there is no joy. Without pain, no healing. So, too, without death, one can never truly live. I would not trade this trueness of spirit, this highest evolution of love, even for immortality."

For several moments, no one moved or spoke. Holcomb wondered if their minds went in the same direction as his own. For humans, immortality could only be a forever of the life they knew. Contemplation of his own death terrified him. To imagine that something of great beauty arose from that fear, to see eternal life as the dull existence of rocks and time, to know that these immortal beings knew little of love and sacrifice, of heroism and bravery, floored him.

"Come with me, changeling," the sprite said softly, her expression every bit as touched as the humans'. "The king will wish to speak with you."

"No!" Mrs. Weingard grabbed her son and wrapped him into an unbreakable embrace.

Mr. Weingard stepped between the pair and the sprite. "No," he repeated, more softly but with equal force. "You will not have him."

Devon's muffled voice held a note of joy despite the tenseness of the situation. "They won't keep me, Mommy. Daddy. I'll come back, but I have to go."

Holcomb wondered whether the boy's excitement stemmed from the opportunity to teach or to rejoin the magical beings who had spawned him. The rifle felt like a lead weight in his arms, nearly forgotten. To his surprise, Mrs. Weingard released Devon as soon as the words left his mouth.

As Devon walked past him, Mr. Weingard reached to grab him, stopped by his wife's gentle touch on his shoulder. "If you love something," she said so softly that Holcomb could barely hear, "let it go." Tears blurred her eyes to pools of emerald.

As the humans watched the sprite and changeling disappear into the tree line, Mrs. Weingard collapsed, wailing. Her husband knelt at her side, holding, rocking, whispering encouragements.

Barnholdt turned to Holcomb, looking equally lost. "So what about the gun?" He inclined his head toward the rifle again. "Have you decided what you're going to do with it?"

Holcomb lowered the barrel, suffering the sting of blood returning to his arms. Glad to discuss a subject other than the family's pain, he explained. "Immortals aren't used to death like we are. I thought if one got killed, they might decide war's not such a great idea."

Barnholdt nodded thoughtfully. "Well, if you're gonna do it, I'd say to get this king of theirs, if you can."

"Yeah." Holcomb bobbed his head in rhythm, no longer certain he could pull the trigger. He had shot his share of raccoons, possums, and skunks; more than 80 percent of the ones in their area were rabid. He had even done in a swamp rattler that had dared cross onto his property. Shooting the sprite, or any being so like a human, seemed too much like murder.

The sprite returned at the side of a creature who closely resembled a skinny, fine-boned man. He shared the sprite's canted eyes, though his were a bright red-orange. He had flat-brown hair that hung in wisps to his shoulders, and delicately pointed ears stabbed through the cascade. Though he bore no wrinkles or gray hairs, he still carried an aura of great age. The sprite made a grand gesture toward her new companion. "This is King . . ." She followed with strange clicking noises that apparently comprised his name.

Holcomb supposed he ought to bow, though he found himself standing frozen, staring. Barnholdt reacted exactly as he did, and the Weingards managed only to decrease the volume of their grief.

The king spoke in a fluid singsong that sounded more like music. The sprite translated. "He says that centuries have passed since the folk of Faery have walked among men."

The king said more, the sprite passing along his words, "In the past, humans have treated us badly. They warded us away with herbs and invoked religious customs and gestures. They slaughtered us in horrific ways, with silver knives, wooden stakes, or fiery pyres. They beat or boiled our changelings to make us rescue what they considered monsters and replace them with the babies they had lost."

Monsters. The words stuck with Holcomb, the same one he had read in the dictionary.

Barnholdt nudged him in the ribs so suddenly that Holcomb nearly dropped the gun. His neighbor jerked his head toward the king.

He wants me to shoot, Holcomb realized, but he was too interested in what the king had to say to obey. Yet.

More translated speech followed, the creatures apparently oblivious to the farmers' exchange. "Humans have changed, and it is finally time that we do the same. Tolerance has grown beyond measure."

Although some humans would disagree, Holcomb knew the words for fact. People of varying colors and faiths who once despised or mistrusted one another now lived, not only in the same cities, but in the same homes as family. Despite persistent cries of racism, sexism, and bigotry, the truth was that the world had clearly and strongly changed for the better, even just over the last half century.

"You have learned to love our children as your own. You made no attempt to harm us, even as we threatened you."

Holcomb's face flushed, and he hastily lowered the rifle's butt to the ground, glad he had hesitated for so long. Had he killed the sprite or the king, an unwinnable war would, in fact, have become inevitable.

"If you can shower this kind of unmistakable love upon us, it seems that we can, once again, interact with at least some of you. Since we can safely come and go from your world, we no longer need to take over a part of it." The king made a flourishing gesture as the sprite formed the appropriate, accompanying words. "We declare this skirmish over before it begins."

With those words, the sprite and the king disappeared without fanfare or smoke, revealing the two small figures standing behind them. Devon held the hand of a thin, blond boy with skin so pale it looked like milk. Before either managed a single step, they found themselves enwrapped in their parents' arms: Mrs. Weingard clutching the new toddler and Mr. Weingard embracing Devon with the same exuberance. The farmers looked at one another. And smiled.

No longer worried for dragons' fiery breathes, for giants stomping cities to splinters, for fairies transforming army tanks into lumbering monsters, Holcomb turned his thoughts to the joy of discovering pixies in the woods and sprites in the treetops. He wondered how the populace would take to these new-found neighbors and hoped the world would handle the fey creatures better than he had. He looked across his fields, at the harvested cornstalks standing like broken soldiers, and nothing seemed less important than working. As the Weingards headed home, Holcomb glanced at his other neighbor. "So, Chris. Is that *National Treasure* movie still playing?"

Barnholdt pulled the pack of Marlboros out of his pocket, stared at it, then returned it without removing a cigarette. Usually, tense situation made a man more prone to smoke, but Barnholdt clearly did not see this as a day for ordinary behavior either. "Naw, it's long gone. But I bet we can find something else interesting at the Coral 1, if you can afford to take off another day."

"I can," Holcomb said, not bothering to consider whether or not he spoke the truth. Regardless of the weather, despite whatever required doing, he needed some time off the farm. "I'll meet you in an hour. I've got this sudden hankering to find a wife and start a family." He looked longingly after the Weingards, who fairly skipped across the field. "Maybe, just maybe, today's my lucky day."

"Graced by the King of Faery," Barnholdt said, smiling, "I think we can count on it."

TEETH IN THE SAND
A TALE OF THE KHAM-RIDHE

by Russell Davis

*"And when the child, so marked by the Moons,
and born beneath the banners of war, be assured
that his father, leader of the Kham-Ridhe and pro-
tector of our people, shall be offered a vision of
peace, and he shall choose that path for generations to come, until the Knights of Shadow and
Light are called upon to defend all from the
sworn enemies of the Spire."*
—FROM CANTO IV, THE PROPHECY OF THE SANDS

THE DEAD MAN'S name was Gaelish and he had
been one of General Seth Rellick's best scouts.
Seth had been waiting for the return of the four scouts
he'd sent into the Gorund Desert for hours, and none
but Gaelish had returned.

And that one was dead on his feet when he staggered into camp.

His armor was gone and his skin was the bright red
of new flame, burned raw by the scorching power of
the desert sun. He was blind and yet somehow had

170

found his way back into camp, and even to his own tent, where he'd scared his wife into hysterics before dropping to his knees, babbling and incoherent. One of the healers was treating her nearby, but Seth could still hear her sobs.

Seth had seen men break in war, but this was something much more disturbing. The strange marks on the scout's skin—raised patches with a white circle in the center—reminded him of bee stings, except that these small marks each wept a thin rivulet of blood. A quick question to his squad leader revealed that Gaelish was not allergic to anything, including bee stings.

Seth watched as one of the healers, an old man named Ikalban, examined Gaelish's still form. There had been little to be done, and none of Ikalban's ministrations had any apparent effect. Carefully closing the eyelids and muttering a prayer, Ikaban slowly rose to his feet, wincing in pain as his knees protested being on the ground for so long.

He approached Seth with the unsteady gait of the very old and very tired. "My lord," he said, by way of greeting.

"Were you able to get anything out of him before he died?" Seth asked.

The old healer shook his head. "Gibberish, mostly. Something about teeth in the sand. He was raving, my lord."

"Then what have you learned?" Seth asked.

"That this is no ordinary death, my lord," Ikalban said. "Not ordinary at all."

"Then what is it?" Seth asked.

"This." Ikalban extended his hand and opened his fist, revealing a tiny object that gleamed golden in the firelight. With the exception of its golden color, the object appeared to be a somewhat larger than average fly.

"Are you trying to say that you think this . . . fly did this to him?" Seth asked.

"No, my lord," Ikalban answered. "Based on the number of stings, I'd say that several hundred or more of these flies did this to him. Except . . ." The old man's voice trailed off into silence.

"Except?" Seth prodded.

"These are not ordinary flies, my lord. They are animagic."

Nearby, one of Seth's personal guard, a knight named Marikus, snorted in disgust. "Bah!" he said. "There is no such thing as animagic, probably never was. Children's stories, used to scare the younglings."

"Animagic . . ." Seth said. "I have heard the stories, of course. Sorcerers from long ago used magic to enhance or change animals and insects, giving them strange abilities, sometimes even combining two different kinds of creatures to create a new, more deadly one."

Ikalban nodded. "Yes, my lord. See here?" He pointed one gnarled finger to the place where the fly's lacy wings ended. "This looks more like a bee stinger. I'll need a closer look to be sure, but I suspect that these are not just flies, but some strange hybrid of a bee and a fly, with a venomous sting."

"But could one fly be that deadly?" Seth asked.

"Not one," Ikalban said. "But hundreds of them together would be deadly."

"My lord?" Marikus interrupted. "You're not going to simply take him at his word, are you? If such creatures were made so long ago, how is that they still exist? Flies aren't known for their extended life spans."

Seth looked questioningly at Ikalban, and the old man nodded. "He makes a valid point, my lord, but there is so little we know about the magics of that time. What we do know, however, is that the stories of animagic are not told as 'tales to scare children,' but as histories. We also know that the Gorund Desert, and the Lake of Fire at its center, were both created by the same sorcerers who are credited with the creation of animagic. Perhaps these flies are all that is left of them, perhaps not. But the flies *are* real, my lord, and if you intend on leading us into the desert, as the prophecy says you must, then we must find a way to contend with them."

"We don't even know that there's any of these things out there!" Marikus interrupted. "You're making an assumption."

Ikalban turned to face Marikus, his eyes sharp and his tone cold when he spoke. "Young man, I've been serving Seth Rellick for too many years not to give him my best advice. I'm not always right, don't even pretend to be, but we are not of this desert. The Kham-Ridhe are a people without a home, where the desert itself will fight us. If we are to survive, then we must learn to adapt to our new environment."

Seth liked Marikus, but he could be impulsive and easily dismissed things he couldn't see, touch or fight. Ikalban was right. They couldn't afford mistakes at this point. The survival of the Kham-Ridhe depended on being able to somehow forge a home in the desert.

He held up a restraining hand. "Enough," he said. "Ikalban, take the fly with you and study it. I'll want a report at first light."

The old man nodded. "Yes, my lord."

"Marikus, I'll want you and my other four guards assembled at my tent by the same time."

"My lord?" Marikus said, accepting the order, while asking a question.

"Four of our best scouts died out there, Marikus," Seth said. "Tomorrow, we will go and find out why."

"Yes, my lord," Marikus replied, anticipation lighting his features.

Seth smiled grimly. *The exuberance of the young*, he thought as he turned and made his way back to his own tent where his wife, Lianre, and their three-month-old son, Drados, were waiting for him.

Stopping just outside the circle of light, Seth watched as Lianre, with her dark hair and eyes shining in the firelight, seated herself in a camp chair near and fed their son. In the three months since he'd been born, Drados had consumed almost all of her attention and time. Just as Seth's had been consumed by the long journey here.

Three short months ago, the Kham-Ridhe were executing the final moves in a war that had swept the western half of the Astran continent. Out of the deepest reaches of the Tulron Mountains, Seth had forged an army of vast size and unstoppable might. The other kingdoms had fallen before them, one by one, until all that was left was the kingdom of the elves. Slowly, one after another, the battles were fought and the elves died. Two cities had been left—Parthanor and the capital of Kathas—and the entire western half of Astra would belong to the Kham-Ridhe.

As the battle for Parthanor raged over two days, Lianre had given birth to his son Drados, and on the night he should have been celebrating his victory, she presented him to his father. The first thing Seth had seen was the twin moons birthmark on Drados' cheek. The second two visions—one, which showed the Kham-Ridhe defeating the last remnants of the elves at Kathas and then falling into despair and eventual death when some future enemy swept out of the bowels of the earth itself to take over; the other, the Kham-Ridhe riding into the desert and taking up the banner of peace until that same future enemy was a cause for them to come forth and defend all the lands.

His people called it The Prophecy of the Sands, but to Seth Rellick, it was the beginning of a long nightmare. The prophecy was hundreds of years old, and to not honor it was unthinkable. At the same time, the Kham-Ridhe were a people of war, and stopping short of victory left a bitter taste of ash in his mouth. Still, there had been little choice.

Seth had led the Kham-Ridhe east, pulling his troops back with him while being hounded at every turn by guerilla fighters who came out at night and slashed his supply lines and people to ribbons. His knights had been ordered, sometimes repeatedly, to defend themselves, but not to give chase. Escape to the desert was their only option if the cause of the prophecy and peace were to be served.

Now, the Tulrons were behind them and Seth knew they could shelter here, fend off the attacks and start life anew. But the prophecy said that the Kham-Ridhe were to make their home in the desert, and Seth meant to honor that prophecy, though to his warrior's mind, it seemed a fool's errand.

Many of his knights agreed, but they were as constrained by tradition and honor as he was. Too many of the prophecies of his ancestors had proven true to deny, and so they had come to the desert and tomorrow he would personally face the first test it had offered them.

He cleared his throat as he stepped into the light.

"Lianre," he said. "How fares our son?"

"Well, my husband," she said, smiling gently at the suckling infant. "He eats like a horse. What was all the noise? I heard a woman screaming."

"One of the scouts returned," Seth said shortly. He unbelted his sword and removed his breastplate before pulling up a camp chair for himself.

"One?" she asked.

Seth nodded. "And he was dead before I could even question him."

"What happened?" she asked.

Lianre was Seth's third wife, and had been a royal-born Skindancer before they'd married. She was the only one of his wives to give him a child and her insight had proven valuable on more than one occasion. Still, the telling of the flies seemed too horrible to contemplate. Trying to keep it short, he said, "Some sort of insect poisoned him."

"In the desert?" she asked.

"Yes," Seth said. "Tomorrow, I will go and investigate."

"You, my lord?" she asked. "Surely Marikus or someone else can do this."

"No, Lianre," Seth said. "They can't. If we're to make our home here, I must find a way for our people to live in this environment. We must adapt."

She nodded, keeping her silence for a long moment, then said, "You are not telling me something."

Seth smiled. She knew him well. "I am worried," he admitted.

"About?"

"Water," Seth said. "We're fine here, but once we're into the desert itself, water will be the most precious of treasures. We must have enough water for ourselves and the horses—without it, all of us will perish."

"Do your counselors have any wisdom from the prophecy on this?" she asked.

"No, Lianre, and that, too, worries me. They speak when it suits them or when they are sure, but their answers are all the same. Riddles and word play."

"What *do* they say?" she pressed.

"Ikalban says that there is magic in the desert from long ago, animagic he calls it. The counselors say it is by magic we will have the water to survive in a landscape where nothing else lives." He snorted in disgust. "I am a knight, a warrior, not a sorcerer. How can I trust to magic?"

Lianre held up Drados in her arms and he stared sleepily at his father. "For his sake, how can you not?" she asked, then rose and kissed him on the cheek before slipping into their tent for sleep.

Staring into the fire, Seth wondered what goddess had gifted women with the ability to speak one sentence and create so much guilt and need. For his son's sake, he would have to trust in magic.

For his own, he would bring his sword. Although what use it would be against a swarm of flies, he had no idea.

Before the sun rose, Seth was awake and dressed and seated before his fire. He had slept fitfully, haunted by strange images of the desert. Finally, he'd given up on the idea of rest and gotten out of his blankets to brew *kalyi*, the dark, heavy drink that he'd discovered in the elven lands and now started every morning with. It had a rich scent and a slightly bitter flavor that he enjoyed.

He held a warm cup in his hands and waited patiently for the sun to come up and Ikalban and the others to arrive. The old healer came first, walking gingerly in the dim light of the early morning.

"My lord," he said, offering a small half-bow from the waist.

Seth looked around. "The others aren't here as of yet, Ikalban, so we can dispense with the formalities." He stood and brought a camp chair over near his. "Please sit down, my old friend, and tell me what you have learned."

"Thank you, Seth," Ikalban said, easing himself into the chair. "I haven't learned much, at least much of value, that I didn't tell you last night. Still, there are some things I think you should know."

"At this point, any information we can get would be helpful," Seth said. "We don't know enough about this place."

"No, we don't," Ikalban said. "That's why I spent most of the night with the other counselors, pouring over the Prophecy of the Sands and seeing if we could come up with anything of value."

"And?" Seth asked.

"We have, reluctantly, concluded that much of the magic from the ancient sorcerers who fought the Mage Wars must still be here, preserved in the sands of the Gorund. After all, they created this desert and the Lake of Fire. There are so few records of that time, Seth, and what we do know is frightening. The ancients had powers that we can hardly imagine."

"So these flies could be a minor magic," Seth reasoned, "with much worse things still out there."

Ikalban nodded his agreement. "But we won't know for certain, of course, until you send more scouts to explore the area."

"No more scouts," Marikus said, hearing the last comment as he approached.

Resuming his more formal approach, Ikalban looked at Seth. "My lord?"

"Marikus is correct," Seth said. "Today, he and I will go and see what we can find out."

"That does not . . . are you certain that's wise, my lord?" Ikalban asked.

"I will not ask the men to go where I would not," Seth answered. "Four have already died, Ikalban. In this, *I* must lead."

"Then wait at least a day or two!" Ikalban said. "There is so much to the prophecy and so many other records we can pursue. Give us the opportunity to arm you, at least, with knowledge before you go."

"Bah!" Marikus said. "We can't sit around here and wait for the counselors to decide to tell us something that has meaning in this world."

Seth stood up, and patted the young knight on the shoulder. "Respectfully, Marikus, please. Ikalban has been my trusted adviser for many years, as have the other counselors. Even if we can't make heads or tails of everything they tell us, their wisdom has guided the Kham-Ridhe through many trials."

"As you wish, my lord," Marikus said, climbing onto his horse. He turned and gave a stiff, half-bow to Ikalban. "My apologies."

Ikalban smiled and said, "You're young yet. In time, you'll learn that not every battle can be won with a sword and shield."

Marikus laughed. "Maybe, but I haven't fought one like that yet!"

Seth climbed onto his own mount as he offered his thanks to Ikalban. "Tell the counselors to continue looking. If we find nothing today, we'll return before nightfall and you can advise me of your findings at that time."

"As you command, my lord," Ikalban said. He looked at Seth directly and added, "Be safe and wary in the desert, Seth. It is a place that has not surrendered to the boot of man."

"I will," he said, putting his heels to his horse. "Marikus, let's ride."

The younger knight followed suit and together they rode out of the camp and into the rapidly growing heat of the day.

Behind them, Ikalban watched and shook his head. "Some knowledge is best gained firsthand," he muttered, then headed back to the counselors' tent to tell them what had happened.

Overnight, the shifting sands had erased whatever tracks the scouts had left on the dunes. There was no way to know for certain where they'd run into trouble, but all the scouts of the Kham-Ridhe followed particular patterns when doing reconnaissance work in an unfamiliar land. Knowing this, Seth used the same patterns, working in slowly expanding arcs.

The desert heat was like standing inside a forge, and both men had removed their armor early in the day. They spoke rarely, keeping their eyes moving over the empty landscape in the hope of finding some sign of the scouts or, more likely, an enemy.

But what truly interested Seth was water. If they could locate a large enough oasis, he could relocate the Kham-Ridhe there and establish a base camp while the rest of the Gorund was explored. Even a few miles into the desert would provide them a clear zone of safety from their enemies and give his people a much-needed rest.

Strangely, when they first spotted the oasis, Seth wondered if it wasn't a mirage. Waves of heat rose from the dunes, making the large palm trees shimmer in the air. Given how their horses were laboring, however, he was glad to realize that it wasn't an illusion. Still, it would be far better to approach with caution, and he said so to Marikus.

The younger knight nodded in agreement. "Let's ride a little closer, then leave the horses and approach on foot," he suggested. "If there *are* more of those flies, they could send the horses into a panic."

For a moment, Seth stared at his companion, wondering where this sudden burst of forethought had come from, then he smiled and said, "A sound plan. I'll take the lead."

Marikus shook his head. "I may not address you in the familiar as Ikalban does, my lord, but I'm still required to be your bodyguard. *I'll* go first." He moved to a position in front of Seth and urged his horse in the direction of the oasis.

"Well, Ikalban has earned that right," Seth said. "He was my first tutor as a boy."

Without looking around, Marikus said, "So that makes him, what? About two hundred or so?"

"Very funny, Marikus," Seth retorted. "I'm not *that* old! Trust me, one day you'll be 'old' yourself."

"Never, my lord," the knight replied, laughing.

They rode on in silence, and when they had closed to a quarter mile, they brought their horses to a halt and climbed down. On the sand itself, the heat was searing, and Seth could feel it through the hard soles of his boots. "Just ground rein them," he said. "In case we have to leave in a hurry."

They both dropped their reins on the ground, knowing that the horses were trained to stay in place. Marikus began walking in the direction of the oasis, and had crossed over several smaller dunes, when he came to a sudden stop. Seth heard his sharp intake of breath and he hurried his last few steps to see what had caused his reaction.

Half-buried in sand, the upper body of one of the other scouts was visible. It, too, was covered in marks from the flies, and burned a bright red from the sun.

"Why do you suppose they took their armor *and* their shirts off?" Marikus asked. "They know better than that."

Seth nodded. "They should've, yes. It doesn't make sense."

"Let's get closer," Marikus said, his alert eyes scanning the area around the oasis.

They moved in, and found the bodies of the other two remaining scouts as well—both in the same condition. "I can't fathom it," Marikus muttered. "What could have possessed them? Where are their horses?" He snorted. "I hate it when I don't understand things."

"Me, too," Seth said. "But the only way to understand is to search for answers. We'll find ours, I think, within the shelter of the oasis."

"Agreed," the knight said, and they both moved forward once more.

There was no sign of the golden flies as the approached the oasis, and stepping into the thin shade of the palms, both men breathed a sigh of relief. While the air was still warm, it was much more bearable here. The sound of fresh water was audible nearby, and they both continued moving in that direction.

When the palms gave way, Seth felt his breath catch in his throat. The center of the oasis was not just a spring, but a crystal clear pool that was an almost perfect rectangle, and large enough to provide water to many dozens of people. At each end, a black stone obelisk jutted from beneath the surface with ancient runes inscribed in white on all sides.

"What do you make of those?" Marikus asked, pointing.

"I don't know," Seth said. "Let's take a closer look."

As they neared the pool, Marikus knelt at its edge and sniffed the water. "It smells clean," he said. "Fresh from an underground spring, I bet." Dipping a hand in before Seth could stop him, he added, "And cold, too!"

"Don't touch anything!" Seth said. "Not until we know more about this place."

Marikus looked around and shrugged. "As you wish, my lord, though I don't sense any threat here. Those obelisks are obviously old—probably built by those mad mages that Ikalban keeps rambling about. There's shade and an abundance of water. It's just about perfect for our needs."

"Let's not lose sight of the fact that those flies, wherever they came from, killed four of our best scouts," Seth reminded him. "We need to be sure this area is safe."

He moved farther along the length of the pool, trying to make sense of the markings on the obelisks, but they were so close together that it wasn't until he was closer that some of them came clear. While Seth didn't make any pretense of being a scholar, some of the images were as clear as words: three wavy lines stacked one atop the other must mean water . . . a simple drawing of a human carrying a bucket . . . and then he saw the images of the flies. Several rows of them, each looking as real as the one Ikalban had found in Gaelish's closed fist, surrounded by symbols that looked like the stars and a moon.

Below that, the image of the man now surrounded by hundreds of tiny dots. The flies?

Were the obelisks a warning of some type? Seth wondered.

Then, farther down, another image: the man carrying the bucket with the symbol of the Spire, the sun, overhead, and beneath that, an inverted v-shaped symbol that Seth couldn't figure out at all. The only thing different about it was that this symbol was carved in a deep, dark red.

Did all this mean that it was possible to remove water from the pool during the day, but not at night? During a full moon, which it was, did the flies defend the pool for some unknown reason? What was this place?

A hundred more questions ran through his mind, but Seth was warrior enough to know that this was a place of magic, and that the ancient mages had left *some* kind of animagic defenses here to protect their water from invaders, possibly tied to the obelisks themselves.

"Marikus," he called. "Come over here and take a look at this." Maybe the young knight would have a different insight into the runes on the obelisks.

Kneeling near the edge of the pool, Marikus said, "One moment, my lord. I just want to refill my waterskin."

"Marikus, no!" Seth said, but the knight had already dipped the skin into the pool.

Instinct told him to run for it, but Seth sensed that the damage had been done. He turned to stare at the obelisk, where the inverted v-shape was now glowing. Above it, the rows of images that depicted the flies had changed from white to golden, and a faint buzzing sound could be heard.

"Damn it, Marikus," he said, backing away from the stone. "I told you not to touch anything!"

Rising to his feet, Marikus started to draw his sword, then let it fall back into the scabbard as he realized it would be useless against the flies.

"I'm . . . I'm sorry, my lord," he said. "What do we do?"

"I don't know," Seth said, watching as the first ranks of flies began to emerge from the obelisk and buzz in rapid circles around it.

Marikus stepped between Seth and the circling flies. "Run, my lord," he said. "If you can get to a horse, you might be able to outdistance them."

"Are you a fool, man?" Seth asked, grabbing Marikus by the shoulder and pulling him backward. "There's no way I can outrun them if our scouts didn't."

"Maybe they didn't see them coming!" Marikus argued. "You have to try, sir. I'll . . . try to hold them as long as I can."

A quick visual estimate told Seth that there were nearly a hundred flies circling the obelisk, with more emerging with each passing minute. From their stingers, tiny drops of greenish ichor were visible—the poison Ikalban had suspected. He had to make a decision and fast. They would attack any second.

"I've got an idea, Marikus," he said.

"My lord?"

"When they come for us, we're going to dive into the pool," Seth said. "We may be safe underwater."

"Sir? How long do you expect us to hold our breath?"

"As long as it takes," Seth said. "Here they come!"

And then he shoved Marikus into the pool, following right behind him as the flies buzzed an angry path directly over his head.

They plunged into the clear, icy water, and Seth immediately knew that if this was going to work, he'd have to figure out something else. He grabbed Marikus by the wrist and gestured up, and both of them kicked for the surface. As soon as their faces were exposed, they took a deep breath and saw that the flies were circling above the water . . . waiting for them.

One landed just above Seth's eyebrow and stung him immediately. An intense, burning seared his skin and he felt it grow hot even as he pulled Marikus back beneath the water. He suddenly realized that the scouts had their shirts off because they'd been filled with flies, and the redness of their skin wasn't from the sun, but from the burning caused by the stings.

They had to go up for another breath, and Seth tried to come up in a different place than before. This time it was Marikus who received a sting, and he cried out in pain as they submerged themselves in the water once more.

We're running out of time, Seth thought. Sooner or later, we'll have to get out of the water. Opening his eyes, he found that he could see readily enough, though the shadows in the water made his vision waver. He peered in the direction of the obelisk and thought he saw a glimmer. Frightened, he wondered for a moment if perhaps the mages had made some sort of water-going version of their fly-bee hybrid, but then he realized that what he'd seen was silver in color, not golden.

Once more, Marikus grabbed his arm and they surfaced, both of them receiving several stings for their trouble. If it weren't for the cold water, Seth knew it would feel like his face was on fire. As soon as he submerged again, he motioned for Marikus to follow him and kicked for the end of the pool where he'd seen the silver flickers of light.

Both men held their breath as long as possible, needing only to surface twice more to reach that end of the pool. Moving gave them some space, and neither man was stung again, though Seth could feel the skin of his face stretching as it swelled in reaction to the poison. Taking one huge breath, he dove down to examine the silver runes etched on the obelisk's base.

Like those above, some symbols made sense, and others didn't. The water symbol was there, as was the man with the bucket . . . but there were no flies. Instead, there were runes that looked a great deal like frogs.

It was ridiculous, but Seth assumed that if the mages made animagic flies, they'd be just as willing to make frogs. The only question was if the frogs were still alive, somehow, and how to get them out of the pillar.

He searched frantically for an answer, when Marikus dove past him, several golden flies clinging to his shirt. The young knight grabbed one off his sleeve and slammed it into the frog design.

Seth waited, his ability to hold his breath much longer rapidly diminishing, then he saw it. The v-shape at the very bottom of the obelisk which was not inverted, began to glow.

Sound carries in water, and it took only a few moments for the deep, *thurr-up* sound of frogs to reach his ears.

Beneath the water, he and Marikus grinned at each other and surfaced once more. The frogs were coming to life and after that long in hibernation, they were bound to be hungry.

Seth felt certain, in fact, that they'd be looking for lunch.

Even creatures of animagic, it seemed, were subject to some of the laws of nature—and that included the one about frogs eating flies with ease. Seth and Marikus stayed in the water long enough for the frogs to do most of their work and explore the confines of the pool.

In the exact center, at the deepest part of the pool, a stone sarcophagus rested beneath the water. Marked with the same runes as the obelisks, Seth felt certain that this was the final resting place of the sorcerer who'd created this oasis and its animagic defenses.

When they'd climbed out of the water and dried off, Marikus gave voice to something Seth had been thinking. "You know, my lord, that this place is nothing like our home. We will have to become a completely new people. Do you think the Kham-Ridhe are ready for ancient magics and living in the desert?"

Seth smiled. "No, Marikus, I don't. But, in time, the memory of our homeland will become a story, a legend passed down to our children. By the time Drados leads, the Gorund will feel like home because he will not remember, nor ever have known, anything else."

Scoffing, Marikus said, "We are the Kham-Ridhe, the Knights of Shadow and Light. We won't stay here forever."

"Not forever, Marikus," Seth replied, "but long enough that men like you and I will be long since dust, and the magic of this place—and all its secrets— will belong to our children's children."

"Do you think there's more places like this one?" Marikus asked. "More creatures of animagic?"

"I think it likely," Seth said. "In fact, I hope to find them."

"What on earth for?" Marikus asked. "This wasn't a close enough brush with such magic for you?"

Seth smiled, thinking of his son and what he would inherit: a kingdom of sand and a prophecy born of it.

He clapped Marikus on the shoulder and they started back for their mounts. There was much to do in the coming days if he was going to create a home here for his people. "I'm beginning to think that we can make a home here, my friend."

"How's that?" the young knight asked, brushing grains of sand off his shirt in irritation.

"I think we'll start by learning the lost magics of this place, and then we'll create something that hasn't existed for hundreds, perhaps thousands of years."

"Oh?"

Seth looked at Marikus seriously for a moment, then pointed to where their horses lay on the sand, dead from the vicious flies.

"We're going to need better horses," he said. "Horses of sand and magic."

For a moment, the young knight could only stare at him in shock, then he shook his head. "As you command, my lord," he said. "As you command."

Together, they started the long walk back to their people, and the beginning of their next journey.

*Author's Note: The first short story about the Kham-Ridhe appeared in *Knight Fantastic* (DAW Books, 2002) under the title "Father of Shadow, Son of Light."

THE TWAIN SHALL MEET

by Bill Fawcett

MEN WITH REALLY big guns always made Thomas Eldersen uncomfortable. As the two very large men in gray jumpsuits carrying very large and likely very automatic weapons escorted him down the equally gray hallway, the small professor kept repeating a number. That number was the fee he had been paid for his acting as a consultant to Humes Aerospace for just one month. The amount was almost exactly three times what he was paid annually to teach Medieval Literature at Smith College, and it was July, so there were no classes.

Yesterday, when Thomas had agreed to accept the consulting contract and check, he had rather assumed they needed him to put together some sort of period festival for their employees. The seven-page confidentiality agreement had made him suspicious that wasn't the case. Two elevator rides and three levels of security checks and a retinal scan later, he was pretty sure that a staff party was not involved.

Thomas Eldersen tried to not look as intimidated

as he felt and repeated quietly to himself that very large dollar amount. The walk ended at what Thomas first thought was the door to a giant safe. For a brief moment he wondered if they planned to give him some more cash, expenses or the like, then one of his escorts pushed a button and spoke.

"General Orgin, Eldersen is here."

There was no reply, but there was a loud click and the three-inch steel door swung slowly open. As soon as Thomas stepped through, both men straightened, appeared like they really wanted to salute, and then walked away.

General Orgin was a large man, just starting to turn to fat. He had to be in his sixties and everything about the white-haired man suggested he had been career military. This made sense to Thomas, as he had just read how many retiring army officers moved into positions at companies they had done business with and Humes Aerospace was one of the Pentagon's largest contractors.

The "general" continued to ignore him, so the professor studied the office to learn more about the man. The office's walls were the same gray as the jumpsuits everyone else seemed to wear. In fact, he realized, the suits tended to fade into the walls. The desk had three phones—one was even red—and several piles of papers. On the walls were two photos, one of the Marines raising the flag on Iwo Jima and the other of a much younger Orgin and three other men standing next to a beaming President Reagan.

"So you are my weirdness expert?" General Orgin asked in a deep voice that sounded used to giving orders. He didn't wait for a reply. "So what is this?"

It took Thomas a moment to focus in the photo the general held up. Then he realized it could not be a photo, but must be a picture taken of an amazingly detailed painting.

"That would be a hippogryph," he identified the beast shown diving toward the camera. "A mythological beast often featured in heraldry."

"Mythological, heh." The general almost smiled, but not quite. "Tough bastards?"

"Yeah, notoriously nasty in most stories about them." Thomas' mind struggled for an example, but nothing came. The general saved him a long silence by bringing up a photo of another exquisitely detailed fantasy monster.

"So what is this, then?"

The creature resembled a snake, but had four short legs and wings. It was painted side on, as if flying past the artist with a long expanse of unbroken forest below it.

"That would be a wyrm."

"Worm, that would be for really big fish." The general looked both annoyed and amused at his own wit.

"No. A wyrm, with a Y," the professor hastened to explain. "A form of dragon, actually, commonly portrayed in England and France. The sort of creature Saint George was said to have fought."

He found himself dropping into lecture mode. "They were fierce beasts who ravaged entire villages. Some were said to breathe fire, others to spread plague with their breath."

"Chemical warfare," the general grunted.

"Most were very territorial. One was thought to guard Merlin's ice cave, another to have provided the fire that forged Arthur's sword Excalibur."

"Could they be killed?"

"Er, sure, I guess . . . in the stories. There are storied of knights skewering them on lances."

"Okay, you'll do," the older man interrupted just as Thomas prepared to give him a detailed account of England's patron saint's battle with a dragon and explain how it was thought to be a metaphor for the conversion of the Britains to Christianity.

Pushing a button on his desk, Orgin once more took up his stack of papers and ignored the literature professor. A few seconds later the door opened, and a younger man with eagles on his shoulders waved the professor from the room.

"I'm Potter," the man introduced himself. Then they began walking down yet another gray hallway. Thomas noticed there was a slight slope to the floor and realized this had been true of the last corridor as well. They had been going lower even as they walked. He realized most of the complex was underground. This certainly fit with the *Dr. Strangelove* feel to the place. Thomas had the uneasy feeling that he had been dropped into a very low budget SciFi Channel special. He was more than a bit frightened and felt like he had lost control of his own life. Once more, the professor repeated to himself the amount of the very high retainer that had already been deposited in his bank account.

"If you will follow me," the slender major explained as they walked down a new windowless hallway, "you will be given a badge and have your clearance processed, Professor Eldersen. Then I can show what is going on."

The clearance process was efficient, though Thomas was surprised to hear several of the men in the office where his badge was prepared speaking Russian.

"Former Spetsnaz," the major explained. "We are a multinational corporation, after all."

It took the professor a few seconds to adjust to that.

The place was so, well, military, he had assumed this was some sort of US Army operation. This was strictly a corporate party, whatever he was mixed in.

Another long walk took them to an underground monorail. The cars were large, and there were no seats. As soon as a car appeared, several large men stepped up and loaded boxes until the car was almost full. When they had finished, Major Potter led him to the front of the first car, where two crates had been set for them to use as seats, and nodded at the operator.

They started with a jolt that almost knocked Eldersen off his feet. Waiting until he had recovered, the young officer then recited what sounded a lot like a canned speech. "I will remind you again of the secrecy statement you signed. If you, at any time, ever speak of what you are about to see or relate anyone else anything that is connected to this project, you will be liable for a massive amount of money and assuredly spend the rest of your life where you can tell no one anything else." He paused for obvious effect, and it worked. Thomas felt himself begin to sweat even though the car was cool. What had he gotten into?

"Is that clear? This is really your last chance to back out."

"Back out of what?" Eldersen realized he was frightened and resented it. And he was getting annoyed at all the secrecy. What the hell kind of party were they planning? An orgy? What else could they need a professor of medieval literature for?

"That is the problem, professor. Once we tell you, you are committed. Leave in ignorance right now, or we proceed and you stay. Last chance."

"And I have to return the retainer if I leave?" Thomas knew the answer.

The major smiled. "Humes Aerospace is a for-profit

corporation. Of course you would be required to return every penny and the confidentiality agreement would remain in force."

Thomas Eldersen once more repeated the amount of money they had paid him. Suddenly it wasn't sounding as large as it once had. On another level, though, he was intrigued. Where was this all leading?

"So, tell me what is this all about," the professor found himself saying almost before he was aware he had made the decision.

About then they arrived and exited the monorail. By way of explanation Major Potter led Thomas into a large cave that opened onto the Atlantic Ocean. It appeared to have been widened and extended, and there were a number of openings on the sides. The sound of the waves alone was impressive enough, but all the professor really noticed was the ten-meter-wide glowing ring of blue flames that hung across half the entrance. Or rather to what was inside that ring, which was a coastline where he knew there should be none. He edged and looked around the side of the fiery ring and saw only ocean beyond.

"Some sort of illusion?" he asked, not wanting to be fooled by a hologram.

"That is a most real portal and a most real place," Potter assured him.

"Portal?"

"To another world." The major seemed to enjoy the open-jawed expression Eldersen achieved. "To a completely different world. A parallel one to our own, it seems."

"How, what, where . . . ?" the professor stammered. His thoughts weren't keeping up with, well, his thoughts.

"The simple version is that what you see is the result of a failed experiment. A mistake. They were attempting to create a new method of communications. One that was so radically different it could not be jammed. The profit would be enormous. Every unit in the armed forces would have to be reequipped with it. So Humes had some quantum physicists working on it, wasting way too much money, a government grant, of course."

"Of course."

Professor Eldersen listened without taking his eyes off the image in the portal. The shore was no more than a hundred meters away. Occasionally, he could see a small bird flitting in the forest that reached almost to the stony shore. Once, he was sure that he heard the screech of a hawk over the crash of waves.

Potter paused to allow the professor to recover a bit, then continued.

"Well, they cranked up the device, which works at something they call the subatomic level. Guess the idea was to change the atoms inside each radio using something called Congruity or a word like that. No real signal, so no jamming.

"The first test was a failure but hinted that there was a reaction. They used ten times the power for the second test. It took all the power from a nuclear station just to open this thing, but that is what they did. It's still straining every generator we have to maintain it."

"What if they shut it down?"

"No idea; maybe it would not open again. Maybe open to some other parallel universe. Maybe the moon next time. No one knows. I would not want to try. Anyone tries to touch this thing or come through it, Orgin has given orders they be shot."

That concept was enough to allow the professor to drag his eyes away again and realize there were half a dozen heavily armed men nearby, most just staring at him and Potter. A few looked like they wanted him to get near the portal or make a mistake. Then the real question slammed into Eldersen's awareness.

"Why are you showing this to a professor of medieval literature from a prominent women's college? My knowledge of quantum physics is minimal at best."

"It is because of where that portal leads to," was the quick reply. Potter must have been waiting for just that question.

"France?" It was sort of a joke. No one laughed.

"Not exactly . . . er, take a look at these." The major passed Thomas a thick book full of photos. It was more photos of the fantasy art, again incredibly detailed. After the fifth shot of the same hippogryph it dawned on the professor that these were not paintings. His jaw dropped a second time and he knew why he was here.

"These were taken there?" He gestured at the land beyond the portal.

"Keep looking," Potter urged.

The next set of photos showed some sort of castle, though the towers were too high and thin to be architecturally possible. That set ended with the pictures of a bearded man standing at the top of one of those towers who must have fired some sort of weapon. The last image showed a round, fiery object just about to hit the camera.

"There are men in armor as well, some seem to be firing lightning from lances they carry," Potter added as Thomas paged past yet more photos of mythical beasts and knights in armor. When he finished, Thomas found he had nothing to say. He was still dealing with the portal; what lay beyond it would take more time to believe.

There was a long pause. Finally Potter spoke.

"Those images cost us almost eleven million dollars in drones. Four went in. Not one made it back out. But they told us what we need to know. We go in tomorrow. You will be accompanying the general as an adviser."

"In? Tomorrow? Some sort of delegation? The general? Me?"

"Not exactly," Potter laughed. "It was determined there is no opposition there that modern technology can't handle easily. I would not want to go up against a .50-caliber heavy machine gun in a tin suit." Then he paused, searching for words.

"The general, some of the boys. They haven't told Washington about this yet. Not sure when they plan to. Guess it will be more of a recon in force. If it goes well . . ."

General Orgin's voice boomed over the conversation as he exited another monorail car.

"Have you any idea what we have out there?" As usual, he was not looking for an answer. "A whole world fresh and full of resources. Not a drop of oil has been pumped, not a speck of uranium mined. Hell, once we are in control, maybe we can ship over our atomic waste and finally shut the liberals up about it."

"You plan to invade a whole world?" Thomas blurted out the question. He wasn't sure if he was outraged or amazed.

"Part of it, at least. They said it was a parallel to this one. From what we could map, the geography is the same. No GPS sats, though. What you see there is an island off the coast of Britain, or what is Britain here. We call it Anglesee or something like that. I sent in a few scouts, but they seem to have had some trouble with the locals. One was hiding in a tree and he sent in the image of a really pretty woman, punk type, with green hair, then went silent. Sneaky bastards, but a few rounds from an M-16 will straighten them out."

"The Holy Isle?"

"Be the perfect place for a base. Once we have it pacified, we can pour in forces. The dividend this year will be incredible. Hmmm, probably make me an executive vice president after all this."

There was nothing Eldersen could say. Or, rather, with his mind on overload, he was having trouble concentrating on one thought long enough to express it. It didn't seem right, invading another world. This needed to be studied, cherished, not attacked. And there was something they had said that had the promise of a hidden menace to it, but he could not settle on what that was. He was only able to reach one solid conclusion, and it was hardly comforting: his retainer wasn't really large enough, not big enough by far for all this. It was also slowly dawning on the professor that he was actually going to see a world where magical creatures existed. But he wasn't going there to study them, they were going to invade them. It not only felt wrong, but even logically it was wrong.

What was he doing here? He had to get out of this mad scheme. The image of that magnificent magical wyrm came back, and somehow the great beast's eyes were accusing.

Maybe if he reported all this to the government? How?

With a sinking feeling, the literature professor realized that his just knowing about the portal meant he was committed. There was no question Orgin would have him imprisoned at best or, more probably, shot if he tried to back out now. Eldersen looked around for a way to escape and realized he had no idea where he was or how to navigate the maze of unmarked corridors.

The general was still speaking.

"The landing craft are arriving now . . . using hovercraft. We go in tomorrow morning. I'll count on you to warn me about anything unusual that we might face," the general finished and then hurried off to supervise a crew mounting some sort of machine gun in a hydrofoil.

"I'm communications officer," Potter offered. "You'll be assigned to me. The general may not need you much. Some of the board wanted a consultant. Orgin tends to just drive ahead. Good man, but very old school. Tougher than the men he leads, and that is saying something. Try to stay away from the mercs. They tend to be a rough crew, mostly former Russian Spetsnatz and South African Commandos, the ones their governments did not want to retain. I'll take you to your quarters."

The room was very military and the bed uncomfortable, but it wasn't like Thomas Eldersen could sleep anyhow. At least three times he convinced himself this was one big practical joke. At one point he was sure the whole thing was something the girls in his Chaucer class arranged. Didn't one of them have a dad in the Pentagon? That—or they slipped something in his coffee and he was in the middle of one astounding hallucination. Those alternatives seemed so much more likely than a magical, alternate parallel world. So it came almost as a disappointment when morning arrived and he was still deep inside the Humes Aeronautics compound. Half an hour later, the professor was on a hovercraft standing next to General Orgin and behind Potter, who was seated at a communications console.

The console was covered in small screens; apparently many of the mercenaries had small cameras in their helmets. At the moment most showed only the inside of other hovercraft where rows of other gray-jumpsuit-wearing men sat in what Thomas felt was uncanny silence. Major Potter's voice was subdued as he ordered the half dozen hovercraft through the portal.

The professor watched, but the fiery edges of the portal didn't change at all as the first hovercraft glided through the fiery ring. To his relief, it continued toward the island without a problem, though a glance around the side of the portal at the empty ocean still gave Thomas a slight shudder.

"Ten top men on each craft, tough and well trained," Orgin commented as the third airboat glided through the portal. "I pity any local yokel who tries to stop them. We should be all done in time for lunch to be catered."

Eldersen felt helpless. He was a part of this insanity, and there was no way out. He looked around for a way to stop the madness and noted everyone had a .45 automatic in their belt except him. Was he a coward to just go along? The professor felt helpless, and all he could do was wait.

Then the fourth hovercraft had passed through and it was their turn. They drifted gently forward and through the portal. Only the supply ship remained at the dock. Thomas braced himself, expecting some sort of feeling at the transition, but there was nothing. A look back reassured the professor that the portal looked the same from both sides. The thought that they were invading an entire planet with less than fifty corporate mercenaries was suddenly very intimidating. It was good to know he could get home. After only a few seconds the whine of the fans subsided.

"We're staying offshore until the perimeter can be cleared and stabilized," Potter informed Thomas when he looked surprised as they pulled to a stop about twenty meters short of the shore. Even as he spoke, the fronts of the other four hovercraft dropped open and the mercenaries moved with intimidating military professionalism onto the island. From one craft a small armored car with a .50-caliber machine gun in its turret rumbled onto the beach behind them.

When nothing reacted, Thomas and Potter both began to breathe again.

"Give me air recon," Orgin ordered without taking his eyes off the men on the shoreline. Within seconds, an unmanned drone and then a two-man helicopter zoomed through the portal and were over the island.

A very unnerving thought pushed its way into the front of Thomas Eldersen's mind. It took a few seconds to solidify, and when it did he had to speak.

"General Orgin, did your theorists say that this was a parallel universe to our own?"

The general's answer was gruff, and he never took his eyes off the shoreline. "Yes, geography, location of cities, lots of things. Less people and those strange critters, but mostly the same."

"But, General, would that not mean that their military, in their own way, would be just as prepared and competent as ours?"

The general almost paused. "I still wonder why the directors saddled me with you. Liberal wimps." He sounded adamant as if saying it made it true. "We have rifles, rockets, an armored car. They still ride horses, for pity's sake."

Potter looked up at the professor, and by the time he looked back at his bank of monitors things had changed.

Three creatures rose out of the forest. They looked like a combination of a hawk and a lion. The professor found he had stopped breathing again as the mythical flyers grew larger on the screen. Potter must have been less impressed. The major popped off a fire-and-forget missile from the drone, and seconds later one gryphon disappeared in a burst of blood and feathers. At the same time a frantic message came over the radio and was broadcast over a speaker in the command post.

"Base, there are three women approaching on— brooms? Can I designate them as hostile?" The minicopter pilot sounded understandably confused.

Orgin grabbed for the microphone and literally yelled into it. "All locals are to be treated as hostiles. Fire at will."

"Charlie can't fire, sir," came a frantic reply in a new voice. He seems to be a frog. Returning to . . . *ribbet*." Seconds later, the feed from the helicopter went black.

Eldersen glanced back at the screen showing the view from the drone. The two remaining gryphons were close. The major sent the unmanned aircraft into a series of preprogrammed evasions, but they were designed more to evade surface-to-air missiles than talons and beaks. Before the drone's camera stopped sending, they got a look at what looked like pieces of the aircraft's ultra-stress plastic wings being torn apart by a foot-long beak.

"Cleared our air cover. Just what I would have done," the general grunted. "We're gonna need some shoulder-launched stuff to handle those big bird things."

"Gryphons," Eldersen interjected. "And I think you may have missed something."

"Forgot more about combat then you'll ever know, professor. I'll run the op. You tell me fancy names," General Orgin snarled. He kept watching the screens. "All units expect an attack. This is a free fire zone, repeat, free fire. If it moves, kill it."

"But, General, didn't they say that this is a parallel world?" the literature professor tried to explain. Potter spun around, and his worried look told Thomas the major understood.

"My world, it's going to be now." Orgin set his prominent jaw and gave another order over the mike. "Proceed inland. Secure your primary objectives."

Immediately, the view from the screens of all forty men changed as they rose and moved forward in short runs. A few times they fired, the sound clear where they stood on the command boat. Nothing fired back; nothing seemed to oppose them. Then an astonished voice said something in Russian that Thomas did not understand. Several other voices joined the first, including some wolf whistles. Standing in front of at least ten of the men were the most incredibly beautiful women, naked except for a very few strategically placed leaves. Then the professor noticed that their hair also was made of leaves.

"Dryads!" Eldersen found himself privately cheering for the defenders.

"Huh?"

"They seduce the men, use their dead bodies to fertilize their host trees."

Everyone had turned to watch him, unable to perceive the danger.

"Psych warfare," Eldersen explained. "They hypnotize men."

Then Potter was yelling that the women were hostiles and to fire on them. Two men managed to do so in time. Those dryads broke apart in a spray of twigs and leaves. The cameras from the other eight were now a mass of static.

It was about then that the horses—no, unicorns, Eldersen realized—burst into a clearing when almost half the remaining mercenaries had formed a defensive circle. They were beautiful and incredibly fast. They closed in on the soldiers in a fraction of a second. From the way images on the helmet cameras bounced and shifted, their single horns were quite deadly. Those who survived the initial charge of the unicorns were saved when the rest of the mercenaries burst from the forest. The horned horses disappeared into the trees, leaving three of their own and several mercs dead on the ground.

"Fire on anything that moves," Orgin ordered. Nothing seemed to be moving, but the mercenaries were near panic. They began to spray the woods around them with short bursts. The firing had just ended when a number of men in robes and cowls appeared. They didn't walk up or emerge from the trees. Suddenly, they just were there without even a puff of smoke.

"Everyone down," Potter ordered while keying in a set of coordinates. The mercs dropped. A few seconds later Thomas heard a *whoosh* as the artillery rounds passed overhead. Looking back at the scenes from the helmet cameras they could all see the robed men raise their hands and begin to chant. Then, explosions filled the screen.

"On target," Potter confirmed. "Stand by." The thunder of the shells landing rolled over the air boat.

When the splinters, leaves, and dust had settled, no one on the air boat spoke. Standing unharmed were every single one of the robed men, surrounded by devastation and fallen trees. One pulled a short stick from his waist and aimed it toward the mercenaries. He said something that sounded vaguely familiar to Eldersen, paused, and then fired. The magic wand spat green flames and the screams filled the command cabin.

"If it moves, fire. Hold for further orders," the general bellowed, slamming his hands against the airboat's rail. "I don't care if the target looks like your gray-haired mommy. Kill 'em all." It was apparent Orgin was beginning to panic.

On the screens men and wizards both died.

"This is a parallel world, General," Thomas tried to explain. He was sure now. "You can't win."

"The hell I can't." Orgin spun and looked as if he was going to hit the professor. It was apparent the mercenaries had given themselves the order to retreat. Soon the screens showed the inside of the hovercraft they had landed in. Looking up, Eldersen could see all four pulling off the beach and running for the portal.

"I'll call in artillery, level the place," Orgin growled.

"Parallel, sir." The professor tried to keep the joy he had in the defeat out of his voice as he explained. "They aren't any weaker than us, just different. You just tried to invade Britain with fifty men and with no surprise since it has been three days after you sent in scouts that were captured. You would have been ready. Why did you expect them to be less competent?"

"But," Orgin started to protest even as Major Potter ordered the hydroplane's pilot to get them back through the portal. Then the younger officer looked out and gestured urgently for them to hurry back to safety. When the professor followed his gaze, he realized why the major was panicking. They had to get out right now, or they would never leave.

But it was too late.

Clad in sea-green webbing, water dripping from the whiskers under their shell helmets, the cold determination of an elite force in their eyes, they rose from the water spewing fire and lightning from wands attached to their flippers. The other side's Navy Seals had joined the battle.

AIRBORNE

by Jody Lynn Nye

"I UNDERSTAND THE new pilot is here," First Underofficer Fili of the Elven Air Cavalcade said as he led his white pegasus Milda through the landing glade toward the stables.

The other elf moved his chestnut flyer's reins into his other hand and pointed into the leaf-wreathed thicket near their stables at the tail of a black horse protruding out a foot or two. The tip of a wing extended up above the tops of the hazel sprays. "There he is. And what a fine-looking animal he is, too," Kauli said, giving it a hearty slap on the flank.

"Watch it, friend," a male voice growled. The horse's behind turned around. To the elves' surprise, it was not attached to a horse's front. Instead, a male torso with muscular arms, tanned skin, and black hair confronted them. A pair of glossy, black-feathered wings joined the back from the shoulder blades down to a few inches below where skin became hide. Kauli gaped. A winged centaur!

"That's a beautiful steed you've got there," said Fili

scornfully to the newcomer, narrowing his green eyes. "Where's the rest of it?"

The centaur tossed his long black hair, and stamped a sable right rear hoof. "I only laughed at that the first thousand times, elf." He threw off a creditable salute. "Pilot Eurwood of the Silver Dale reporting for service."

"Welcome," Kauli said, extending a hand upward, for the centaur stood head and shoulders above him. "Second Underofficer Kauli. This is Rabena." The mare danced shyly behind her rider's shoulder.

"Nice to meet you," Eurwood said. He reached out a friendly hand to scratch the mare behind her pointed ears. She nickered with pleasure. "Where's the commander?"

"This way," Fili said. He turned his back on Eurwood and headed toward the captain's tent. Eurwood gave him a startled glance, but fell into step behind the first officer and his steed. Kauli, too, was taken aback by the curt dismissal of a new comrade-in-arms.

Kauli kept glancing curiously at his new companion as they walked. The Elf Kingdoms extended across roughly two thirds of the continent they called Shoi'ana, and the dwarves in their third called Caragrok. Centaur herds roamed the southern reaches beyond the mountains, in plains that were too empty for the elves and not filled with enough interesting minerals for their shorter brethren. The three races usually did not mix much with one another or with the other species who lived there.

Times, however, were changing. The elves' war against the Blood Host, already almost eight years in duration, had caused so many casualties that they found themselves appealing to their neighbors for aid, both to stop the influx of vampires, harpies, and werewolves from Mori'ana across the sea, and to keep them from spreading farther across Shoi'ana. Most of the dwarves who had joined the forces preferred to be ground troops and cavalry, mistrusting the pegasi. Naiads and dryads refused to leave their forests, but had been giving good service by changing the paths and setting confusion spells all throughout the woodlands, which had driven some of the enemy mad and had done a lot to damage their opponents' morale all around. The few centaurs that had come forward were used as shock troops, combining their superior size and strength with mobility that Kauli could not help but envy. He never dreamed one of them would join the elite flyers of the air corps. Still, he felt that there was something wrong with a centaur with wings. He knew Fili felt the same as he did. The Free People were fighting against species perverted by evil, and now they would be fighting alongside one perverted by nature. They had seen other creatures suffer after being bespelled by the evil invaders, even some members of their own airborne force. Some of them had been terribly deformed, growing horns, or a third eye, or suffocating as their mouths and noses were sealed under a layer of flesh. Perhaps that was the cause of Fili's dislike. Still, this was wartime, and they should be grateful for any allies who would help them rid the continent of their enemy. They should do all they could to get over their uneasiness.

"Captain Bakolli!" Fili saluted. The silver-haired elf sitting alone at the small camp table underneath the trees signed to the trio to approach.

"Our new recruit," Bakolli said with a smile. Eurwood saluted and handed him a silver acorn. Kauli knew that it contained an introduction from either a centaur captain or chief of a herd. "Thank you, Pilot

Eurwood. Glad to have you here. We are at rest at the moment, as you see. It will give you a chance to acclimate to our company. I'll review your records. In the meantime, my officers will show you around."

"Yes, sir," the centaur said, eyes forward. "Thank you, sir."

"That is all, pilots. Get some food. I will see you at the evening sing."

Elves did not stable their animals in between four walls and a roof as the dwarves did. Pegasi preferred a calmer, more open setting, through which the soft night wind could flow. Plantwise elves had brought forth a garden suitable for equine companions that was comfortable enough that Kauli thought he wouldn't mind living in it himself. Narrow whips of hazel and rowan had been woven into flowers and thick vines bent to form bowers up among the branches of the huge trees in which a winged animal might find peace. They were hung with fragrant honeysuckle and mum's ivy, a plant that drank sound. Pegasi were nervy beasts, as likely to kick down the bowers as stand or nest in them, and needed a bit of soothing to calm them after a hard day's flying. The other elves were already there, sitting on smaller branches beside their winged friends, speaking quietly to them and feeding them tidbits and fresh flowers.

Fili glanced sideways at Eurwood as they walked through the aisle in between the two rows of trees. Rabena danced a little impatiently and nibbled at Kauli's ear as he paused before her stall. He took off her tack and gave her a pat on the side. The chestnut gathered herself and winged upward, alighting on the woven platform.

"There's nothing for you here. You won't be needing to linger," Fili said curtly to the centaur.

"Wait," Kauli said. "What is he going to do when we settle our mounts for the evening?"

"What, do you kiss them good night?" Eurwood asked scornfully.

"Yeah," sneered Fili. "You can kiss your own backside then, too."

Eurwood leered at him. "Why don't you kiss it for me?"

"Enough!" Kauli exclaimed, and immediately lowered his voice as several of the pilots glared at him past their animals' sides. "Eurwood, this is a bonding exercise, caring for our animals. It is an important facet of our training, and our daily routine. Afterward, we sit together and tell stories, listen to one another, try to learn more about each other to form a stronger corps."

The centaur snorted. "Then I guess when you're putting your animals to bed in the treetops, I'm going to go straight to the bar and start drinking. How about that for a bonding exercise? I should be drunk enough by the time you get there to think that you are civilized beings. I can find the sleeping quarters by myself." He stalked off, leaving the two officers exchanging glances.

Kauli studied his friend. "This is not your usual custom, to dislike someone on sight, Fili."

The senior elf shook his head. "Something about him makes me think of our foe, Kauli. I find myself unable to restrain my tongue. He is so prickly that it does not help me to accept him. It's not as though he is really an elf."

The small, leafy glen where the pilots gathered at the end of the day was filled with tension. Eurwood

had indeed gotten a head start on the barrel of mead
set on a bracket near the table of victuals. He sat on
a high branch above the others, glaring down at them
when Kauli offered introductions. Fili poured them
both mugs of the honey wine and made a few choice
comments on the intelligence of centaurs as he flopped
down into a comfortable seat made from a clump of
thornless briars. The others laughed, so Fili enlarged
upon his topic.

"And especially half-breeds," he said loudly enough
to be heard above the derisive noises Eurwood let out.
"Anything stupid enough to breed with horses can't
have much upstairs."

A stream of mead poured down on Fili's head. He
leaped up, sputtering. The others snorted into their
mugs. Even Kauli smiled secretly into his drink.

"Got this upstairs, anyhow, elf," Eurwood's voice
came out of the leaves.

Just after sunrise, Captain Bakolli held his saber in
the air while his silvery steed Mercury hovered fifty
feet above the ground, fluttering only his wingtips.
"One pass, loose three arrows through the rings and
into the targets. Your aim must be perfect every time,
our enemies do not allow for second chances. We need
to keep sharp, pilots! The wyrm is coming, and we
will have little time to stop it!"

"What's this wyrm?" Eurwood asked.

"Silence in the ranks!" Bakolli bellowed.

Kauli surveyed the crossed vines strung from the
tops of two tall birch trees down to the ground.
Along each one were tied a series of rings as wide
as an elf's head. Beyond them, attached to the trees
themselves, were hay-stuffed targets. If and only if
one maneuvered one's steed into the proper place,

one could shoot through the rings and strike those targets.

"The wyrm is the Blood Host's secret weapon," he whispered to Eurwood. "It's killed hundreds."

"All right," Fili said, turning around in his saddle and starting straight at Eurwood. "Let's see whether you belong with this unit, pilot!"

"Fine," Eurwood said, saluting smartly. "Sir, permission to make the pass?"

"Granted," Fili snapped out, returning the salute.

Kauli knew the maneuverability that he could get on Rabena's back. She took care of the flying, responding to his gentle knee pressure and verbal orders. By comparison the centaur seemed clumsy as he galloped into the sky, flapping his great wings. He had to handle both flying and fighting at the same time. Still, once he was airborne, the awkwardness passed swiftly. Eurwood flicked through the hanging vines with remarkable speed, never touching a single one. At the first officer's signal, he whisked the bow from the baldric across his chest and an arrow from the quiver on his back, joining the two in an instant. A quick pull and loose, and the first arrow winged through the top ring and smacked into the center of the target with an audible pop!

The pilots of the Cavalcade murmured admiringly among themselves. Fili shook his head. "One arrow, with no distractions. Any junior pilot should be capable of that. Kauli, you next! Fly cross-pattern."

"Yes, sir." Kauli nudged Rabena, and she was off. He drew his bow. The winged mare responded to his knees, weaving in and out of the obstacles. He reached the first ring at the same time Eurwood was crossing beneath him, aiming for the second. Their arrows hissed from the bow at the same moment. The watching pilots let out a sigh and a groan. Kauli looked back. His arrow had not struck the center. He felt his cheeks burn with shame. Rabena nickered, the vibration reverberating through her barrel so that he could feel it in his legs, as she sympathized with him.

But one arrow did not lose a battle, despite what their captain said. Kauli swung around, ready to take aim at the next target. Eurwood was below him, heading for number three. Another elf, Brauxen, brought his bay horse over their heads. The shadow obscured the opening of the ring, but Kauli had already marked its location. He loosed, and knew the arrow found its true mark. Eurwood, too, had taken his third shot, and returned to the line on the ground, his bow held over his head in triumph.

When Fili and Kauli examined the targets, they found that all of the centaur's shots had found the center. Kauli had to grant Eurwood his arrogant celebration. None of the other pilots had done nearly as well. Fili nudged Milda to land. The mare tilted her great white wings and sailed gracefully to the ground. She trotted up and down before the ranked pilots. Kauli noticed that his companion's shoulders were taut under his leather tunic as he stopped before Eurwood.

"Good shooting, pilot," he said, his tone grudging.

Eurwood kept his eyes forward. "Yes, sir."

Kauli searched the long face. "Who was your teacher, pilot?"

"Is that an official question, Second Underofficer?" Eurwood asked.

"No, just friendly curiosity."

"Then, with all due respect, none of your business, Second Underofficer."

Eurwood's subsequent passes at the targets were as

flawless as the first. The elves watched with growing
admiration and applauded the final pass. Any one of
the Cavalcade would have been flushed with pleasure
at the approbation, but the centaur continued to look
bored and hostile. He rebuffed friendly comments and
ignored compliments. Kauli thought that perhaps Fili's
abrasive reception of him the night before had put
him into a sulk from which he had not yet recovered.

Kauli caught up with him when they broke for
lunch.

"I did not mean to offend you with my question,
Eurwood," he said.

"No offense taken, Second Underofficer." The centaur continued trotting along, rapidly outpacing the
elf. Kauli broke into a light run to keep apace of his
taller companion.

"Please, call me Kauli when we're not on duty."
Was the fellow walking even faster? "Come and dine
with us. We'd like to know you better."

"If you wish." Eurwood didn't sound as if he re-
lished the offer.

"I do. You must forgive Fili. He has been at war
so long that he does not readily accept newcomers.
We have been betrayed at times, by those we thought
we could trust."

"Not my problem," Eurwood said curtly.

"We are grateful for your service. Please accept
that."

"I'm not here to please you, Second Underofficer.
I have my own reasons."

Kauli kept trying. "That's a handsome bow you
carry. Did you make it?"

"What would it matter if I did?" The centaur
opened his stride and plunged into a thicket of bram-
bles. The prickly shoots swayed shut before Kauli
reached them. He decided not to follow.

Kauli was undeterred. They had had elves from many tribes join them, each with his or her own customs, and often with a chip on their shoulders, but they all served the greater purpose of keeping Shoi'ana free.

But by lunch's end, neither Kauli nor his friends knew anything more about the newcomer than they had before. He gave them his tribe's name, the Silver Dale, and allowed that he was twenty-eight years old, but nothing else, not even his reasons for joining the Cavalcade. Fili was scornful, as always.

"Let him be alone," he said. "With an attitude like that, he will probably get killed in the first onslaught by the enemy."

"He's come freely to join us, Fili," Kauli said, frowning. "If he risks his life for the country, he deserves our respect and support, if not our friendship."

"He certainly can shoot," Brauxen said, grabbing another handful of arrows from the fletchers' table and refilling his quiver.

"And fly," added Trasbre, an elf from the southern reaches. "I think my stallion was jealous of him! Did you see him turn on his right wingtip around that tree? He never touched a leaf! And he flew straight up and *over*. A marvel. With his shape he can do things we may not dream of."

"Such a shape! I've heard of an elf becoming attached to his steed, but that's ridiculous," Hobri snickered.

"You say he's crossbred," Brauxen said. "Do you know with what? Where did he get those wings?"

"Harpy," Fili said with grim satisfaction. "I knew he reminded me of something evil. His life story was there in a nutshell. Captain Bakolli let me see it. Mother's a centaur. Father's a harpy. He put a love spell on her, but they stayed together for more than thirty years. Freaks."

"Aye, yes," Trasbre agreed. "He's a freak. But I still wish I could fly like that. I asked him to teach me that wingtip turn, and he told me to . . ." The southern elf made a couple of hand gestures that made the others gasp, then snicker.

"Let him alone for a while," Kauli said. "Just show him some respect, and he'll come around."

"There's no time for being soft in warfare," Fili said. "If he takes orders, that's all I care about."

"Why are you being so hard on Eurwood, Fili?" Kauli asked, once the others had disbursed. "He's proving to be a worthwhile addition to the squad. Give him a chance to feel as though he belongs here."

"We have no time for coddling," Fili said curtly. "The enemy is everywhere. And if he can't take a little banter, then let him go back to whatever warped nest spawned him."

"It's more than ordinary banter. You're picking on him, Fili."

"And what if I am? Have you forgotten the bloody battles we have fought against the harpies?" Fili asked.

Kauli shook his head. "He's not one of them. He is our ally. He may be the product of an unnatural mating, but he has come to fight for our cause. It would serve you better to remember that."

Fili looked down upon him coldly. "If we're speaking about memory, Second Underofficer, I outrank you, and that freak told you to mind your own business, did he not? We have more to think about than the happiness of a half-harpy."

"Won't you come join us, Eurwood?" Kauli asked. The centaur had fluttered up among the high branches of the tree above the glen, and Kauli had climbed up after him, determined that he should not spend another evening alone. Below them, the nightly sing was in full spate. The other pilots were vying with one another with new poems. Some were scurrilous, others solemn. Laughter and applause filtered up to them through the thick green leaves. For a moment Kauli saw a wistful look on the centaur's face, but it passed swiftly.

"Thank you, but no," Eurwood said.

"We come from many tribes here, and many different walks of life. My mother is the queen's chirurgeon, and my father is a listener."

"An unusual profession." Eurwood eyed him curiously. More than mere sound, listeners could hear cracks at the heart of a stone, plants growing underground, or a wound healing inside an elf's body. At that moment Kauli wished he had more of his father's skill, but he sensed the centaur might be willing to open up a little.

"Tell me about your parents," Kauli said, settling himself in a comfortable niche between branch and bole with his legs propped up. "I know very few centaurs well."

"You mean, how could one of them take up with a harpy?" Eurwood asked. "You wouldn't understand."

"I will try," Kauli said.

Eurwood seemed to struggle internally before he allowed himself to speak. "Not all harpies are ugly, misshapen beasts. It's the evil they do that warps their bodies and their spirits. My father did not look like the ones who serve the Blood Host. He appeared as noble a creature as you. If he was evil, it would have shown. He loved my mother. He played a trick on her with a love potion, but they lived together joyfully long after it wore off. She made him pay for that little ruse, I promise you."

Kauli laughed. "I can well imagine. An elf maiden would exact the price of her pride before forgiving."

Eurwood tossed his head like a stallion. "The same for a centaur filly. My mother might have forgiven him, but the others of our herd never did. You have admired my skill in the air. *He* taught me how to fly. Would you still have given me even grudging compliments if you knew the source of my skill? Probably not. He was a man of honor and a hero. I am here in his memory."

"He is dead, then?" Kauli asked sympathetically. "What became of him?"

Eurwood glowered. His horse's hooves gathered beneath him, and he sprang up to take wing. His black wings and pelt rendered him instantly invisible against the night sky.

Kauli helped himself down thoughtfully. Fili saw him climb out of the tree.

"And what of our misshapen recruit?" Fili asked, waving him over.

"An interesting fellow. It sounds strange to say, but his family sounds quite normal. He could have been raised as an elf."

Fili snorted.

Kauli looked around at the others seated nearby. "He came to join us in honor of his father's memory."

A few nodded respectfully, but Fili gave him an odd look. "Harpies have no honor."

Kauli knew what he was thinking. Not two years past, the Cavalcade had gone after a flock that had attacked a small village to the southeast of their camp near Woth Forest. When it was over, they went into the village to see if they could help the wounded. There were no wounded, only dead. All the elves within had been gutted by harpy claws, including chil-

dren. He had a keen memory of Fili sitting on the
ground holding the still-twitching body of a small
child.

"Why would he come to us, then?" Kauli demanded, dispelling the horrific vision. "He will risk his
life beside ours. You cannot doubt that a centaur
would be our ally. I sense no falseness in him."

"We will see whether his heart's with his horse half
or his vulture half," Fili said carelessly as he rose,
dumping out the last dregs of his mead. "I'm for bed."

Kauli and a few of the elves continued to try and
make friends with Eurwood, but most of the Cavalcade followed Fili's example, and made fun of the
centaur when they couldn't ignore him. Some of it was
rank jealousy. Eurwood was an incredibly good flier
and a deadly archer. The centaurs had invented the
art, for all that the elves claimed it. Kauli had been
taught the truth, and he knew his fellows had, too. He
and his friends openly showed their admiration for
Eurwood's skill. He hoped that all of the elves would
come around and stop treating the centaur like a
stranger. The war *was* approaching. They needed to
be united. Their survival depended upon it. The seers
among them had begun to have terrible dreams of
scaled faces with lidless eyes, and hungry, fanged
mouths forever reaching for their throats.

"Tomorrow," Bakolli confirmed at dinner on the
third night. As usual, Eurwood sat at the end of the
glen, paying heed only to the captain's announcements
and nothing else. "The battle returns to us, my friends.
Sharpen your knives and make sure all your arrows are
straight. Tomorrow a new enemy force arrives. I have
seen it, and I have received messages from my fellow
commanders at sea and on the western shore. They have

driven past the armies of the deep, and they will land at the river mouth of Irensis. We overfly the army at the Pass of Tryiora, and may Nature protect us all."

A huge force assembled a mile west of Tryiora. Of those present, the elves were the most plentiful. Five regional armies had met and melded under one flag at the beginning of the war, but in few circumstances had the force ever massed together as they did now. Contrary to the belief of dwarves that all elves looked alike, Kauli saw the tanned faces of the southern elves, the solid black faces of the forest elves, nut-brown complexions common to the central mountain range, the pale elves of the far north and the biscuit-tan of his own people, who hailed from the region under attack. Most of them were infantry, trusting more to their swift feet than to any landbound steed. Kauli waved greetings to the few he knew. Some friends were missing. He would wait until after the battle to find out their fate. It would not help him in battle to know he had more loved ones to mourn.

The hundred or so dwarves, armored in shining ring mail with axes and hammers at their sides, bearded to a man, rode stocky ponies, short-legged bullocks, and curly-headed rams that pawed the ground impatiently. The centaurs, for there were a few of the equine race present, towered over their strong allies. Like the elves, they carried bows as well as swords. A few dry-ads nipped in and out between the slender trees, disappearing into the substance of the wood and emerging on the other side. Kauli found it fascinating. Fili was too tense to study his fellow countrymen. After his superior had snapped at him a few times, Kauli kept his observations to himself. He admitted that part of his scrutiny was to keep his own mind off the coming battle.

The Elven Queen's generals decreed that this pass was the best place to engage the new army of the Blood Host. As it had chosen to land at Irensis, it must come this way if it wanted to attack the queen's forest-city of Crenn, the most likely target foreseen. Many of the enemy force did not need roads, such as the vampires, but the wyrm could not fly. Its exhalations were so caustic they burned the flesh off one's bones. Its claws were so sharp they cut the air into ribbons. Its body was strong enough to crush any unfortunate being caught in its toils. If only they could stop it here, they would save so many lives. Kauli feared it, but he would give his life to protect his homeland.

The flutter of wings brought everyone's eyes up to the treetops. A messenger in blue livery mounted upon a huge eagle came circling down to land at Bakolli's feet. He leaped from the bird's back and dropped to one knee.

"The Blood Host is but ten miles distant, Commander. The giants have lost half their number. We are the ones who must halt them."

Bakolli turned to his officers. "This is it, then. Muster your forces. We join in battle within the hour."

Waiting was the worst part. Kauli on Rabena and Fili on Milda hovered at the head of the file beside Bakolli. The pass was a mile behind them. Two hundred archers, elves, and centaurs, along with two dozen wizards, were arrayed in the hills to provide coverfire and to act as the last line of defense should their opponents break through. The others held ready, waiting for the enemy to swarm the narrow river valley.

Kauli's bow began to slip in his hands. He palmed the sweat onto his pants leg. He had two quivers on his back. The left was full of ordinary arrows; the right, silver-tipped to kill the undead invaders.

Suddenly, the air was full of twisting snakes. The fangs that he had seen in his dream were all around him. Kauli grabbed for his knife. Rabena let out a shrill whinny of fear and began to kick.

"Up, up!" Fili yelled, striking at the foe. He spurred Milda upward. "Get above them!"

Kauli followed. He slashed at the snakes. They recoiled, hissing. Luckily, none of them had bitten him yet. He feared for his mare's well-being. The pegasus bounded around with fear.

"Calm down!" Bakolli shouted. "It's all illusion! Hold steady!"

Around them, other commanders yelled orders. On the ground, the dwarves pressed forward, swinging their axes. Not all of the attackers were illusions: unearthly screams rose as sinuous bodies flew into the air, black ichor dripping from their wounds. Kauli guided Rabena back into line, chanting soothing rhymes and stroking her neck. The poems, drawn from ancient lore, even calmed a few of the butterflies in his stomach. He soon saw the snakes for what they were, and sheathed his knife. Best to wait for a real target.

A white light suffused the air, and the illusions disappeared. The pegasi stopped kicking and calmed down. The only steed that hadn't panicked was Eurwood's lower half. The centaur hung in the air like an effigy. Kauli began to envy him his detachment. Once the spell had been broken, he could see how few snakes there had been. Below them, the last few were crushed to death under the hooves of the dwarven cavalry.

Trasbre, the scout, came flying back, leaning low

over the neck of his steed. "The wyrm approaches, Captain!"

Bakolli nodded. He cocked his arm and beckoned the Cavalcade forward. Below them, the infantry and cavalry were already on the move.

Like a black cloud on the horizon, the vampires swept down upon them. These were real. The gray-skinned undead carried with them the miasma of the grave. Many of the horses, already panicked by the illusion of the snakes, shrieked. A few fled, carrying their hapless riders toward the mountain pass. Kauli was proud that not one of the pegasi tried to desert.

Bakolli brought up the saber and dropped the point. At the command, the Cavalcade zoomed out of the sky, firing silver-tipped arrow after arrow at the pale undead. Kauli saw the first bolts strike. The bodies exploded into dust. The captain gestured again, and the winged horses stroked their way back into the sky. The pilots divided into two groups, and plunged down once more in two streams that crossed over the leading edge of the enemy's line. They destroyed many of the foe before the two armies met.

The dwarves engaged the vampires, striking them with their great war hammers. The undead recoiled as they realized that the crushing weapons were clad with silver foil. Alas, their wielders were not. The vampires dodged with unearthly speed and lighted upon the backs of their enemy, clawing away the mail coifs, seeking the large artery in the neck. The dwarves divided into pairs, each striking at the parasitical beast upon his partner's back.

Some of the vampires rose into the sky after the pegasi. The saber swept upward. Kauli led his pilots up and around into their primary defensive formation. Eurwood, unfamiliar with the patterns, was left hanging in the air with a dozen vampires rushing toward him with avid eyes and outstretched claws. Fili and his wingman were closest. They peppered the undead with arrows until the hapless centaur was at the center of a cloud of gray and black dust. Fili emerged from it with Eurwood on his tail. The newcomer wiped the dust from his eyes and regarded the First Underofficer with respect.

"My thanks. I owe you, elf."

Fili waved a hand. "Nothing to it, centaur."

Eurwood shook his head. "I never forget a debt."

Below them, what vampires remained had passed pushed past the dwarves and into the path of the elven army. The fallen warriors were necessarily forgotten for the moment in the teeth, literally, of the onslaught of werewolves who followed. The hairy, gray-pelted creatures each wore a jet medallion with a round, gleaming white gem at their center—a moonstone! It permitted them to retain their cursed shape no matter what the phase of the moon.

These did not march so much as swarm. With the moon madness upon them, they recognized no authority. Trolls with whips drove them from the flanks. They fell upon the doughty dwarves with ululating howls. The dwarves, well-organized and well-armed, dealt with these so well there was no need for the Cavalcade overhead to do anything but kill the trolls at the sides. Without their keepers, many of the werewolves fled, scrambling off into the forest that lined the hills. Bakolli gestured to let them go. The trees and their guardians were waiting.

They had no time to watch. A sharp pain lashed Kauli's face. He gasped and turned, reaching for his knife. A harpy! The female, hovering above Rabena's head, let out a shriek of delight and tasted her claws. Kauli was disgusted by her ugliness. They had the head and torso of an elf, but the wings, back, and talons of a great bird. Their size made them formidable foes, and their huge, black wings allowed them to fly as silently as owls. All at once, the other battles they had fought against her kind came rushing back to him. He struck out at her.

"Pay no attention, pay with your life!" she shrilled, and flicked her powerful wings so she was just out of his reach. She dropped again the next moment, landing on Rabena's neck. The mare whinnied in terror as the harpy's foot-claws slashed, drawing lines of blood on the bronze pelt. Kauli reached for an arrow, but before he could nock it, another took the harpy in the throat. With a yell, the ugly creature fell out of the sky, trying to pull the arrow out with her claws. Kauli soothed the wounded mare, chanting a healing spell to close the wounds. True healing must wait for the end of battle. Fili flew close. It was his arrow that had saved their lives. Kauli saluted his friend in thanks.

"Here's his family," Fili shouted, pointing at the harpies. "We'll see whether he defects or remains true."

The hot red flush of Eurwood's face told Kauli he had heard Fili's jibe, but the centaur stayed in formation with the other pilots in Kauli's line, lending a hand to wingmates on either side. A huge male harpy harried him from above. He closed his wings and dropped several yards to give himself range to draw his bow. The male followed him, trying to light on his back and tear out his spine.

"Mutation! Crossbreed!" the harpy bellowed.

"Pilots!" Kauli shouted. Elves nudged their pegasi around and harried the black-winged male. He withdrew a few more yards, but came rushing back, claws out, yelling a war cry.

"The Blood Ho . . . !" was all that came out before

an arrow buried itself to the feathers in his chest. He looked down in surprise. His wings went limp, and he fell like a stone, disappearing into the melee below. Eurwood's cheeks burning red as he lowered the bow.

"Guess he's one of ours after all," Fili said, "but one kill doesn't make a hero. Cavalcade, aloft!"

The cry went up from beneath them. "Wyrm! Wyrm!"

Suddenly the valley seemed filled by a twisting, writhing body. The long, scaled body was the color of red river clay or scarred flesh. At its widest point, it was more than ten feet across, and Kauli estimated it at over a hundred feet long. When it raised its head, it opened a sharp-toothed maw big enough to engulf an entire pegasus. It crawled along on four thick, jointed legs, and its stubby, knobbed feet were armed with curved talons that glistened with the blood of its victims.

Dwarves and elves surrounded the creature, pounding or slashing at it with their weapons. The wyrm lifted the center of its body and slammed it down on whole companies of soldiers, smashing them and their steeds to the ground. Cries of pain tore at Kauli's heart.

Bakolli signed to the Cavalcade to begin their crossflight attack. The pilots separated into three lines. While one stayed aloft to protect their backs from the harpy flock, the other two spurred their pegasi downward. Kauli felt the rush of wind in his face, and it stirred his blood. He drew and loosed arrows as fast as his hand could move. Their orders were to aim at the wyrm's eyes, its most vulnerable features. If they could blind it, they would gain a huge advantage.

One bolt, marked with Fili's colors, lodged in the beast's left eye. It let out a bellow and thrashed around in pain, causing more confusion among the wyrm's defenders as well as its attackers on the ground. The pilots cheered. The monster could be beaten!

Most of the arrows bounced off the overlapping plates on the creature's back.

"Aim under the scales," Bakolli shouted.

The crossflight changed direction for its second pass.

"Aim for its neck!" Fili commanded. Kauli echoed the order. As the beast flexed its muscles, the heavy scales rippled upward. The interval during which its pale underskin was visible was brief, but long enough. Even arrows that rebounded were enough to distract the creature away from the forces mustering around it. A dwarven contingent surged forward and attacked the wyrm's exposed throat and one of its feet in a dual sortie. They managed to chop off a toe as large as one of their number by the time Kauli came around for another pass.

"Again!" Bakolli commanded. Fili signed to Kauli. The two of them led their winged forces down over the wyrm's back. It twisted more energetically now, beset as it was by many enemies. Elves dodged nimbly around the huge feet, slashing at the softer scales of its belly. Suddenly, the wyrm turned its head and breathed. Kauli's eyes watered from the caustic smell. He could almost *see* the exhalation. Dozens of elves staggered and fell to the ground. A few stopped moving altogether. The pilots set their jaws grimly. This was its chief weapon. The claws and teeth they could manage, but the poison of its breath could kill more than any of those.

Bakolli watched the hand signals of the commanders on the ground, then directed the air cavalry around in another pass at the monster's neck. Arrows thwacked into the flesh underneath the scales. Most of the hits, Kauli noted, were black-banded arrows fired by Eurwood. He signaled praise to the winged centaur. The others had not missed their new companion's prowess even under fire. They began to make way for him, protecting him from the remaining harpies and vampires that plied the thermal gusts in the narrow valley. Eurwood scored again and again. The wyrm began to show signs of distress, tossing its head wildly.

Fili raised his hand and led his line of pilots downward. Instead of remaining to the rear, he brought his force around and under the writhing head, aiming at the paler, thinner scales of its throat. Milda's hooves narrowly missed the helmet of the dwarven captain, who gave him a dirty look, but Fili shot two arrows that lodged deep under the wyrm's jaw.

But fortune was not smiling upon the First Underofficer. As he urged Milda upward, the heavy head came around and knocked the pegasus heavily to one side. The mare fluttered madly, trying to regain her equilibrium. Fili's bow went flying as he held on tightly with both knees and hands. The wyrm sniffed audibly, seeking the thing that it had struck. Milda pawed the air, seeking to gain altitude, but she had no time. The wyrm breathed. Fili slumped over the mare's back. Milda's head tilted upward, her wings went limp, and she began falling.

"No!" Kauli cried. Already he and the rest of the Cavalcade were winging down to rescue their companion. The wyrm roared as the elves shot it with dozens of arrows, trying to get it away from the distressed pilot and his steed.

"Cover me!" a hoarse voice cried.

Eurwood broke out of the ranks and shot downward, his huge black wings almost closed in a controlled fall. Kauli hoped that he would not lose control. He ordered the rest of the line to distract the beast—anything—to prevent another casualty. They did not fail him.

The centaur dropped below the belly of the falling mare and ducked his head underneath her barrel. She landed across his back. The two of them fell another twenty feet before he opened his great wings and flapped with all his might. The wyrm heard the commotion, and swung its head back to kill whatever was troubling it.

Kauli ordered Rabena close enough to the wyrm to dance on its head. The mare kicked at the beast's one remaining good eye, then sprang upward, eluding the fatal breath by the width of a hair. He ordered her to circle around.

With an escort of half the Cavalcade, Eurwood set down his burden near the tree line. Healers converged upon the three of them: the wounded mare, the unconscious pilot, and the rescuer, whose face was red, and whose wings fluttered limply along his back.

The rest of the battle blurred in Kauli's mind. He knew more from report than from memory that the dwarves and elves, given the protection of the Cavalcade, managed to slash open the wyrm's throat. It died only a quarter mile from the mountain pass. The other enemy combatants were hunted down one by one over the countryside. Shoi'ana was saved—until the next onslaught of the Blood Host.

Eurwood sat in his accustomed place in the glen, a mug in his hand. The joints at the base of his wings were bound in linen bandages. They had been so badly sprained that the healers instructed him and

Kauli, as his commander, that he was not to attempt so much as a flutter for at least ten days.

"I'll spend it drinking, then," the centaur declared.

There wasn't an elf that would deny him the pleasure. Nor did Eurwood lack for company in his indulgence, little though he seemed to relish it. He had but to drain his mug, and one or more of his admiring comrades would be on hand, ready to refill it. By the second night's sing, two of them had come up with songs extolling Eurwood's deed. The centaur made a few gruff comments about their quality, but Kauli suspected he was secretly pleased.

Fili had been under the healers' care for several days, but as soon as he recovered strength enough to stand, he demanded that Kauli help him to the centaur.

"I owe you my life," he told Eurwood. "More than that, I owe you thanks for saving my mare. She is dear to my heart. Be assured of my eternal friendship. I am sorry if there has been a misunderstanding between us."

"It's nothing, First Underofficer," Eurwood said shortly. "Go curry your pegasus or something."

"I offer you my friendship," Fili said, his pale cheeks red. "Why do you continue so hostile?"

Eurwood looked him straight in the eye. "Because I heard you call me freak. That was not lost upon me. You made many remarks about harpies, always so I could hear them. My father was a man of honor, elf, perhaps more honorable than you. You know the length of their marriage, but never thought to ask why they are no longer together. He flew out to resist the first incursion of the harpies of the Blood Host. He died in battle six years ago. I joined the Cavalcade to honor his memory."

Fili had the grace to look deeply ashamed. "I knew nothing of this, Eurwood."

"And never asked, not once. Kauli asked, but I was too full of anger to tell him all. I am accustomed to being alone, First Underofficer. I have never belonged anywhere. The harpies won't claim me, the centaurs reject me as an abomination, and when I find the first place where I would think it would be natural to fit in, you push me away out of hand. I will continue to serve, but I expect nothing from you. Beneath your gratitude, you are the same as you were before the battle."

Fili sat down heavily beside him. "I assure you, I am not. I have had much time to think during my convalescence. I have fought against harpies many times in the past eight years. I saw only the destruction they wreaked, and the pleasure they took in it. I never knew that any of their kind were creatures capable of love or honor. I found myself wondering if, in your place, I would have sacrificed myself to save you as you saved me. Your heart was greater than mine, and I am humbled.

"I have let my past experiences color the present. I do not excuse it. I apologize, with all my heart, Eurwood. It is true that I react to anything that is different with suspicion. But quite often our suspicions are true."

Eurwood snorted into his mug. "They will always come true if you greet any new experience with scorn and bad blood. I am used to it. Let it pass."

"No," Fili said, extending his hand. "You are right. I should have welcomed you. Kauli, here, was far wiser than I. Let us give each other another chance. I have much to learn from you. Will you allow me and teach me?"

He held the hand in place while Eurwood finished his drink and poured another one. At last, the centaur put down his mug and clasped the hand. "Very well. You might mean what you say."

"I do," Fili said.

"And I," Kauli said, letting out the breath he didn't realize he had been holding. "I would be proud to be your friend. We may not have had much in common to begin with, but we are all proud to be airborne."

"Yes," Eurwood said, with a sheepish grin. "Though you ought to know better than to trust a relationship built on air."

The three of them laughed together. For the first time, Eurwood looked truly at ease. Kauli sensed something like a wound closing in the centaur's heart.

"Come!" Fili called to the other pilots. "Join our new friend in a toast to the Cavalcade. May we always be airborne together!"

Kauli drank that toast gladly.

DEMON'S TOUCH

by James Barclay

AUUM DROPPED LIGHTLY to the ground, rolling on impact and rising swiftly to his feet. The tiny clearing was hemmed in by typically dense Calaian rain forest foliage. It was one of a network of insertion sites spread throughout the forest, kept clear by RingFence wards.

He stepped to the tree line and nodded up into the darkness. The two mages hovering above him soared away, ShadowWings whispering against the night. One after another the team flew in, carried by mage pairs. Soon, the six of them stood together. Auum gave a small prayer of thanks to Yniss for their safe arrival and led his Tai forward, silent over the dense undergrowth covering the rain forest floor. The canopy above held in the humidity of the day gone by and in the gloom, the forest was alive with the sounds of life and sudden death. This was the land Auum knew, his land. Land he would give his life to rid of those who did not belong.

A few paces in, Auum sensed movement. He held

up a hand and they stopped, dropping into a crouch. From the east it came, padding easily through the undergrowth. A panther, sleek and black, intelligence and recognition in its eyes. It nuzzled Auum's hand.

They relaxed and stood, waiting. An elf emerged from the trees in front of them. His panther went to him. The eyes of the forest: she, jet black; he, tall, very slim, and with a face painted half white, half black. They were ClawBound, mind and senses melded to one another. The perfect scouts. The ones the enemy termed *death-watchers*.

"Care," said the elf in a voice unused to speech.

"Always," said Auum.

"The nest is large. It offends."

"Purification is at hand."

"Travel north. You will know when you are near." The ClawBound pair vanished into the forest, lost in moments.

Auum indicated left and right, and the two others of his TaiGethen cell, Rebraal and Ciisker, slipped soundlessly away to flank and observe. Behind Auum, three mages of the Al-Arynaar calling tracked his footsteps. He would take them where they needed to be. The execution was their task; and none would be more challenging than this.

The war against the demons had been won, but pockets of the enemy remained trapped in the Balaian dimension. And, deep in the rain forests of Calaius, enough had escaped detection to present significant threat. Dozens of temples to Yniss, Gyal, Shorth, Tual, and any number of elven gods lay hidden in the vastness of the forest. Places where demons might use the power they possessed to reopen the dimensional gateway once more. That could not be allowed to happen. Balaia was too weak to repel another invasion.

Auum ran on, his eyes piercing the darkness, his ears listening for any sound that clashed with the natural ambience of the rain forest. It was fitting that tonight's target had chosen to cower in a temple dedicated to Shorth, the god of death; benevolent to his own, tormentor of his enemies.

In less than five hundred paces, the feel of the rain forest changed. Auum stopped and dropped to his haunches, the mages with him. Rebraal and Ciisker appeared at his side, wraiths from the dark.

"Rodent, lizard, and bird grow silent," said Auum. "We are close. Rebraal, report."

"We are on the defensive perimeter," he said. "The temple is sheathed in vine and moss, little more than ruins on the outside. Strike-strain, reaver, and seeker demons are airborne."

"It is the same left," said Ciisker, her voice low and husky. "Their flight grid is tight. Ground is cleared all around the temple. There is light and movement inside."

"Many to send to Shorth," said Auum. He looked at the mage trio. Dila, Geth, and Jaru. All from the Heth tribe and handpicked by Auum himself. "We need a way in."

Dila nodded. "We'll take care of it. Get us closer. I need to see what we're up against."

"Tai, we pray."

Each TaiGethen painted the face of another. Dark greens and browns completing the camouflage of their clothing. A ceremony for focus on the verge of battle and to remove any last vestiges of uncertainty. The mages knelt by them, heads bowed, reverent.

"Tual, lord of forest denizens, let your children guide our senses. Shorth, protect our souls should we fall. Yniss, lord of all, we exist to do your work. Today we take one small step. Tomorrow, the end of our journey is closer. TaiGethen and Al-Arynaar will never fail you. Our eyes will pierce the dark. Our ears will hear every sound. Our hands and feet will kill. All in your name. Yniss, we beseech you, show us the path."

Assent was murmured. Auum nodded.

"This master is ancient and powerful. He is an implacable foe. Do not be fooled by his stature. His strength is immense. He is Hiela, and he is to be respected but not feared. Heth mages, when you have the opportunity, you must be quick. Remember what his death means to us and to the humans of Balaia. Tai, seek the calm. Trust your instincts. Without each other, all are lost. Tai, we move."

In front of the temple, the ground was cleared for thirty yards until the forest closed in. Auum knelt in deep cover. Tual's children were quiet in the trees and in the undergrowth. He studied Dila, watching her follow the flight patterns above the temple. She was frowning.

"Problem?"

"No," she said. "Just takes a while to realize it isn't random. A mistake on their part. Give me a moment."

She spoke quickly to the others. Auum saw them understand.

"The EarthMask will only last a count of twenty, or we'll be too drained. You'll have to move fast," she said.

Auum raised his eyebrows. "Just show us the marks."

"One chance. We'll be Cloaked," said Dila.

"Yniss will protect us. He will work through you."

"Your path takes you on an arc across the patch of

dead strangler vine ten yards ahead right, the balsa tree stump a further fifteen yards right center and last into the lee of the door overhang. Keep your elbows tucked and run low."

Auum nodded. Dila turned to her mages, and the three of them studied the tight corridor she had described. Every leaf, every clump of earth, blade of grass, and strand of vegetation registered in the shape they built in their minds with mana, the fuel of magic. The backdrop, the stars in the sky, everything. The shape was incredibly complex, incredibly draining on a mage's stamina. Of all the spells that had been developed in the aftermath of the demon invasion, this one alone impressed him.

Dila turned a face lined with strain to the Tai cell. She blinked once. Auum felt a shiver in the air. The projection snapped into place.

In line order, the elven warriors tore across the open space. Half-crouched, counting. Above them, the demon seekers cruised and turned. Auum made the distance before the count had reached fifteen. He ushered Rebraal and Ciisker in and motioned them to examine the door, a solid iron-bound wooden double portal with a heavy lock mechanism.

To his right, the briefest shimmering and the illusion fell. He tensed. Up in the sky, a seeker demon was drawn. Some tiny sudden movement out of kilter with the rhythm of the forest. It broke from its flight pattern and swam down, fluid. Its sinuous net of optics resembled a sparkling cobweb in flight.

Out on the open ground, the mages approached under CloakedWalks. Auum could see the slight depressions in the sodden muddy undergrowth. Before long, the seeker would see them, too.

The creature floated down, followed by a dozen rat-sized strike-strain. Reavers followed a little higher, lazing in the sky, their body colors swimming from deep gray to a warm, pulsing blue.

Rebraal was at Auum's shoulder.

"We must distract them," he whispered.

Auum put up a hand. "Trust, Rebraal. Panic, and we are lost. Their footfalls are slowing. They can see the danger."

And they could. No new depressions were made. The mages had not ceased forward motion, but progress was slight, like flowers opening on a new day. To stop would be to become visible. Balance was everything.

The seeker floated lower. Auum retreated into the deep shadow, peering through a net of vines. Out in the open, the mages could only make their minute body moves forward and pray the seeker did not collide with them. Auum offered a prayer to Tual to protect His children. The seeker's flanks flashed with white and blue. It moved in a quick circle. An alien sound pierced the night. One of frustration. It peeled off and soared away. Auum nodded his thanks to the god of forest denizens. The mages appeared one after the other, all crouched low, all with mud on their hands. The fear in their eyes was mixed with exhilaration.

"Good work," said Auum. "Ciisker, what of the door?"

"Elven construction; they have not adapted it nor strengthened it," she said. "A FlamePalm will melt the workings."

"Get to it."

Dila indicated Jaru take the task. Auum assessed the flight patterns. Demon suspicion had been raised. Reavers were gathered almost directly above their position. Behind Auum, the dome of the stone temple rose into the canopy which reached down to embrace it. It was of classic construction. Temples to Shorth contained a wide area for worship beneath the dome and led away down a single corridor to reading cells, private chambers, and the blessed fountain where the dead were cleansed. Hiela, if he really were here, would be at the seat of the temple's power.

A muffled metallic thump sounded at the door.

"We're in," said Jaru.

He edged backward, allowing the TaiGethen access. "Remember your positions, remember your kill spot. Guard the mages."

Ciisker placed a hand on the left door and pushed. The merest creak and it moved inward. Inside, the shapes of benches along each side of a short hallway formed from the darkness. There was light spilling beneath a second set of doors. They moved in, closing the outer door behind them. Jaru placed a WardLock on it. In the dome, there was movement. Auum held up a hand.

"Be ready," he said.

The Tai cell grouped by the left-hand door, the mages in the shadows at their shoulders. Ciisker moved the handle of the right-hand door down and pushed. The door swung inward, light flushing into the hallway. Auum's heart rate increased, and he used it to drive focus through his mind and muscles. He relaxed, waiting. The sound in the dome ceased. There was a series of chitters and calls. Feet padded toward them. A shadow grew in the doorway: humanoid, well-muscled, and with a long, loping stride.

A face edged into view. Gray and white swirled across a blue face that writhed and twitched. The creature had dark pools for eyes, flat slits for nostrils and a wide mouth ringed with needle-sharp teeth. It stank of rotting vegetation. A reaver.

Auum flashed across the gap, diving low and grappling the creature's legs as it took a single pace into the hallway. Ciisker and Rebraal moved as he did, Ciisker at the demon's arms and chest, Rebraal at its head. Its skull cracked into the doorframe as it went down, stunning it momentarily. It was enough. Rebraal rolled aside, Ciisker dragged one arm away from its body, and Auum plunged a dagger up into the nerve ganglion in its armpit. It quivered and died.

Already the mages were looking into the main worship area. It was empty, its benches and finery long since removed and destroyed. Spells were ready against an attack from the shadows that shrouded the passageway to the blessed fountain.

"Good," said Auum. "But tread carefully. Miss nothing."

Moving around the edge of the dome toward the passageway, Auum had to fend off his own anger. It threatened to cloud his mind. Years after so many of his friends had given their lives in an alien dimension far from Balaia to end the war, and still this desecration occurred. Every defaced frieze, every torn canvas and excreta-smeared carving was an insult to their sacrifice and achievement. He wanted so badly to let the fury take him, but brief satisfaction would betray the future. If they were to rid the rain forest of their enemies, elves like Auum had to stay alive. He blinked his eyes to clear an unbidden mist and forced calm on himself.

"Auum?" It was Rebraal.

"Never forget, never forgive, never lose control," said Auum.

Rebraal placed a hand briefly on his shoulder.

Auum focused on the passageway. It was dark though light crept out from cracks around three of five doors. And it was quiet. Still. Like nothing existed there or in the forest surrounding them. It was unsettling.

"Straight to the blessed fountain," said Auum. "Be quick, be vigilant, be sure. Tai, we move."

The cell spread across the wide passageway a few paces in front of the mages. Their feet ghosted over the cold stone, their breath clouded in the cool air, their bodies were flickering motes in the darkness. The door to the chamber of the blessed fountain was plain, made from rough-cut timber. A cool blue was edging beneath the door, indicating the fountain's inner luminescence triggered by the light of torch and brazier.

Auum held up a hand and slowly closed his fingers into a fist. Each of them thought a brief prayer, commending their souls to Yniss. He nodded. Dila's two mages prepared spells. Ciisker tested the door with the gentlest of pressure. It was not locked, merely latched.

"Disease is within. We will purge it," said Auum. He took a single pace back.

Ciisker edged the latch up and pushed the door aside. A sparkling, shifting blue light washed out and the sound of the fountain lifted their souls. The two mages stepped into the room, ready to cast. Auum was at their back. There was Hiela, beyond the fountain with his back to them, hovering a foot or so above the ground. His arms were outstretched to either side, legs together, feet pointing down. His skin was a deep, dark blue and his head was completely bald though veins writhed and twisted across his skull. Deep in meditation, he appeared not to have noticed them.

A chill stole across Auum's back. Something wasn't right. Yet if this was truly an opportunity to kill Hiela silently, surely they should take it.

"Don't," whispered Rebraal. "Cast and run."

Auum concurred. "Cast."

FlameOrbs shot away from the hands of the two mages, hissing through the fountain and turning water to steam, crashing into Hiela and the wall behind him. Yellow fire cascaded down as the orbs exploded, eating into flesh, burning and cleansing. And when the afterglow had dimmed, nothing remained.

But Auum felt no sense of satisfaction, and the smiles of the mages faltered when they saw his face.

"This is not victory," he said.

And in the next moment, the temple filled with demons.

"To me!" shouted Auum. "Rebraal, Ciisker, Dila, to the fountain."

The elves grouped and ran for the center of the chamber. The demons came from everywhere— floating down from the ceiling, materializing from the walls, walking through the door, ascending through the fountain stream. Dozens of them in a kaleidoscope of color. Powerful reavers, tiny strike-strain, hammer, and spike-limbed karron, and the one master, Hiela. Undamaged. Smiling indulgently. His was a face unbearably human. He even sported a beard in deference to Balaian myth art.

Auum felt the fear growing around him. They were searching for what they had missed. The clue that would have seen them escape the trap. But there was nothing. Nothing but the unsettling quiet of the rain forest.

"Focus," he said. "We are TaiGethen, we are Al-Arynaar. We are not lost, we are in Shorth's temple." His voice calmed them. "Seek the opportunity. Do not let them provoke you. Move as one."

The demons made no sound as they approached.

There was no aura of anger, more of curiosity. They closed to within a few paces. Only Hiela moved nearer, coming to rest before Auum who stood in front of his people. He hovered, hands steepled under his chin. Arms tucked in.

"Well," he said. "My nemesis. I see you met my double."

Auum stared back at him, gaze never faltering. Hiela projected fear, but he would not let it affect him. Neither he nor his people could afford a moment's doubt.

"The great Auum," said Hiela. "And Rebraal. You should both know how good the souls of your friends taste through the passing of the years. Evunn, Thraun, Ark. Hirad Coldheart."

"You do not own Hirad. He escaped you even as you reached out your hand to claim him," said Rebraal, snapping at the bait. "He was like an elf. His soul is strong."

Auum gestured minutely. Rebraal relaxed.

"We will release them," said Auum. "And any pleasure you feel will be repaid in pain. Shorth will teach you so much you could never dream."

Hiela ticked a finger once. "You're brave, I'll grant you that. And elven souls are indeed hard to take. But so prized as a result. Elven mages particularly."

"Prized because you barely taste them," said Dila.

"Enough," said Auum.

"Yes," said Hiela. "It is best that you surrender yourselves respectfully. Dignity at the end."

"You are confused," said Auum. "Tual guides us, Yniss protects us. It is you who is alone. And Shorth awaits you."

Hiela's expression flickered momentarily with doubt. It was enough.

"Dance," said Auum.

The TaiGethen blurred. The mages needed time and space to cast. The demons were fast, but Auum saw them as if they moved through water. Hiela had reacted more quickly and was out of reach, but he had left his cohorts badly exposed. Auum's right hand whipped out, his blade slicing deep into a reaver's face. He followed it up with a front kick to the midriff. The creature squealed and fell away, wound already healing. Auum's left hand battered into the body of a strike-strain, sending it spinning into a wall where it clung and shook its head, dazed.

On his flanks, his Tai fought with calm and purpose. The cell moved into the gap they'd forced. Karron were moving up, hammer and spike limbs cocked and ready, mats of sensory hairs over their bodies guiding them. Behind him, flare and detonation. Yellow fire rained down, eating demon flesh. There were screams.

Auum spun, delivering a roundhouse kick to the chest of a karron. The demon roared frustration and swung his hammer limb. Auum saw it coming and swayed back, feeling the rush of air past his face. He was upright and striking in the next heartbeat, blade chopping up into the karron's face. The demon wailed and lifted its spike to protect itself. Auum switched his blade to his left hand and rammed it up into the exposed armpit. He had turned to defend Dila before the body had hit the ground.

"Ciisker, take our backs. Don't be drawn out."

Strike-strain were gathering in the rafters above. Twenty or thirty, poised to attack. They were in front of Hiela, who cruised the spaces under the roof, directing his servants. Auum rocked back and kicked out straight into the neck of a reaver threatening Dila. His blade weaved in front of him, cutting and slashing.

The wounds might not kill, but demons still felt pain and fear.

"Al-Arynaar, kneel. Dila, target Hiela. Jaru, Geth, area defense castings. Keep the pressure off."

Auum had the defense the way he wanted it. The mages knelt at three points of the fountain, drawing strength from the flow at their backs. The TaiGethen moved in a circle around them, presenting a shifting barrier.

Hiela had been surprised at the speed and ferocity of the elven assault, but he was reorganizing now. His few karron kept up a frontal assault supported by reavers coming in at head height. Above, strike-strain looked for opportunities to dart in and threaten mage concentration, wear down their belief.

Jaru pushed out a ForceCone, driving a wedge through the demon ranks and pinning two reavers to the back wall of the chamber. He moved it high, left, right, and overhead, sweeping the enemy aside, forcing them to scatter and reform, keeping Hiela on the move. It was a brave casting. It might just force the master demon into Dila's compass. But it also made him a target. Two karron pressed an attack that Ciisker struggled to repel. A reaver missed tearing out his throat by a whisker, Rebraal's two-footed kick driving it aside at the last instant.

The former Raven elf landed atop the reaver, seized his chance, and drove his blade into the creature's armpit as it flailed for purchase. But he was unprepared for the hammer limb of a karron to his left that battered into his arm and chest, flinging him into the base of the fountain.

"Ciisker! Tai down."

Rebraal's unconscious body had caught Jaru a glancing blow and disrupted his concentration. The

ForceCone dispersed and the demons surged again. A dozen strike-strain poured down.

"Jaru, above you." Auum's warning was too late. He tore a huge gash in the flank of a karron, moved left, and swept his leg over Jaru's kneeling form. Still, six demons struck the Al-Arynaar mage, arcing through the fountain, claws raking shoulders, neck, and head before they cleared back to defend Hiela.

Auum took off, spinning in the air and catching a reaver in the face, sending it tumbling away, wings thrashing to restore its balance. He landed by Jaru, ripping the last strike-strain from his back and tearing an arm from its socket, casting the body aside.

Ciisker forced a moment's breathing space, her limbs and blade a smear in the air, while Geth had launched a second ForceCone behind them, desperate defense against their open flank.

"Hang on, Jaru. Tual will protect you."

"Cold," gasped Jaru.

Auum could see the multiple wounds, blood seeping into his robes and down his face.

"It's the demon's touch," he said. "It will pass. Do not waver. Do not leave your soul vulnerable."

"They track me," said Jaru.

"They will fail."

Auum stood. Strike-strain were coming in again. He stretched his hands and breathed deeply. Behind him, Ciisker's dance was mesmerizing, her movement too much for the lumbering karron whose limbs were more risk to the reavers around them than the elves in front of them.

The TaiGethen leader stood astride Jaru and within reach of Geth. His gaze relaxed and he widened his perception, identifying the pattern of every strike-strain on its way down.

"Don't be too long, Dila," he said.

"I won't."

Auum struck out. Left arm up and around, batting a tiny demon aside. Same arm down, fingers crushing into a shoulder, biting into the armpit. One down. Right hand straight out. Punch. Three times, three cleared aside. He felt a rake over the back of his skull, ice spreading across his head. Right arm back. He grabbed his attacker, hurled it into another heading straight for him.

"Remember yourself, Jaru. Stay with me."

From across his vision a reaver crashed into Ciisker's unprotected back, dodging Geth's ForceCone on the way in. The Tai sprawled out of the circle. Karron turned. Spike and hammer limbs fell. Blood sprayed into the air. Demons exulted. Auum felt her passing like a knife in his own chest.

"Dila. Two Tai down. Area solution. Let's take them with us."

"Way ahead of you, Auum."

Auum would be overwhelmed. Demons pressed in on all sides. They chittered and called, sensing victory, sensing the sweet taste of TaiGethen and Al-Arynaar souls. Dila cast, and the atmosphere changed immediately. Light bloomed across the length and breadth of the fountain chamber. Moments later it scattered, forming drops of pure yellow mana fire. HotRain. Everything beneath the deluge would be destroyed. He had not meant it to be this way, but with half of his team down and Hiela still right above them, knowing they would not cast over their own heads, Auum was out of options. He dropped his head and commended all their souls to Yniss, sparing them the eternal touch of pure ice.

He heard the screeches and screams as strike-strain

were caught in the torrent, reavers darted for the door
and karron panicked, too slow to escape. ClawBound
would come with the rededication team, and only then
would the TaiGethen know if Hiela had perished.

"SpellShield up."

Geth's words were raindrops from a clear sky.

"Yniss bless you," said Auum.

With the heat of the rain blooming on his skin,
Auum grabbed Dila's armor at the neck and dragged
her next to Geth. In the next instant, the rain began
peppering the ground, hissing and spitting in the fountain, spitting on Geth's spell and melting demon flesh.

Dila hauled Jaru's leg inside the shield, her hands
swatting at the flames encasing it. Rebraal, curled motionless around the fountain, was safe from the fires
though surely close to death. Ciisker was lost.

Auum searched the chamber. Burning demons' bodies were falling to the ground. Husks smoldered.
Those that survived were crowding the door, their
howls of panic bouncing from the walls as they rushed
to get out. But of Hiela, there was no sign. Inside the
shield bubble, they had respite, but it would be brief.
Auum laid a hand on Rebraal's neck. His pulse was
still strong though blood was flowing from inside his
armor.

"What can we do?' said Dila. "They will be back."

"I—"

Auum's back crawled. He spun on his heels and
rose to his feet. There was Hiela. Scarred but un-
bowed and flying in hard. Too fast for Auum. The
demon caught him by the throat and forced him back
against the bowl of the fountain. Auum gasped at the
touch. Fear flooded down Hiela's fingers, threatening
to overwhelm him. In the doorway, the few surviving
demons turned back. They were unwilling to enter,
but their cries had turned to taunts once more.

"Exit solution," managed Auum. "Dila, Geth, you know what you must do."

"Auum . . ."

"Do it. Don't try and approach."

"And they will leave without you," hissed Hiela.

All pretense at calm superiority was gone. The master was in pain, and he was furious.

"But you are damaged," said Auum. His hands grabbed at Hiela's outstretched arm, but the demon's strength was extraordinary. It tightened its grip. Auum choked, "We will return, and you will not repel us."

"Shield down," said Geth.

Hiela looked over Auum's shoulder, momentary confusion on his face.

"Immediate extraction," said Dila, voice faint with concentration on her Communion spell. "Expect enemies at exit point."

Hiela growled, and his eyes registered his understanding. "Scatter!" he shouted.

"Too late," said Auum.

A sheet of light washed across the chamber. A FlameOrb shot away. Auum heard it detonate through the chamber door. Demons screamed.

"Run!" ordered Dila. "Take Jaru."

Hiela did not move. He focused again on Auum.

"Your friends are running into eternal torment," he said. "And now you are alone."

A blade thudded deep into Hiela's exposed armpit. Rebraal's pale, agonized face appeared in Auum's eyeline. Hiela's eyes widened, he gasped, and his skin rippled through a rainbow of color. Outside, demons howled anguish

"You are mistaken," said Rebraal. "A TaiGethen is never alone."

Hiela spasmed and dropped to the floor, releasing Auum, who coughed and wiped a hand across his face.

He took a moment to calm his breathing and his pulse. He jabbed Hiela's body with his foot. The carcass was already decaying.

"Yniss has plans for you, Rebraal," he said. "You have struck a decisive blow."

"We need to leave," said Rebraal.

"We'll be faster together. Put your arm around my shoulder."

Rebraal did, wincing. The two of them half ran through the door and down the passage to the main worship chamber. The temple was all but deserted. No karron remained, and inside a handful of strike-strain tracked them from high rafters, not risking an attack.

Auum ignored them, following the trail of the escaping mages. The WardLock had been blown on the main doors and in the rain forest, the sounds of the pursuit were loud in the otherwise still night.

Rebraal was struggling, every footstep accompanied by a grunt of pain.

"Let me carry you," said Auum.

"No," said Rebraal. "Too slow."

Auum nodded and ducked into the welcoming canopy of the forest. Strike-strain were no use here, unable to travel within the shroud. And reavers were forced to run, wings folded away. Auum felt a grim satisfaction. This was elf terrain. And despite Rebraal's injury, they were gaining.

Driving headlong to the insertion point, they could hear more pursuit behind. Auum muttered a prayer that every vine would tangle them, every root trip them. Ahead, silence fell, and Auum's heart missed a beat. They were near the clearing. His senses pushed out, searching for threat. Nothing.

He ducked under a branch, and hands were around

him, helping him forward. Rebraal was taken from him. A TaiGethen cell stood in the clearing, mages behind. The bodies of three reavers lay at its center. Dila and Geth knelt nearby, tending Jaru.

"Down!"

Auum ducked and rolled. DeathHail roared over his head. Flechettes of ice hammering into the foliage, mana-fueled freezing thorns shredding leaf and branch and flaying the skin from helpless demons. The cries were brief. Shorth took his victims quickly.

The TaiGethen leader came to his feet and looked behind him. The forest was quiet. Above, clouds gathered for the next downpour, he could smell it on the air.

"Good," he said. "Good. Tual bless you, Geeran."

He clasped the arm of the Tai who stood before him. Geeran bowed.

"The ClawBound reported before Dila's Communion. It is an honor to protect you," he said.

"And now you must work. Hiela is down, but some remain. Cleanse the temple and ward it. The ClawBound will guard it until it can be rededicated. See that Jaru and Rebraal get the attention they need. Jaru is sick. The ice is deep within him. I will not lose him, Geeran."

"You will not."

There was a whisper on the wind. Auum glanced up into thickening rain. Al-Arynaar mages landed, eight of them. Auum cocked his head.

"More work?' he said.

"If you are able," said one. "The ClawBound have sighted a nest not far from here. A scout operation."

Auum nodded. "Dila, Geth. With me. In the names of our injured and our fallen, we will not rest this night."

Al-Arynaar mages stood by him. ShadowWings sprouted at their backs. Auum grasped the carry belts at their waists, and they rose quickly into the roiling sky. The rain was torrential.

"Yniss is angry, and Gyal's tears fall," he whispered.

The flight turned to the south and picked up pace, the ClawBound calls echoing, calling them to battle.

DISPATCHES FROM THE FRONT: NUMBER SIXTY-ONE

by Kristine Kathryn Rusch

Winter, Year Five
Near the Cascann Mountains

THE SHELTER IS little more than a snow-covered hut. The centaur who brought me up here cannot fit inside. We cover him with blankets to warm him up, give him hot mead and the last of some richly scented stew, and send him back to his troops.

All the way up, he complained about letting a human ride his back, even though he is the media liaison for this part of the war. He doesn't like answering to a woman, particularly a woman once known as a unicorn tamer, a woman whose only real magical skill—besides her learned ability to put pen to paper— is to get equine creatures to do her bidding.

He made me swear I was not charming him. I swore. He did not believe me.

The journey up the foothills was treacherous, and one I was glad I did not have to make alone. He remained silent through most of the trip—afraid, he told me when it looked like we wouldn't reach our destination—that I would report every word he said.

I reminded him that we had censors. Before any parchment gets tied to the feet of the carrier pigeons, it is copied by the monks attached to each unit, and dispatched to headquarters. The monks remove things; the officials remove more.

So I try to be vague while being descriptive. I'm told by my editor that the censors don't mind harsh talk, just specific talk, talk that will give away positions to the enemy or allow him to divine battle plans.

I've heard that the Scralle have lost their diviners and are now relying on general wizardry, but like all rumors, there is no way to confirm.

What I told my centaur—what I tell all of the media liaisons—is that being a battlefield correspondent is like being a soldier. I only see pieces of the war, not the whole. I leave the analysis for the historians of whichever side survives.

Those historians will not know what to make of this—the entire magical world at war with itself.

The hut has only one room. Pixie Air has divided it into two using a gossamer blanket that is sturdier than it looks. The main area, with the large fireplace, is filled with pixies. Those back from the latest mission have the closest pallets to the heat. The rest must rely on blankets so small that they wouldn't cover my feet.

The second room is for the lumbering nonmagical humans—mostly young women or boys who have not reached their full growth. They wear furs and lined boots against the cold. While they wait, they play card games that I have never seen before or ask me and the unit scribe to write letters to their loved ones back home.

I was told, back at base, that I could go on the next

mission, but the pixies object. I am twice as tall as the tallest human here and three times as heavy. I am the only adult over the age of twenty-five.

It doesn't matter that I have kept my so-called innocence so that I can retain my small magic. What matters out here are height and weight restrictions. If I get into one of the crafts they call pixie boats, there will be no room for the bomber, and that will compromise the mission.

The centaur will not return for me for three days. During that time, I will eat the meager rations of food, probably taking something from someone who has an actual purpose in this raid, and I will try to be useful.

The pixies sit in the farthest corner of their section of the room. The leaders—none of them above a colonel (and I get the sense these ranks may be honorary or self-chosen)—do not know what to do with me. They want to comply with headquarters, but they are frightened and tired and not used to making decisions.

They're also not used to the cold.

This pixie troop comes from the tropics. They volunteered as a unit—straight out of flight school, one of the older men told me—and fought their original missions in the jungles near their homes.

But after the destruction of the Pegasus Fleet, most of the winged fairies defected. Only a few remained, and those who did had greater uses as attack planners rather than raid commanders.

The pixies continued to move north, until someone discovered—quite by accident—that pixies flying against a gray sky over a snow-covered landscape were nearly invisible.

The air troops got sent here, along with the pixie boats—painted by artist mages to resemble clouds—and sent on their first raid.

Headquarters say Pixie Air has changed the course of the war. They believe that the pixies, with their delicate wings and quiet voices, are the ultimate in stealth weaponry. The Scralle do not know how to find them, let alone bring them down.

Rumors say that dragons have been sent against pixie fleets and have failed. Even if the dragons open their mouths and spew fire against what seems like—to them—an empty sky, they cannot defeat the pixies. They generally fire away from the fleet—dragons being the blindest of all flying creatures.

I mention this late my first night to the commander. She is a delicate woman who has been in the war from the beginning. She volunteered before her country ever got involved, and she initially attached herself to the First Eighty-second Flight Unit, back when they took multiple ethnicities.

For a short time, she was paired with a pegasus—a good team, she said, because he could fly her into enemy territory and she could invade the headquarters, as unnoticed as an insect, operating as a short-range spy.

When I asked her about the destruction of the Pegasus Fleet, she turned away. Later, her second, a man who has known her since childhood, says she blames herself for the poison. She smelled the mash as the brownies heated it, and it nearly made her pass out.

I say, there is no way she could have known what it would do, and even if she did, she wouldn't have been able to stop it. Four thousand pegasi on the western front died as vampire troops, posing as humans in the late-night hours, replaced the good mash with foul.

Her second nods. "I know," he says, "but that does not alleviate her guilt. There are always some friends we cannot bear to lose."

I say nothing. Each unit I embed with thinks I am new to the war. I am not. I, too, have lost my share of friends, and some of those deaths will haunt me forever.

But I spoke to her second after I spoke to the pixie commander. She listened to my talk of dragon fire and invisible pixie boats, and looked at me as if I were crazed. Then she held out her right hand.

The fingers are blackened and swollen. The tops of her wings are bandaged, the tip of her nose gone. Even though the pixies wear the warmest clothes they can find, even though the wool they receive from the weavers is spelled against the chill, it is not enough.

These small bodies are used to temperatures one hundred degrees warmer than the warmest days in these foothills. Add elevation, and the temperature drops even more.

The commander must send double, sometimes triple, the number of pixies it takes to keep the boats aloft in case part of her troops lose consciousness or worse.

She figures they have only five more raids up here before the enemy finds our hut. She implied, in our shortened conversation, that my presence might have threatened even those. The centaur and I were visible against the snow. Even though we wore white—also spelled to take away lines, and ease visibility—his hooves left prints, and our scents carried on the chill breeze to the orcs on the other side of the mountain.

She will not approve me for a raid over the next target. I cannot say I blame her. I am getting in the way. My understanding of the way the pixie boats worked may have been right for the first few years of the war, but it is not right now.

So I go to the far corner of the room—the half for

the humans. Outside, the wind howls. It has gotten dark. Lanterns hang from the wall, but it is cold back here. The gossamer curtain blocks more than sound; it also blocks heat.

In the far back corner lie the wounded. They will get evacuated as soon as the raids are over. An oxendrawn transport will leave tracks in the thick snow. Eagle runners can only carry a stretcher between them, and are also quite visible, particularly as they struggle with something that weighs as much as a young human.

Fortunately, most of these injuries are physical. Cursed or charmed injured must go to the barn, as far from the others as possible. We all know that anyone who is taken to the barn will die—it is not warm enough to live there for more than a few days—and while we have compassion for them, we cannot risk being contaminated by them.

Curses seep. They invade dreams, travel in body fluids, or shared utensils. Sometimes they are airborne, although the air here is too cold to keep most curses alive.

Only the house medical mage treats the injured who have been moved to the barn. Before she can reenter the hut, she gets scrubbed with lye (her skin is so raw, I have no idea how she bears it) and rubbed with herbs that supposedly protect against a curse's spread. The other mage—brought to create the weapons— says some kind of charm over her coming and going, and everyone hopes that is enough.

I have brought my quill, ink, and precious paper. I sit in the far corner with the gravest of the ill, and take dictation. After a few moments, we realize that I must clutch the inkwell between my legs so that the liquid remains warm enough to use. As the ill talk, I can see their breath.

Only it is not fair to call them "the ill." They are so much more. There's Tanre, a boy of thirteen years who has been fighting for the past three. He has just started to hit his growth spurt. The first sprouts of beard form on his chin.

They embarrass him. He wants to remain young forever, so that he can stay with the pixies. But his hands are gone—lost when the last *alcana* opened as he dropped it through the trapdoor. His flying partner managed to tie off his wrists and do a rudimentary spell to keep him from bleeding to death. The pixies had already turned around, and the mage who invented the *alcana* happened to be near the hut.

No one could save Tanre's hands, but they were able to save his life. He believes the witches in his village will be able to make new hands for him, but no one has the heart to tell him that our side does not use that kind of magic. That kind of magic—which revives dead body parts and uses bits of the darkness in all of us—is what started this war in the first place.

Instead, we leave him with the hope that he will get well, he will live a useful life, and he will fight again.

He sends a letter to his mother, and it is an adult's letter, filled with nothing but the beauty of the countryside, the courage of the various peoples he's met, and the strangeness of a woman who can write.

People like Tanre, from countries so remote they are only sites on poorly drawn maps, have borne the brunt of this fight. My people stay in the cities, plan the attacks, make changes as the forces grow or diminish. But Tanre and his kind are on the edges of the crisis, seeing the destruction firsthand, and believing they make a difference.

His letter is lovely—he is articulate for a boy his age—and it says nothing. The next letter I write, for a young woman named Quay, is not articulate at all, but it is filled with anguish. She has lost fingers, and her face—once beautiful—is black with frost. There are poultices that can help her, healers from the cold communities who know how to treat such damage, but I do not tell her this. I don't know if she will reach them in time.

Instead, I let her dictate a blunt letter to her fiancé, freeing him of his obligation to her, and letting him marry the woman he has always loved. Tears fall across her dead skin as she says this: she has been promised to him since they were infants. She is letting go of a dream.

I ask her why she does not wait, why she will not let him make the choice after he sees her. She turns away from me, and for a moment, I think she will not answer. Then she says, "It is not fair to hold him to a promise his parents made. The world differs from the one we were born into."

The world differs.

She says this with simple understatement. The world she was born into, maybe fifteen years before, was in the last days of the Interim. I have lived twenty years longer than she. I was born in the last days of the last war, and saw the veterans return home. I was old enough to go to the flaring conflicts—the firestorms, the politicians called them—that could so easily put out with arrogance and a bit of so-called diplomacy.

I thought war was that: simple conflagrations among peoples not meant to live together—elves moved from their small woods to houses in the city; sea nymphs forced to work in rivers; the were-creatures, brought to so-called zoos so that they could be studied and tamed.

Whenever a nonnative population rebelled, it was seen as an isolated incident. We were raised to believe that all beings could get along. But the hatreds between the dwarves and the trolls; the natural enmity between vampires and humans; the unwillingness of ghosts to leave their traditional haunts, were more than flare-ups. They were the result of too much tampering. Politicians thought diplomacy could solve all—that we would learn to get along, that we could deny our natures—not realizing that this strange idealism created even stranger bedfellows. Believers in dark magic affiliated with practitioners of even blacker magics, and bribed the greedy, like the dragons who normally affiliated with no one.

When the actual war came, it caught us all by surprise and yet shocked no one. It was a logical extension of all that had come before.

But I say nothing of this to her. The world does differ for her. Because she had those early years of calm, when it seemed like all the bloodshed would remain in the past—or at least in distant places with names none of us could pronounce.

In those days, she would not have been able to envision herself here, on this cot, her beauty gone, her dreams shattered, her future the only gift she could give to the man she loved.

In the other room, the pixies plan the next raid, their voices rising in agitation. We cannot make the words out in here—they are lost to the gauze and to the high-pitched tones that the human ear can acknowledge but not truly hear.

I take the letters I have finished, unrolled and drying, to the company clerk. It is better for the letters to go through official channels. If they go back with me, they're subject to all the censorship that my dispatches must face. The letters might not arrive home before the wounded do.

Then I push past the gauze curtain and step carefully into the pixie area. The pixies are so small that I could easily hurt one if I'm not careful. Their wounded lie on pallets nailed into the wall like shelves. I have not talked to them. I have not tried. Most are in comas induced by too much effort, a loss of magic, and the deep, destroying cold.

"Humans are not welcome," the commander says to me, "and you cannot report on our conversations."

I nod. But I know what they're discussing. It has been the subject of everyone here—the high casualties, the impossibility of maintaining these raids much longer, the future missions. We all hope for five, but the medical mage in the back told me in confidence there are barely enough for one more.

"I have a suggestion," I say. "Since you're planning strategy, I thought you might want to consider it."

The commander puts her hands on her hips. Her wings flutter in the heat waves from the fireplace.

"Speak," she says. Even in her tiny voice, the word sounds like the command that it is.

"Let me release an *alcana*," I say a bit too eagerly. "Then you won't need anyone else in the boat with me."

"You're not to serve," she says. "We have had strict instruction about that."

From the centaur? Or from his unit commander? Or have the orders come from even farther up? I do not know and I do not ask. I've found that it's better for me to take action on the front than it is to go through channels. Channels are starting to disintegrate anyway.

(It is amazing to me to write a sentence like that, knowing it will be cut. Why do I write it anyway? Because I have to? Because I'm daring them—you, poor censor, who must read these words? Or because I hope that these reports, all of them, of which this is the sixty-first, will be published some day, some day in an Interim, where a young girl can grow up and think a lack of conflict is normal, where she does not face the loss of her beauty at twenty or the loss of her hands at fourteen.)

"Nothing is strict anymore," I say to the pixie commander.

She studies me, damaged hands still on her hips. I wonder what else she has damaged, what I can't see, what she can't see yet. And I wonder if she will survive long enough to take stock, to know what faces her in the years ahead.

I wonder that about all of us, in my most despairing moments. I wonder if any of us will survive long enough to understand what we have seen.

"You have magic," she says after a moment.

I nod.

"You might lose it. The *alcana* can destroy magic around it."

Which is why the pixies cannot touch it, why the boats are reinforced with some kind of metal, made in the mountains a thousand miles from here and flown, at great risk, to these isolated places.

"My magic is small," I say.

She shrugs. "It is magic. I cannot destroy that."

"I have the power to charm equines," I say. "It is supposed to vanish with my innocence. I haven't tested it since the war began."

She leaps onto a human-sized stool, left in here as a table. Her wings flutter as she leans toward me. I wonder if that flutter is a form of palsy, the beginnings of a pixie's loss of control of her various limbs.

"You rode a centaur here," she says.

"He is the media liaison. He is under orders."

She sighs. "Innocence is an old-fashioned term for virginity. Have you lost yours?"

"In all the ways that matter," I say.

She laughs. The sound tinkles, like water across rocks, gentle and beautiful and terribly out of place here. If she were my size, she'd clap me on the back. Instead, she reaches out her small hand and takes my littlest finger, shaking it as if we have just become comrades.

She thinks I am being coy. She thinks I have been with a man. But I am not being coy. I believe there are all forms of virginity, and they can all be lost. Does it matter whether I have made love when I have seen mermaids sliced from waist to tailfin? Or children, orphaned, homeless, and starving, destroyed by the breath of a single brown-eyed dragon? Or men, leaping to their deaths, because they believe their own lives are more worthless than the world they are fighting for?

I did not charm the centaur to get him to come up here. I did not even try.

I believe my innocence to be lost long ago, the day I first trudged into the Rhines, volunteering for duty with my papers, my pens, and my bottles of ink.

"We leave before dawn," the pixie commander says, her smile fading as suddenly as it arrived. "Someone will make sure you're awake."

She floats off the stool on a current of hot air from the fire. That small movement seems like it takes a lot from her. When she lands on the floor, she puts a hand to her back, hunches for a moment, then, thinking she's unwatched, winces. Finally she stands upright and walks among her troops, a proud woman ready to face another day.

* * *

I report to the weapons mage. He is not the inventor of this *alcana*, although the inventor once lived in this hut. The *alcana* is a newer weapon, one developed for the cold regions, designed to work at lower temperatures than most evil charms.

We have had a dilemma from the moment we started using magical weapons against our opponents. Too much darkness in the weapon itself, and we become like our enemies. Our violence, our bleakness, our lack of compassion will only be a matter of degree—and we will no longer be fighting for all that is good and true, but that which isn't quite as bad and not quite as false.

There are rumors, unsubstantiated of course, that the weapons makers must return to the labs for a debriefing. One maker, on his way out of a camp south of here, told me he feared that he would be put to death upon his return.

"How else can they control us?" he whispered. "There's no way to test for incipient darkness."

The *alcana* inventor has trained his apprentice and left three days before I arrived. Weapons inventors are privy to a kind of invisibility so that they might pass from one region to the next; the centaur and I might have passed him on the trails and never have known.

The weapons mage has long black hair, tangled from the harsh winds, and a beard badly cropped below his chin. His eyes have a desperation to them. He seems more afraid of the weapon than I am, perhaps because he knows what it does.

We are inside what must have been a chicken coop before the winter storms came, before the war found its way up here. The air still smells of dung and

chicken feathers. It has a dryness that makes me want
to sneeze.

The mage does not let me touch my *alcana*. That is
what he calls it: mine. While I stand there, he charms
it to obey only me.

It is smaller than I expect, although twice the size
of an adult pixie, and it is shaped like a giant robin's
egg, although it is not blue. It is an iridescent white,
a color I have never seen in nature.

It will fall from my hands, silently against the gray
sky, landing with a little poof in a pile of snow. Then
it will burrow to the frozen ground, and the magic will
leach from it, absorbing other magics, turning them
and changing them ever so slightly—just enough so
that their users can no longer summon them. Unsum-
moned, the magics will wither, and eventually die.

The only thing we do not know is the range of the
alcana. We do not know if magics ten miles away will
wither as well or if only the magics in the near vicinity
will wither.

"We are protected in any case," he tells me. "The
alcana only steals the dark magics."

"Then why warn me away? Why warn me that I
might lose my magic?"

His smile is slight, bitter. He mutters, "I wish she
had not told you that."

I wait, in silence, and he finally adds, "Because we
do not know how many of our magics have their origins in darkness. They have turned light. But light has
various shades, and one of them is the gray of twilight.
Which side does gray belong to? Both? Neither?"

He wears gloves while he handles the *alcana*, and
hands me a pair just before I leave. He gives me specific instructions which I cannot repeat here—not because I know you'll delete them, my friendly censor

(you will, of course; I would), but because I do not want to trust them to the page even as far as headquarters. If I did, this would be the dispatch stolen, this would be the turning point of the war: the enemy would learn the basis of our weapons technology, and would, then, know how to spell against it.

I cannot give them this gift, even in theory.

Suffice to say my duty is easy enough. Little more than dropping the *alcana* from the pixie boat. Painfully little, but just enough to cost me my hands should I do it wrong.

And because I will be in the boat alone, no one will be able to tie my wrists. I will bleed to death, trapped in a boat painted like clouds, held up by a fleet of pixies, flying courageously toward their doom.

It is disingenuous to say I am awakened before dawn, just as it is disingenuous to write this in present tense when it is clear by the act of writing that I have survived enough to tell this story to someone. It is just there are few words to describe the moment when someone tapped my shoulder. I was not asleep, but I was not exactly awake either. I had been lying on a filthy cot, thinking of the day ahead, cold and trembling, and then I am awake, following a young man I have not met yet into the boat barn.

The pixie boats are misnamed. They are boxes large enough to hold a platoon of pixies but so small I wonder if I can actually fit inside. The outsides are painted like clouds, or were, but are now so scratched and damaged from use that they look like bits of unusable cotton.

My adviser—I don't know what else to call him; he never gave me a name—shows me where to lay, how to hold the *alcana* until I need to release it. My breathing is shallow; I regret begging for this assignment now.

I will be trapped inside that box—alone—until a pixie crawls through one of knotholes in the side and shouts the heads-up at me. Then I release a lever, open the trapdoor beneath me—with nothing to hold me inside the box except my legs braced against the walls—and hold the *alcana* over the emptiness. Then I activate it, and let it go.

I'm not even supposed to watch it drop. I let it go, pray it hits silently in the snow, and then close the trapdoor. The sound of the closing door will notify the pixies that I'm done. Then they'll turn around and head for home.

It almost works like that. I do fit inside the box—although how two humans fit inside at the same time, I'll never know. I have to lie in a fetal position on my left side so that my right arm can reach the lever. The mage has given me a holder—like a little stand—for the *alcana* so that I do not have to hug it to me. He worries that I might get some permanent damage if I do that.

I'm worried I'll get permanent damage no matter what. Within a few moments—or so it seems—my entire left side falls asleep. I wish I could follow it—the time in the box is excruciatingly long. Before we even take off, I'm chilled through. By the time we're done, they'll have to check me for frostbite, if I don't fall asleep and die first.

I have no idea how the pixies fly in this—their wings so thin I could shove a fingernail through them. They hold gossamer strings attached to the box. The commander assured me before we left that the strings have the power of a spiderweb, which does not reassure me. I have broken through spiderwebs many times.

It is surprisingly light inside. The wood is thin and the box poorly constructed; light comes through all sorts of cracks. That's good; I'd been afraid I'd be flying in darkness.

Liftoff seems surprisingly easy; it's the midair part of the flight that's hard. The box rocks—partly with wind currents but partly, I later learn, as the pixies drop away, one by one, victims of the cold.

By the time we reach the drop zone, only half the squad remains.

I do not know this inside, blissfully. I am cramped in the small space, unable to do much more than raise my head. I want to move a little, but I'm afraid the pixies won't be able to handle any great shifts in weight. So I move my fingers on my nerve-deadened arm, and pray that the sleep won't kill it. I waggle my toes, and count, and, under my breath, recite every poem I learned as a child.

The interior of the box warms a little, due to my body heat and the air I breathe out. But I am still frozen through and through. I cannot believe that some of the human team have ridden on eight or more missions. I do not know how they endure this.

Finally, a pixie squeezes herself through the knot-hole near my head. Her features are strained, which I attribute to the difficulty she has getting inside, but which I later learn is due to the team attrition. At this point, she doubts we will ever make it back.

"It's warm in here," she says in her tiny voice.

"Only in comparison," I say.

She smiles, but the smile is distracted. "It's time."

I nod, and she squeezes out—all going the way the instructors have told me it would. I pull the lever with my good arm and for a moment, I fear that the trap-door is frozen shut. Then it squeals open, letting in air so cold that I think I will flash-freeze like a drop of water on a crisp midwinter day.

With a shaking right hand, I reach for the *alcana*. I do not trust my left. I remember the boy with no hands, wonder if he had a malfunctioning limb, wonder if he tried to activate the *alcana* with only partial control of his dominant side.

I scooch against the wall, feeling the rough wood send splinters into my back. I use my knees to hold the *alcana*, having been warned not to activate it in the holder (in case I can't remove it, I think).

Then I lean over the trapdoor. Beneath me, I see sundazzled snow, and tops of trees and chimneys belching smoke. All seems peaceful, like the valley I came up with the centaur.

Do they know what's coming? Do they realize the threat?

Do they care or are they as sick of this war as we are?

I shove the activated *alcana* through the hole, and reach for the lever, promising myself I will not watch.

I almost make it. I see the puff of snow as the *alcana* slips beneath the surface, between several buildings and near a tramped-down bit of land. The door closes slowly enough that I see someone—human-shaped, although I cannot be sure the person below is human—emerge from one of the buildings and walk in the opposite direction from my little missive.

Then the trapdoor closes, shaking the entire box. For a moment, it slips toward the front, sending me sliding toward the lever. More splinters go into my cheek—and probably into the numb left side, although I cannot tell for sure.

I think I hear chatter—screaming, maybe?—although I might be making that up.

Finally the box rights itself. I feel the turn as we head back, and I believe I do doze, in the silence, in the frozen air that suddenly feels hot, in the strange interior light.

When I wake—and this time, I do wake from a real sleep—it is as the box thuds to the ground, back at the hut. The lid comes off, other humans bundle me out and carry me to the human room where the injured lay. Someone rubs my limbs, paints an ammonia-scented ointment on my skin, and whispers soothingly at me.

I go back to sleep, asking no questions, which is so unlike me.

It is not until the following day that I learn only twenty of the pixies made it back from that trip. The other eighty died, falling away like the *alcana*, too small even to make puffs in the snow.

When the centaur returns, I go to him carrying only my parchment for this dispatch. I have given my pens and ink to the scribe, my envelopes to the clerk. The papers are mostly gone, used to write letters home for the humans remaining in that hut.

There are barely enough pixies for one more raid. The commander tells the centaur that, and he nods gravely.

Then he gets on his knees, camellike, to let me climb on his back. He does not grouse this time, nor does he mention my abilities.

"I hear you released a weapon," he says.

"Yes." I do not want to talk about it. Even now, my skin tingles with the cold, and I have no feeling in my left foot.

"Did it go off?"

How should I know? I want to snap at him. He knows better. He is a soldier. We only see pieces of the war, never the entire part. Each action we make might be futile; each life lost, lost for nothing.

Then again, we might have made the decisive blow that changes everything.

Only the historians will know.

"Did the weapon work?" he asks with a little more emphasis, as if I had not heard him the first time.

"I hope so," I say. For the sake of eighty tiny people I never really met, for everyone in that hut, for all the people scattered along our side of this mountain, I truly hope it worked.

WILDEST DREAMS

by Michael A. Stackpole

T HEY CAME FOR their tribute on the night of no moons. They appeared out of the twilight, one minute dim ghosts in the distance, then corporeal nightmares seeping into the vale below. The *suraitha* spread out to ward both flanks, and the *trondukhai* hulked along in the center of the horde. The *lomai* flittered about as was their wont, but the *Maeruunne*, their masters, came on in a disciplined formation. Their ranks ordered, their footfalls were as thunder, and the precise crack of scabbards on armor came as one crisp sound.

Their advent was as it had always been—the way they assumed it would always be.

They were mistaken.

This time *their* blood would spill before any tribute would be paid.

The *Maeruunne* leader, Goronock, marched ahead of his line, and a small retinue followed him. Of the hundred people they had taken two centuries before, fewer than a dozen remained. Less than half of them could walk. Only one kept pace with Goronock.

Even at this distance, in the half-light, I knew him. Danasal, my brother, my twin. Born minutes apart and now separated by centuries.

The *Maeruunne*'s clawed hand rested on his neck, in a gesture a father might use when encouraging his son. My brother did not shy from it, nor did he warm to it.

The *Maeruunne* are not so different from us, save being larger and stronger. Their leathery flesh has a greenish hue which becomes gray in the twilight. Their fingers and toes end in talons, their lower jaw sprouts black tusks, and their ears are mounted high on hairless heads. Their red eyes have no pupils and never close, as the *Maeruunne* never sleep.

I descended to the road to meet Goronock. Neither of us carried a flag of truce, and both of us came armed. I had a buckler bound tightly to the stump of my left arm, and a sword rode in a scabbard over my left hip. He carried a black iron spear in his left hand—it was twice his height and nearly thrice mine in length. As I approached without the tribute trailing in my wake, he contemplated throwing that spear at me, but then a slight grin tugged at the corners of his mouth.

He stopped and squeezed Danasal's neck. Goronock sniffed once, his slit nostrils pulsing, then he sniffed his charge. His eyes narrowed as his head came up. "Ah, yes, you are the one I did *not* choose. I see the blood-ties to your twin have preserved your life beyond your normal span. Don't you wish, Danasal, your brother had grown wiser with his years?"

My twin stared at me. He'd been gone a year by *Maeruunne* reckoning, but two centuries had passed here. Taken when he was ten, in form he was only eleven. His eyes, however, were older than mine. He could not recognize me, and this was just as well. The greater part of the hell he had lived through had been of my doing.

The *Maeruunne* leader again sniffed the air, then licked his lips. "You have them waiting for us. Why don't you bring them and save yourself trouble?"

I slowly shook my head. "You heard my vow when you took him. Never again."

"I have heard many vows in many places. Your father vowed the same thing, from behind tall palisade walls. They afforded neither him nor his troops protection." He rose on tiptoe and smiled. "You've built a castle of stone, but it will avail you nothing. The bargain between our people still stands, and will endure forever."

"You are mistaken. Return our people. Repudiate the bargain. Depart this place." I lifted my chin and gave him as cold a stare as I could muster. "Or is this where you wish to die?"

The *Maeruunne* looked at me curiously, then threw his head back and laughed. A moment later his people echoed his mirth, then the others took it up. The *suraitha* barked, their riders hissed, the *trondukhai* huffed base bursts and the little *lomai*'s laughter ascended into tones no man could hear.

"You think you can defeat us?" He stroked his chin. "Why would that be?"

"Men are unlike all the other creatures you've conquered on the various planes. We *dream*. You value us for it. You sup on our nightmares."

"They are far more piquant a vintage than any wine could possibly imagine, manling."

I ignored the pleasure washing over his features.

"To haunt us, you have driven *vampyr,* lycanthropes and their illnesses, into our world. You plague us with demons and other foul beasts, then through the children you take, you distill our fear and anxiety."

"You *have* learned. You've not been idle after all." Again he looked at me, more closely this time, his curiosity become wariness. "Your name is Colerayne."

"Once it was."

He nodded slowly, recognition making him grin. "Ah, of course." He bowed his head to me. "You are the Gray Lord, the Master of War."

"I am what you forced me to become."

"And when you destroy us, it will be my fault?"

"All of this is your fault, Prince Goronock." I shrugged. "Your defeat is just a consequence of it."

His nostrils closed as he raised his head and peered down at me. "Your legions may have conquered half this world, but that does not mean you can defeat us. I tell you now that if you believe you will, you have wasted your life." He waved a hand back toward his troops. "You are correct, we savor, we *devour* your dreams, the more horrible the better. We have driven monsters into this plane to frighten you, but *you,* the Gray Lord, you have been better at terrifying your people than anything we visited upon you. You have brought war to many lands, and fear of your coming has produced the most exquisite nightmares.

"In fact, I would thank you, nay, honor you, save you are withholding our tribute." Goronock smiled, revealing uneven ebon teeth. "And yet they wait for us, dreaming, afraid of what will happen when you fail. Potent stuff."

"You covet spoils of a battle you've yet to win, my lord." I gestured with my half-arm. "From the *vampyr* and others, we have learned much about you. We have dreamed of defeating you. We shall. I've waited for two hundred years. The time has been wisely spent."

"How can that be true? All you have is your little stone fortress? From the potent taste of your dreams, I thought they were far more grand."

"Realistic trumps grand when one dreams of battle." I half-turned away from him. "It's your tribute. Come. Take it."

My brother whimpered.

Goronock towered over me. "If you have learned anything about us, you know that no man can defeat my *Maeruunne*. You may kill some of the others—in fact, some of them need killing—but the *trondukhai* will destroy your fortress, and the rest will kill your people. After that, I will range farther, kill more people, just so we are not inconvenienced in the future."

"Leave now, Prince Goronock. The only inconvenience here will be wiping *Maeruunne* blood from our swords."

"Arrogance can choke the life out of you."

"Remember that when you cannot breathe."

The *Maeruunne* gave my brother a light cuff on the back of the head. "Go with him, Danasal. You've been a good pet. I shall remember you fondly."

I raised my right hand and a company of bearers came forward. They collected the returnees, then left Goronock and me alone downslope of my fortress. "This is your last chance. Go home. Leave us in peace."

"You, the Gray Lord, asking for peace." He laughed again. "If only irony tasted as good as fear. Tell me, was it the hope of seeing your brother again that kept you alive all this time, or the desire to fulfill your childish vow?"

"Both. More."

"Ah, the wish to see me dead." His eyes slitted. "No, not just that. It was the desire to kill me yourself."

"Among other things." I gave him a curt nod. "You have an hour to withdraw."

"In an hour, you will be dead."

"I've been dead for far longer than you know. In an hour you will join me." I turned and left him laughing behind me. I trailed after the bearers and my adjutant met me on the twisty road up to our stoutly-walled fortress. Though Dayris had been with me for two decades, she still had the youthful enthusiasm for war that had first caught my eye.

"All is prepared, my lord. We will destroy them."

"Make certain the men share your confidence, Dayris."

"Their confidence is in you, my lord."

"And you have mine, Dayris. Go, ready the second line."

"As you order it." The tall woman turned and ran off, her mail surcoat rustling.

Two centuries to plan the coming battle had once seemed an eternity, but the time needed for certainty had long since run out. The *Maeruunne* and their allies had a serious advantage in that they came from dark planes. Our night was as day to them, and this benefit was not one they would surrender lightly. Though we had means for making light, and I had trained my troops in night maneuvers, we would never be as good in the night as they were.

Moreover, their troops were well suited to fighting us. Men use tools efficiently, but it is because we must. Lacking fang or claw, in absence of speed or strength or a carapace, tools are all we have. Even the fabled sorceries of Far Nathei and nations beyond the Blood

Sea, were they available to us, would be of marginal use. What a sorcerer cannot see, and does not understand, is something immune to his enchantments.

I did recall the battle before my brother was taken. Tall wooden walls had been shattered. Men had been cleaved in two, torn to pieces, and died screaming sounds later echoed in thousands of nightmares. The *suraitha* and *lomai* had done the worst once the *trondukhai* had broken the walls. Yes, the behemoths had dashed men's brains out and crushed them beneath heavy hooves, but the deaths they caused were mercifully swift.

Not so those wrought by their allies.

And the *Maeruunne* had never broken their formation. They watched their subordinates savage the men opposing them. They remained there, silent and strong, a brooding presence armored with arrogance. Goronock had stood to the fore, his face implacable throughout, save when his eyes widened and he listened to the symphony of agonies that was our defeat.

I'd made my vow while anointing myself with my father's blood. Later, tears shed for my lost twin washed stripes through the stains, but my resolve remained. Just because nothing had defeated them before did not mean they could not be beaten, and I would be the one to do it.

What passed as a year for them was lifetimes for me, and I used every one of them to advance my goal. Armies had been raised and slaughtered. Cities sieged and razed. Empires gained, sundered, and recreated. There had been times of peace, brief respites, but then the relentlessness began again because I had seen how the *Maeruunne* would be.

I strode through the gateway and gave a signal. The massive doors creaked as men turned capstans to close them. Heavy wooden beams dropped into place to bar the doors, and others sank into pits to brace them. Goronock would send his *trondukhai* to break them, and I meant for it to take them a long time.

Between that outer wall and the inner lay a cobbled street ten yards wide that ringed the fortress. Arched stone bridges connected the outer wall with the inner; broad enough to let men reinforce or retreat, but narrow enough that a few brave souls could hold off besiegers. If the battling got to that point, we would be fighting the *Maeruunne*, and my people knew forcing them to engage was a victory in and of itself.

Beyond that inner wall, nestled deep within precincts of towers and barracks, hidden in a blocky building filled with narrow twisting corridors, the sleepers rested. A hundred of them, children of every nation under my control, writhed and twitched in thrall to nightmares. Though not a drinker of dreams, I could almost feel the torrents of anxiety pouring off them.

Bait, for our trap. Bait, and more.

I mounted the battlements just east of the gates. Below, in the narrow vale that led up to the mountain pass my fortress warded, the *trondukhai* lumbered forward on short legs and long arms. Impossibly tall and broad of shoulder, their bodies narrowed to tiny hips, furred hind-quarters and feet with cloven hooves. Two horns curled back from their temples, and not in some grand and regular way. They seemed blasphemies against nature, and were heavy enough that the *trondukhai* were forced to assume a posture of subservience. A single eye rode beneath a thick brow ridge, beards decorated their chins and their muzzles did protrude. Only their three-fingered hands and the

great curving claws seemed at odds with their basic
nature.

Huge targets though they were, my finest archers
would be useless against them. While their prodigious
strength made them engines of destruction, it was their
impenetrable flesh that perfected them as warriors.
Arrows glanced away, and they shrugged off stones
tossed by siege machines as a man might ignore a light
rain. I had no idea if burning oil or molten metal
could hurt them, but it was something I meant to learn
before the night surrendered to dawn.

As they marched up the hill, claws gashing green-
sward, I drew my sword and raised it. Goronock sent
a half dozen at us—keeping two in reserve. Spotters
along the walls yelled back to compatriots on the inner
wall, and they relayed the information to the men in
the courtyard below. Men shifted on the walls, mur-
murs rose, prayers were offered and black jests
wrested short laughs from the terrified.

Closer they came, closer. Behind them, the *suraitha*
began to maneuver. They were to lizards what wolves
are to dogs. Ten feet long from nose to tail, with uneven, ragged teeth and patterns of bright dots and
stripes over their scaled flesh, they appeared to be
nothing more than beasts. Every tenth one of them
bore a rider—a sharp-toothed cherub some took to be
Maeruunne toddlers—and it was assumed the riders
gave orders to the *suraitha*. I discounted that idea.
The riders were pets, and the lizards were intelligent.

Intelligent enough to revel in slaughter. Able to gal-
lop faster than any horse, they would be into the
breach as soon as the *trondukhai* broke the walls
down. They would still need them to breach the inner
wall, though the possibility they could scale the walls
with their claws had not escaped me. We would deal

with that when the time came. Regardless, though their flesh could be pierced, from what I recalled they took a lot of killing, and the loss of a pet just seemed to make them fight more savagely.

The *trondukhai* finally made it into range. My sword fell. Men yelled orders and those orders were echoed below. Snaps and clacks, cracks and thumps fill the inner courtyard as catapults launched their cargoes into the sky. We had practiced for months and years to know where our missiles would fall. Stones had been sown on the slope so the *trondukhai* would bunch themselves on easier paths.

So they would put themselves where we needed them to be.

The first missiles hissed and rustled as they flew overhead. Vast nets fitted with spring-loaded jaws and hooks unfurled themselves and descended. They draped themselves over the horned giants. The jaws snapped shut, pinching flesh. Hooks caught in nostrils and mouths, tangled in beards. Some nets hung from horns, lashing other *trondukhai*, catching, linking two of them. Though their flesh could not be torn, the giants bellowed angrily and tore at the chains. Fur came out in clumps, and hooks did tear through flesh from the inside of mouths.

In dealing with the chains, the giants paused long enough for other loads to rise through the air. Wooden casks filled with oil exploded like overripe fruit on heads and shoulders. Showers of burning coals arced through the night like dying stars. Their caresses ignited the *trondukhai*. One of the giants roared, expelling a great gout of fire, then fell to the ground thrashing with his lungs burning. Others, panicked, battled each other and one ran back down the hill, scattering a *suraitha* formation.

Two others, however, possessed of intelligence or so devoid of it that even panic could gain no purchase in their minds, came on uphill. Heedless of other missiles flashing past them, they reached the roadway and sprinted at the doors. Both of them, burning but curiously undiminished by it, slammed into the siege doors.

The impact dropped me. I scrambled to my feet again, and men helped me up, but the giants' continued pounding almost upset me again. One of them raised burning claws overhead, then raked them down into the oak. Flaming splinters fell in curls around him. Raising my sword once again, I made for the nearest bridge and my men came with me.

On the inner wall, Dayris shouted. "Hurry, my lord. Goronock sends the *lomai*."

"Make haste, men." I pointed my sword at my subordinate. "You know what to do. The *lomai* are yours."

To be afraid of the *lomai* almost defied logic. It was akin to being afraid of a starling or a squab. The raven-winged creatures stood no taller than the forearm I'd lost, and though mostly having the form of a man—save for a crow's head and wings—they were quite light. A stiff breeze could have held them at bay and a crone armed with a broom could have crushed one easily.

The difficulty was that *lomai* flocked; they did not travel alone. And small though they were, they bore bows and shot small arrows, fashioned from thorns native to their plane. A dart might not go deep, but the poison on it would cause pain and, in sufficient quantity, hideous hallucinations which the *Maeruunne* would drink with great pleasure.

And now, to sweep us back from the walls, Goronock had released his *lomai*. Visible only as blurred movement that momentarily eclipsed stars, flocks of them rose. Thousands of them came. Some groups flew high, twisting and curling around to dive down, while others raced in directly. So thickly they filled the air, no one of them could fear death, since the chances of his dying were so small.

Behind me, windows snapped open and bells in towers began to peal. Trumpets blasted loudly enough to wake the dead—though our drugged sleepers would barely register the sounds. Men shouted, defiantly and encouragingly. Though *trondukhai* pounded mercilessly against the doors, the men tasked with stopping the *lomai* were not to be cowed.

Black-winged nightmares drove in at us, but rising to meet them came snowy phantasms winging silently through the night. Deadly whispers, great owls slashed through the *lomai*. Larger, faster, with sharper beaks and razored talons, the owls did as they were trained. *Lomai* blood spattered us. Black feathers fluttered down. Bodies thumped to the ground, with darts and bows clattering beside them.

Though sending the owls against the *lomai* was equivalent to setting *trondukhai* on men, the *lomai* did outnumber them, and owls were not impenetrable. I had known that from the start, and no matter how valiant my birdmen and their charges, in a war of attrition, the owls would lose. As went their battle, so would go ours.

And we could not lose.

Our second wave rose and attacked the *lomai* just as they regrouped to deal with the owls. Bats, thousands of them, *hundreds* of thousands, rose in grand tornadoes of leathery wings and piercing shrieks. They poured from hollow towers that extended down to caverns beneath my fortress. Some were tiny, preferring insects to larger prey, while the biggest, the flying foxes, would have gladly made a meal of the owls themselves. The bats fell on the *lomai*, wrapping them in their wings, sinking fangs into their flesh.

The battle in the air amazed me. White ghosts flashing, *lomai* rising, freezing to draw a bow, being hit before they could release. A burst of feathers, arrows and bow spinning away. A bat whipping about, shrieking, body stuck with a dart or two, falling from the sky but still managing to capture a *lomai* in its wings. The melee in three dimensions moved with strong currents that would fragment into eddies of slow murder, that would again speed up, twisting and curling into a torrent that ripped more of the enemy from the sky.

I watched for almost too long, and might have lost myself in the battle, save for a splinter whistling past my face. Goronock had dispatched his last two *trondukhai* to bring the gate down. Their assault snapped thick planking and twisted metal. The braces bent and bowed, then burst. One of the massive doors cartwheeled inside to disintegrate against the inner wall. Another *trondukhai* reached in with both hands and ripped the other door free. It flew and battered a burning giant to the ground.

Even before the *trondukhai* could enter the fortress' outer precincts, the *suraitha* slithered in past them. Leaping and weaving, they flooded roads and raced along over cobblestones. Their claws clicked against them with a rasping cadence. Some came halfway up a wall, more because of velocity than finding any purchase, but archers sent shafts crossing through them. The *suraitha* did fall back to the ground, but multiple piercings seemed to slow them only slightly.

My archers found a wealth of targets. The bronzed men of Vangxia let fly with powerful recurve horn bows. They shot arrows with wickedly-barbed heads. Not to be outdone, the Garandella crossbowmen shot in volleys. Their heavy arbalests put bolts completely through *suraitha*. One nailed a lizard's skull to a wall, while another cored one from cloacae to throat. While all took joy at hitting *suraitha*, each archer knew the carpet of lizard flesh meant they could not miss. Killing the lizards proved as difficult as hitting them was easy, and this caused no little consternation among my men.

The two *trondukhai* entered the courtyard and split, one heading east, the other west. They did not scruple at treading on their allies. For the most part the *suraitha* were nimble enough to dart from beneath the giants' hooves. Those that were not—ones either stuck solidly with arrows or, in one case, nosing a beheaded pet—became smears on the cobblestones. The *trondukhai* moved along the road, intent on reaching the offset inner gates that would loose their army on the center of my domain.

The one moving east hit a trap first, though only a heartbeat or two before his companion did likewise. The roadway collapsed beneath his bulk. His hooves punched through the planking buried there, then hit the slanted slab of stone fifteen feet below the surface. The *trondukhai*'s face smashed against the ground, dazing him, then the creature slide back and down. The hooves entered an open space and the giant sank into the hole past his waist, stuck firmly and fast at the lower edge of his ribs.

He bellowed loudly and long. As he exhaled he slipped a bit farther down. He clawed at the sides of the pit, but only succeeded at pulling loose rubble down on himself. The debris packed in around his chest, further tightening his breathing. He bellowed again, defiantly and yet with a trace of fear. He slipped lower and the bellow ended in a squeak.

Two hundred yards away his compatriot had likewise become fixed in a pit. Impenetrable flesh or not, the *trondukhai* had to breathe. With their ridiculous physique, fashioning a trap that would slowly suffocate them had taken little thought. Throughout my fortress such traps had been sown. I could have dealt with two dozen of the giants easily.

But I did not want them to die easily. Looking down upon the one, I gave the signal. Below, from within the depths of the walls, men opened murder-ports and molten lead gushed into the pits.

Being unable to breathe meant their pitiful screams fell to silence well before the *trondukhai* died.

Behind me, the rhythm of the pealing bells changed. Flaming pits of molten lead cut off avenues of *suraitha* retreat. Not being stupid, the lizards knew we had trapped them. They also knew they were faster than we were, heartier and certainly better suited to war. Many of them bristled with arrows, but they did so defiantly, hissing loudly and displaying teeth sharp enough to saw the limb off a man in a heartbeat.

Yet before any sort of organized resistance arose among them, other ports opened in the interior walls. Through them poured a rustling avalanche of beasts that leaped immediately to the attack. *Suraitha* hissed and charged, lunged and snapped, but their efforts appeared as slothful as I would have trying to outrun one of them.

I'd thought on the problem of the *suraitha* longest of all, and it had inspired much of my early career. I knew no man would ever be able to stand against those creatures, but I also knew they were far from invulnerable. It took me fifty years to solve the mystery of their undoing, and I spent a century and a half perfecting the weapon we now employed against them.

Hounds, massive hounds, sheathed in steel mail, with spiked collars, went after the *suraitha* almost playfully. I'd taken the dragon-hunting dogs of the Baraltai Mountains and bred them with the saber-fanged wolves that had once warded the nobles of the Teyrah Empire. The resulting beast, while gentle in nature, massed more than most men, and were possessed of a loyalty no man could match. Bred for size and speed, silenced by design and trained to hunt, there was no game they could not bring down, and no predator they feared.

In a flash of gray a warhound caught a *suraitha* by the throat and shook it. The pet flew from its back, smashing its skull on the wall, while the *suraitha*'s spine snapped. The hound tossed that one aside and went for another, eluding a bite to catch it by a foreleg and tear the limb free.

The *suraitha* fought hard, but when they went for a throat, they got a mouthful of spikes. Their teeth did penetrate mail, but not deeply. Some of the hounds did die, but more of the lizards perished. A few did try to leap the bubbling pools of lead. One made it, at the cost of its tail, and slithered back to its master. Mostly, though, the lizards retreated into piles against the far wall, mouths pointing in all directions, teeth bared. The hounds isolated them and archers rained missiles down, slowly killing them in layers.

I watched the slaughter, ignoring the rising cheers among my men. For so long I had planned and dreamed. I'd seen this battle fought for ages, for lifetimes. It had gone better in some dreams, but seldom; and worse far more often. Despite nightmares, I had never doubted the outcome of this part of the battle, but it was only a prelude to ending *Maeruunne* predation.

I looked over at Dayris. "Now comes the hard part."

"He could listen to reason?"

"Pride won't let him."

She smiled. "And it won't let you either, will it?"

I nodded slowly. "You know how this has to be done. I am counting on you."

"Yes, my lord."

I strode boldly and alone over the bridge to the outer wall, side-stepping a feeding owl. I opened my arms and raised my voice to Goronock. "Your army is destroyed."

He reached down and grabbed the surviving *suraitha* throat and tail-stub. He raised it up, then placed a knee in its back and snapped its spine. "*Now* my mercenaries are destroyed. Not so my army."

Oh, how I longed to fly from those battlements and destroy him as the bats had the *lomai*. I ached to watch his smugness evaporate. I wanted him dead and I would have him dead, but his death was not my only goal. It would have to wait.

For a moment, at least.

I lowered my arms, but not my voice. "Leave now, Prince Goronock. Are our dreams worth your life?"

The *Maeruunne* tossed the broken lizard aside. "You have done better than I expected. I should have expected this of the Gray Lord. The dreams you spawned, the empress herself found intoxicating, very much so. Too much.

"She would want me to keep you alive, so she could

again and again enjoy them. It will disappoint her for me to kill you, but it will be for the best."

I laughed. "I'll not be dying here today."

"Put no great stock in your minor victory."

"I don't. It's your fear that give me heart."

"Me? Afraid of you?" Goronock chuckled and shook his head. "The *Maeruunne* fear nothing, but I understand what you are doing. You style yourself a hero, and you wish for the heroic. An epic battle, you and me, something to inspire dreams that won't be worth the time to sample? I'll give you that battle, Colerayne, but not the result you desire."

I leaned forward on a crenel. "And when I kill you?"

"You want a prize? You *do* ask much; but since you will never collect it, I will acquiesce to what I know you must desire." Goronock looked at his troops, all thousand of them, pennants fluttering in the light evening breeze. "If you win, we shall return home."

"And never to come back. You go home, forever."

"Return and rob your feat of its heroism? Of course not." He picked up his spear and spun it over his head, then rested the butt by his left foot. "Come, Colerayne. The dreams my tribute offers are too delicious to be denied me for long."

Dayris followed me through a small sally-port and placed a round helmet on my head. "You need not do this. The fortress will hold. We will break them."

"I'm counting on that, but Goronock is the key to their discipline. Without him, they will not fight nearly as well."

She raised an eyebrow. "Then you don't believe they will depart when you kill him?"

"No more than you do." I glanced back through the port, but could see nothing of the building where the dreamers slept. "Everything is ready?"

She nodded. "They will not get through us, but if the unexpected happens, the dreamers will die."

"Good." Turned toward the broken gate, but she laid a hand on my forearm. "Yes?"

"Danasal is with them. He went there. He's dreaming."

"Don't let them spare him, just because he is my brother."

"No, my lord." Her eyes tightened. "Go. Finish this."

I nodded once, solemnly, then stalked from the fortress. My mail surcoat wrapped around my legs, lapping like waves against my calves. I checked my buckler and tightened a strap, then drew my sword and marched past the fires of a *trondukhai* corpse.

From the fortress came a half-dozen handcarts filled with wood, which men took down to the place I'd met Goronock earlier. They stacked the wood in piles equidistant around a circle and lit them. Where we would fight, night became day.

After the fires had been lit, two thousand of my soldiers gathered on the hillside before the fortress. We outnumbered the *Maeruunne* two to one, but Goronock's troops showed no signs of fear. They had drunk of our worst nightmares, and many nightmares addressed this day of their return. Those dreams usually ended badly, and the *Maeruunne* were more than willing to make them come true.

Goronock regarded me coldly as I entered the circle. "You know they will be as nothing before my forces."

"They serve as a rein on treachery."

"I'll not take offense at that." He raised his spear over his head and pumped into the air. "I do you the honor of meeting you as an equal, one warrior to another, even though you are inferior."

"You refer to my only having half an arm?" I forced myself to smile. "This is an inequality I can soon remedy."

"If you are going to grow an arm, do it quickly." His spear snapped down, pointing at me, quivering. "Are you ready to embrace death?"

"Death holds no fear for me."

"Good. Better you fear me." Before the last syllable had trailed from his thin lips, the *Maeruunne* struck. He came in quickly, unbelievably so. His spearpoint dipped low as if he meant to stab the ground between my feet, then it came up. It shifted slightly to my right, the triangular head meant to stab through the inside of my thigh and open an artery. Before I could move, before I could blink, I'd get to watch my life pulsing out from a dark hole in my leg.

I twisted left, pivoting on my right foot. My thigh pushed his spear wide. My buckler came up caught it, deflecting it from my face as he tried to lash me with it. Then I spun, continuing my pivot, working in toward him.

Before he could retreat, I stabbed with my blade and hit him over the stomach. My point caught in his mail and the sword bent, but he leaped away before all the rings could part enough to let my blade taste his flesh.

Goronock took another step back, and I retreated as well. His right hand probed where I'd hit him and jerked back. A drop of black blood welled up where a split link cut his finger. He sucked at the wound for a moment as a cheer rose from my men.

My bowed my head. "You face the master of half this world."

The *Maeruunne* snorted. "You face the master of many worlds."

He drove at me again, harder and faster, his spear defined by fiery glints and the ringing of iron striking steel. Some blows I parried, and others I blocked. Those I caught on my buckler were heavy enough to knock me aside, but I never lost my footing. He came again and again, relentless and indefatigable, an avatar of war.

And the Gray Lord, as much as he was feared, was but his pale shadow.

Goronock gave me no respite, no chance to rest, and certainly no chance to attack him again. His spear's point popped rings on my mail and scraped paint from my buckler. The heavier end of his spear battered my shield into a misshapen lump. One stroke would have taken my head off, save that I ducked. Instead, it batted my helmet away, crushing it.

Of the *Maeruunne*, I had heard many stories. Always they were fearsome and implacable. They'd mastered the *trondukhai* and, as children, hunted *suraitha*. They fought on more worlds than could be counted, and while there might be a *vampyr* here or a demon there who recounted a distant victory, nothing had defied them for long.

Goronock knew no man could stand against him. While I had come to the fight with the hopes that he was wrong, my best efforts at battling him evenly had drawn but one drop of blood. The *Maeruunne*'s confidence surged when I lost my helmet, and from that moment on I fought only to survive.

Which is to say, as he and I both knew, the fight had ended.

He circled to my left side and poked the spear at my chest. I knocked it away with what was left of the buckler and realized it been too easy. Before I had any chance to leap back, Goronock swept the spear down and around, whipping into my left leg. It caught me fully and hard.

My left leg snapped.

He never even allowed me to fall. With his next thrust the spear's head punched through my mail just beneath my left breast. The triangular point spread ribs, sliced through heart and lungs, then caught on the way out. Goronock screamed in triumph and lifted me high in the air. I hung there on the point of his spear. My feet dangled. My sword dropped from my hand.

He looked up at me then shook the spear. I felt the point grate along bone, then pop out through my back. Slowly, I slid down the spear until stopped by his hand against my chest.

The *Maeruunne* growled in a low voice. "You can cry out. It will make me think no less of you."

I said nothing.

"Fool. You dreamed defeating us. " Goronock spat in my face. "You should have dreamed of stopping at *nothing* to destroy us."

I smiled slowly, his saliva dripping from my chin. "That's exactly what I did. I stopped at *nothing*."

My right hand came up and caught him by the throat. I gave him a second to think before I squeezed. I don't believe, even in that moment, even as I crushed his throat and spine, he understood what I *had* embraced to fulfill my vow.

He accepted that the blood my twin and I shared was what had allowed me to live two centuries. It wasn't. Not that. Not even my vow would have been enough to sustain me for so long.

His troops would come to understand.

As he fell, as I slowly thrust his spear all the way through me, they started forward. Even though mild intoxication broke their straight ranks and loosened their gait—for they had been sampling the dreams that would be theirs once we were undone—they were magnificent. With Goronock at their head, they would have easily destroyed an army of men.

But it was not an army of men they faced. Long ago the *Maeruunne* had driven *vampyrs* into our world to terrify us. Men had fought against them, destroying them and their spawn. *Vampyrs* were hated and feared. Most saw them as unalterably evil, and were glad when they died, but I had an entirely different vision of them.

My troops, those before the fortress, braced for the *Maeruunne* attack. Two thousand of the best troops mankind had fielded over the last two centuries. Two thousand men and women who had vowed, as I had, that *nothing* would stop us from destroying the *Maeruunne*.

Not even the loss of our humanity.

We, the *vampyr*, did not fight alone. Catapults launched more casts of oil and chains and stones into the *Maeruunne* formation. Archers and arbalesters peppered them with missiles, cutting great swaths through their ranks. Even my warhounds harried their flanks. And though the *Maeruunne* did fight well, and more of us fell—man, *vampyr*, and hound—than had earlier in the night, dawn lit a broken *Maeruunne* host.

A few of the *Maeruunne* survived. We blinded them and hitched them to a wagon bearing the heads of their comrades. We sent a message with them.

"Our world is no longer the land of nightmares. We

dreamed of a way to defeat you. Do not give us cause to dream of a way to exterminate you."

I have no idea how that message will be received by the *Maeruunne* empress. I do not care how she reacts. But my brother, when he dreams about it, smiles.

ABOUT THE AUTHORS

Jean Rabe is the author of more than a dozen novels and more than three dozen short stories. She usually writes with two dogs wrapped around her feet, and sometimes with a cantankerous parrot nested on her shoulder. In her spare time she visits military museums, pretends to garden, and tries to put a dent in her more-than-considerable stack of to-be-read books.

Writing under his own name as well as the pseudonym A. J. Matthews, Rick Hautala has written more than thirty published novels and over sixty short stories that have appeared in a variety of national and international anthologies and magazines. His most recent books under his own name include *Bedbugs* and *The Mountain King*. As A. J. Matthews, he has published *The White Room*, *Looking Glass,* and *Follow*. He has two collections forthcoming—*Occasional Demons* (short stories) and *Four Octobers* (novellas). His original screenplay *Chills* was recently optioned by Chesapeake Films.

Fiona Patton lives in rural Ontario, Canada with her partner, a fierce farm Chihuahua and inumerable cats. She has five novels out with DAW Books: *The Stone Prince*, *The Painter Knight*, *The Granite Shield*, *The Golden Sword*, and *The Silver Lake*. She has twenty-odd short stories published in various DAW/Tekno anthologies including *Sirius the Dog Star*, *Assassin Fantastic*, and *Apprentice Fantastic*.

Tim Waggoner's novels include *Pandora Drive*, *Thieves of Blood*, the *Godfire* duology, and *Like Death*. He's published close to eighty short stories, some of them collected in *All Too Surreal*. His articles on writing have appeared in *Writer's Digest*, *Writers Journal*, and other publications. He teaches creative writing at Sinclair Community College in Dayton, Ohio. Visit him on the web at www.timwaggoner.com.

Alan Dean Foster's writing career began when August Derleth bought a long Lovecraftian letter of Foster's in 1968 and much to Foster's surprise, published it as a short story in Derleth's biannual magazine, *The Arkham Collector*. His first attempt at a novel, *The Tar-Aiym Krang*, was bought by Betty Ballantine and published by Ballantine Books in 1972. It incorporates a number of suggestions from famed SF editor John W. Campbell. Since then, Foster's sometimes humorous, occasionally poignant, but always entertaining short fiction has appeared in all the major SF magazines as well as in original anthologies and several "Best of the Year" compendiums. Six collections of his short form work have also been published. His work to date includes excursions into hard science fiction, fantasy, horror, detective, western, historical, and contemporary fiction. In addition to publication in English, his work has appeared and won awards throughout the world. His novel *Cyber Way* won the Southwest Book Award for Fiction in 1990, the first work of science fiction ever to do so.

Tanya Huff lives and writes in rural Ontario with her partner, four cats, and an unintentional Chihuahua. After 19 fantasies, and two space operas, *Valor's Choice* and *The Better Part of Valor*, her newest novel is the thrid in her *Valor* series. *The Heart of Valor*. In her spare time she gardens and complains about the weather.

Mickey Zucker Reichert is a pediatrician and the author of twenty-plus novels and fifty-plus short stories, even though she is still young, vivacious, and knockout gorgeous. Her most recent release from DAW Books is *The Return of Nightfall*, the long-awaited sequel to *The Legend of Nightfall*. Currently, she is working on a third trilogy of the Renshai. She claims to have neutered cats and men, and no one is waiting around to find out if it's true or not. Buy her books, please. It's safer.

Under a variety of names and in several different genres, Russell Davis has written and edited both novels and short stories. Some of his recent short fiction has appeared in the anthologies *In The Shadow of Evil*, *Gateways*, and *Maiden, Matron, Crone*. He lives with his family in Arizona, where he's hard at work on numerous projects, including keeping up with his kids. Visit his website at http://www.morningstormbooks.com or his irregularly updated blog at http://russelldavis.blogspot.com for more information about his work.

Bill Fawcett has been a professor, teacher, corporate executive, and college dean. He is one of the founders of Mayfair Games, a board and role play gaming company. Bill began his own novel writing with a juvenile series, *Swordquest*. Anticipating cats, he wrote and edited the four novels, beginning with the *Lord of Cragsclaw* featuring the Mrem, which appear in *Shattered Light* as a hero class (all rights owned by Bill). The *Fleet* series he created with David Drake has become a classic of military science fiction. He has collaborated on several novels, including mysteries such as the *Authorized Mycroft Holmes* novels, the *Madame Vernet Investigates* series, and edited *Making Contact, a UFO Contact* handbook. As an anthologist Bill has edited or coedited over fifty anthologies. Bill Fawcett & Associates has packaged well over 250 novels and anthologies for every major publisher. Bill is the editor of *Hunters and Shooters* and *The Teams*, two oral histories of the SEALs in Vietnam. His most recently published work is as coauthor of *It Seemed Like a Good Idea, Great Historical Fiascos* and *You Did What*; both are a fun look at bad decisions in history. Also available is *How To Lose A Battle*, a modern look at how bad generals lose battles.

Jody Lynn Nye lists her main career activity as "spoiling cats." She lives northwest of Chicago with two of the above and her husband, author and packager Bill Fawcett. She has written over thirty books, including *The Ship Who Won* with Anne McCaffrey, a humorous anthology about mothers, *Don't Forget Your Spacesuit, Dear!*, and over eighty short stories. Her latest books are the humorous military SF novel *Strong Arm Tactics*, and *Class Dis-Mythed*, cowritten with Robert Asprin.

James Barclay was born in Felixstowe on England's East Anglian coast in 1965. Following college in Sheffield, he went to London to train as an actor in 1987 and has lived there ever since. *Dawnthief*, his first novel concerning cult hero The Raven, was published in 1999. Five more have followed in a very successful series, now available in eight languages. After years of juggling writing and a full-time job, James became a full-time author in 2004. He married his wife Clare in August 2005 and published the first of a new series, *Cry of the Newborn*, in October 2005.

Kristine Kathryn Rusch has won or been nominated for every award in the SF/F field. She's also been nominated for several mystery awards and has won a few of those as well. Her most recent SF novel is *Buried Deep*, and her most recent mystery is *Days of Rage*, written as Kris Nelscott. To keep up on her ever-changing career, go to www.kristinekathrynrusch.com.

Michael A. Stackpole is an award-winning author, game and computer game designer and poet whose first novel, *Warrior: En Garde* was published in 1988. Since then, he has written forty-one other novels, including eight *New York Times* bestselling novels in the Star Wars® line, of which *X-wing: Rogue Squadron* and *I, Jedi* are the best known. Mike lives in Arizona and in his spare time spends early mornings at Starbucks, collects toy soldiers and old radio shows, plays indoor soccer, rides his bike, and listens to Irish music in the finer pubs in the Phoenix area. His website is www.stormwolf.com.

C.S. Friedman

The Coldfire Trilogy

"A feast for those who like their fantasies dark, and as emotionally heady as a rich red wine." —*Locus*

Centuries after being stranded on the planet Erna, humans have achieved an uneasy stalemate with the fae, a terrifying natural force with the power to prey upon people's minds. Damien Vryce, the warrior priest, and Gerald Tarrant, the undead sorcerer must join together in an uneasy alliance confront a power that threatens the very essence of the human spirit, in a battle which could cost them not only their lives, but the soul of all mankind.

BLACK SUN RISING	0-88677-527-2
WHEN TRUE NIGHT FALLS	0-88677-615-5
CROWN OF SHADOWS	0-88677-717-8

To Order Call: 1-800-788-6262

DAW 18

MERCEDES LACKEY

The Dragon Jousters
Book Four

Aerie

Kiron has secretly gathered an army of dragon riders
in the abandoned desert city they have named
Sanctuary, from where they will join with other dragon riders to rid their world of magical domination.
But it is also a time to build a new society in Aerie:
an ancient city that seems to have been designed for
dragon riders and their mounts....

"It's fun to see a different spin on dragons...and as
usual Lackey makes it all compelling."—*Locus*

0-7564-0391-X

To Order Call: 1-800-788-6262
www.dawbooks.com

DAW 24

Tad Williams

THE WAR OF THE FLOWERS

"A masterpiece of fairytale worldbuilding."
—*Locus*

"Williams's imagination is boundless."
—*Publishers Weekly*
(Starred Review)

"A great introduction to an accomplished
and ambitious fantasist."
—*San Francisco Chronicle*

"An addictive world ... masterfully plays
with the tropes and traditions of
generations of fantasy writers."
—*Salon*

"A very elaborate and fully realized setting
for adventure, intrigue, and more
than an occasional chill."
—*Science Fiction Chronicle*

0-7564-0181-X

To Order Call: 1-800-788-6262
www.dawbooks.com

DAW 45

Melanie Rawn

"Rawn's talent for lush descriptions and complex
characterizations provides a broad range of drama,
intrigue, romance and adventure."
—*Library Journal*

To Order Call: 1-800-788-6262
www.dawbooks.com

TAD
WILLIAMS

Memory, Sorrow & Thorn

"THE FANTASY EQUIVALENT OF *WAR AND PEACE*...
readers who delight in losing themselves in long complex
tales of epic fantasy will be in their element here."
—*Locus*

THE DRAGONBONE CHAIR
0-88677-384-9

STONE OF FAREWELL
0-88677-480-2

TO GREEN ANGEL TOWER (Part One)
0-88677-598-1

TO GREEN ANGEL TOWER (Part Two)
0-88677-606-6

To Order Call: 1-800-788-6262

DAW 42